THE RELATIONSHIP COACH

BY SYLVIA MCDANIEL

Books by Sylvia McDaniel

Contemporary Romance

Standalones
The Reluctant Santa
My Sister's Boyfriend
The Wanted Bride
The Relationship Coach
Her Christmas Lie
Secrets, Lies, and Online Dating
Paying for the Past
Cupid's Revenge

Anthologies
Kisses, Laughter & Love
Christmas with you

Collaborative Series

Magic, New Mexico
Touch of Decadence

Western Historicals

Standalones
A Hero's Heart
A Scarlet Bride
Second Chance Cowboy

The Cuvier Women
Wronged
Betrayed
Beguiled

Lipstick and Lead
Desperate
Deadly
Dangerous
Daring
Determined
Deceived

Scandalous Suffragettes
Abigail
Bella
Callie
Faith

The Burnett Brides
The Rancher Takes a Bride
The Outlaw Takes a Bride
The Marshal Takes a Bride
The Christmas Bride

Anthologies
Wild Western Women
Courting the West
Wild Western Women Ride Again

Collaborative Series

The Surprise Brides
Ethan

American Mail Order Brides
Katie

The Relationship Coach
Published by Virtual Bookseller

Cover Design by Kim Killion
http://thekilliongroupinc.com/

Edited by Andrea Dickinson
http://www.qualitybookservices.com/

Formatted by Laurelle Procter
laurelleprocter@gmail.com

Short Description: Reed Hunter is ordered to expose relationship coach, Lacey Morgan, but she's not quite the swindler he thought…

ISBN: 978-1-942608-38-7 (paperback)
ISBN: 978-1-942608-39-4 (e-book)

{Contemporary Romance – Fiction}
{Romantic Comedy – Fiction}
{Romance – Fiction}

www.SylviaMcDaniel.com

Synopsis

Sometimes exposing the truth about love can leave your own heart exposed.

Documentary filmmaker Reed Hunter is ordered by his boss to expose relationship coach, Lacey Morgan's Twelve Steps of Dating program. Discovering the matchmaker is not the swindler he thought, catches him off guard.

Lacey twists him in knots, revealing the value of relationships and shattering his bachelorhood philosophy. But when she learns the truth about the documentary, Reed must choose between reaching his career goals at the expense of Lacey's or receiving the love he never expected to find. Which will he choose?

Table of Contents

Chapter One

Relationship coaches are no more than glorified witch doctors making money off people's emotions.

Reed Hunter stepped into the back of the glitzy, hotel ballroom in Austin, Texas, to catch the last few moments of relationship coach Lacey Morgan's *Twelve Steps of Dating Seminar*.

Reed received a lot of satisfaction from protecting underdogs who are unable to defend themselves from the many scammers in life. Like a crime fighter, he focused his camera on swindlers and cheats, revealing how they stole hard-earned cash from innocents. Con artists like Lacey Morgan.

A beautiful, professionally attired, longhaired blonde, wearing a short skirt that exposed boundless legs, owned the stage. Despite the fact she was going down, two things impressed him. Her Miss America smile and her mystifying ability to screw with people's relationships-first his boss's and now his.

She strode to the edge of the stage. "Today, we've learned to recognize your expectations in a mate. You've learned you need to find someone who matches your lifestyle. Someone who challenges and makes you think about life differently. Someone who likes to do the same things you do, but encourages you to try new experiences."

Reed coughed to stifle the sound of laughter rumbling deep within his chest. People bought into this psychobabble crap?

Lacey Morgan, dating guru, had convinced his girlfriend, Blair, to end their convenient sexual relationship. Since he wasn't promising her a ring, a honeymoon or his last name, she'd decided to move on. And she had. Packed up, moved out, and left with a *so-long-sucker* text message.

"I know many of you were dragged here by a friend, coworker, or the significant other in your life. However you got here, I hope you learned something today that will help make your relationships stronger."

Waving to the crowd, she strode from the stage. The audience stood and cheered, paying homage as if she were a rock star, not a therapist.

Blair's leaving had brought Ms. Morgan to his attention. And he enjoyed nothing more than exposing shysters like Ms. Morgan who earned their often opulent lifestyles by feeding off people's emotions. After he exposed Ms. Morgan's devious ways, Blair would probably return and thank him.

Shaking his head at the number of gullible people who believed her spiel, Reed stepped into the hallway, leaned against the wall, and stared as the audience streamed out of the door. Most of the women stopped to purchase a book or CD or DVD. He watched her assistants take their money with a mobile card reader. If the cunning cheater had a cash register, the *cha-chings* would have echoed through the hall.

Yes, she was stealing from the lonely and vulnerable.

Ten minutes later, her assistants began packing up the merchandise while he stood waiting, waiting, waiting.

A door opened.

There she was, Lacey Morgan. Charlatan. Chiseler. Cheat. Her gorgeous face and knock-me-to-my-knees body sent the air in his lungs packing for a short vacation, leaving him gasping like a man in need of a ventilator.

Per her online bio, she was in her late twenties and only had two letters behind her name-not psychologist, psychotherapist or counselor, just a B.A. And he was living proof any dumb schmuck, that goofed off for four years, could still get a Bachelor's degree.

Reed moved away from the wall and stepped in front of

Miss-I-Know-Everything. "Excuse me."

She turned and he switched on his best trust-me-I-want-to-help-you smile.

One of her assistants, a short brunette, stepped in front of him. "Can I help you?"

"I have a question for Ms. Morgan." He completely ignored her employee and averted his eyes from the swell of Lacey's breasts that were no longer hidden by her suit jacket.

Lacey laid her hand on her employee's shoulder and locked stunning blue eyes on Reed.

Any other time, those lovely blue eyes would have had him in full pursuit of the hot Ms. Morgan.

"Yes?"

He held out his hand and used a deep timbre that always scored him a woman's number. "Reed Hunter. I'd like to discuss your business over dinner."

"Sorry, I'm not available." Her response was quick, cold, concise, and held no consideration.

This could be a tough sell.

"I'm producing a film. A documentary on relationship coaches, and I'd like your business to be the main focus."

Few people could resist being on camera. Few people realized the power of film. Few people knew Reed Hunter's skills to expose imposters with a camera.

"Why would you want to include me?" she asked, her voice direct, her gaze cautious, like she might be immune to his charm.

"I want you," he said, upping the charisma. "You're the best relationship coach in the country."

Her face visibly relaxed and her scrutiny morphed into at least consideration and at last earned him a smile.

"Thank you. Who else is part of this film?"

He named two other relationship coaches he'd found on the internet, never intending to film either of them.

"What other films have you produced?" she asked.

"I'm not as well-known as Michael Moore, but I won an IDA for my film on the Russian sex trade." He left out the other films he'd done on people who conned and cheated their way through life.

"The IDA?"

"The International Documentary Association. It's the industry's best film award."

"Nice." A soft sigh lowered her shoulders and the tiny tension filled lines around her eyes relaxed. The barriers she'd erected between them slid down a notch.

"Within the documentary film arena, the IDA's are as prestigious as the Oscars." Someday he'd win that golden statue, but not with a film on dating.

"Tonight, we return to Dallas." Lacey glanced at the woman standing beside her before she returned her attention to Reed. "Amanda is my marketing rep. Send me a DVD of one of your documentaries. Call her and make an appointment. We can discuss your offer," she paused, "after I see one of your films."

Success pumped like a narcotic through his veins, swelling his chest and head. Lacey Morgan was no different from all the other women he'd coerced over the years. Once she signed the release, Reed would reveal this scheming swindler and save men's sexual arrangements from the likes of this relationship coach.

His camera would reveal how she made a living off susceptible, defenseless women with unrealistic promises.

Amanda placed a business card in his hand. "Our office hours are on the card. Call me."

His jilted boss, Graham was right. Reed would film the lovely Ms. Morgan as a crusader for dating and then reveal her as a fake using people for their money.

"Thanks, ladies. See you soon." He strolled away, the familiar pursuit of the hunt spiking his heart rate faster than running a marathon. *Game on, baby. Game on.*

~

Lacey watched Reed stride down the hall, his walk confident, determined, and oh, so masculine.

"He wants to do a documentary!" Amanda's voice rose a notch away from a full squeal, her eyes wide, as an oh-my-God smile spread across her pixie face.

Lacey cautioned, "Documentaries can make us paupers or millionaires. We need to know how Reed intends to film Mate Incorporated, before we make a decision."

She wanted to join Amanda in a fan girl squeal while jumping up and down like they'd seen a rock star, but there was a certain decorum she had to maintain, and she didn't know enough about Reed Hunter to make a decision.

"But it would give us lots of free publicity!"

"It could." Lacey's business had come a long way from that first meeting with her friends in the university library three years ago after she'd watched them make horrible dating choices.

"This documentary could propel Mate Incorporated right into television." Amanda could hardly contain her enthusiasm.

Best friends since college, together they'd built Lacey's small practice into a growing business that finally paid the bills.

"Your meeting with the television producer is next week," Amanda reminded her.

"I'd rather do the television show. Besides, there is something about this guy. For some reason, my internal alarm is shrieking danger, danger, danger."

Amanda frowned. "Maybe it's not alarm bells. Maybe your body isn't shrieking danger, but rather hunk alert."

"Doubtful." Lacey pursed her lips. "Google Reed Hunter and see what you find."

"You haven't seen Dean in a while."

Lacey smiled at the idea of seeing her nerdy lover again. His image triggered a zinger of excitement, anticipation and stimulation, straight from her heart to between her legs. "Dean's coming home tomorrow night. I can't wait to pick him up at the airport."

"How long have you guys been apart this time?"

"A month."

Amanda's hazel eyes narrowed in disapproval, and she reached over and grabbed Lacey's arm. "How can you tolerate him being gone so long?"

"Dean's job involves a lot of traveling. He loves what he does." Lacey had already gone over every danger, playing out every scenario in her head a million times.

"What happens if you get married and have kids?" Amanda released her arm and gave a little shrug as they walked down the hall towards the door of the hotel. "Sorry, kids. Daddy missed your birthday because of work. He was off in the Congo, searching for a rare species of plants. *Risking his life*," she drawled.

Lacey tried to be pragmatic, but she was growing tired of him being gone so much. A month was a long separation for a couple dating. "Dean's job is important. His company finds new plants to use in pharmaceuticals and they need him to explore the jungle."

Part of her hated his job. Hated him risking his life and feared for him every time he got on a plane.

"Girl, I just hope he doesn't get kidnapped or sick in one of those God-forsaken countries."

All the fear she'd kept carefully locked away, now lay exposed and bleeding in her mind. Amanda had catalogued all Lacey's fears, except for the one that had Dean finding another woman. For some reason that wasn't a concern and she didn't understand why. "I try not to think of the danger he might be in, and instead, I concentrate on the positives.

He's doing what he loves."

"Tomorrow, I'll mark my calendar-do not call-Lacey while she's getting laid for the first time in a month." A smile lit her heart-shaped face.

Warmth chased the fear away, spreading through Lacey like sunshine at a fourth of July picnic. She couldn't restrain the smile that filled her face at the thought of seeing Dean-her dark-haired, handsome, geeky guy who fit all her criteria. The man was her perfect match. "It's been a while. I'm looking forward to spending time with him."

"Have you told your mom and sister you're apartment hunting for you and Dean?" Amanda asked, her forehead scrunched into an oh-crap expression. "Your mother is known for her strong opinions."

Lacey loved her mother, but there were times when facing the woman could be like walking into a blizzard, dark, dangerous, and dreadful.

"Oh God, Mother will be horrified we're living together. Her philosophy is if you love them, marry them. And she's got five marriage licenses as proof."

"Your mother is a weird character," Amanda said, her eyes wide as she shook her head. "I'm just saying."

"Character? I'd say character is a mild description of a woman married that many times. A woman who still believes in true love and is fixated on finding husband number six." Lacey loved her mother, but her childhood had been more like a rerun of *Eight is Enough* with a revolving Dad door.

"Wow."

"She's already approached me about our dating service. I lied and told her our agency didn't have any men her age. She's had enough husbands." Lacey's shoulders shuddered involuntarily. And her stomach warned of impending nausea at the thought of matching her mother with one of her clients. Finding her mother husband number six felt incestuous.

Amanda shook her head, her chestnut curls quivering. "But how much longer can you postpone telling your mother and sister about you and Dean shacking up? You're practically engaged to the guy."

Lacey had grown up with multiple fathers, siblings, and aunts and uncles, men who'd walked into and out of her life before the ink on the wedding license dried. "As long as possible to put off the lecture on marriage. When we're both ready, we'll get married. No one is forcing me down the aisle. I'm doing this once and only once."

"Great! The relationship coach is hiding her feelings from her mother," Amanda said quietly as they continued down the long hall past other exhibit rooms in the hotel.

Lacey vehemently denied what she knew was true. "I'm not hiding my feelings. I just haven't chosen my battlefield yet. Because, believe me, once she learns we're moving in together, there will be a bloody battle."

~

Reed lifted his right arm and slammed the racket against the tennis ball. Ty Ward, his best friend, college roommate and now cameraman, returned Reed's serve, smashing the ball onto the court. Reed raced to return the volley and knocked the ball out of bounds.

He leaned over, rested his hands on his knees, and tried to catch his breath. "Damn. That's game-set-match. I guess drinks are on me today."

Ty slapped his hand on Reed's shoulder. "It's not often I win, so hell yes. Drinks are on you."

Still fighting to control his breathing, Reed straightened and contemplated his friend. "Let's shower and go see who's hanging out at the club this afternoon."

"You mean, see if Blair is working today." Ty's sly grin filled his thin face. His appearance was more like a child of the sixties with his tied back dark hair, yet the ladies loved his big brown eyes and long lashes. With just a smile, they seemed to flock to his side.

"No, man. She gave my ass the boot."

In a nanosecond, Ty's jaw dropped like a tennis ball and bounced back up to his lip. His eyes widened. "When did this happen?"

"Blair attended a *Twelve Steps of Dating* seminar, and afterwards, we had the 'what are your intentions' talk."

Ty grimaced in that universal man connection of oh-no-not-that-talk. "I hate those."

They walked toward the men's side of the clubhouse, passing the empty swimming pool. "We dated for six months, and she wanted to know where we were headed, which is chick speak for how soon can I expect an engagement ring."

"Did you tell her when people in hell manufacture ice chips?" Ty asked.

"I tried to play it cool. I told her it was too soon to start talking about marriage. But she unloaded me the next day via text," he told Ty, his chest squeezing his lungs until his breath felt labored. It wasn't that he loved Blair. He thought she'd bought into his lies. He thought they would be together for several more months. He thought he'd be the one to call it quits.

"A text! Really?" Ty laughed until his face flushed red and tears shimmered in the corner of his eyes.

"It's not funny. It's the first time I've been dumped since college. I'm the dumper, not the dumpee." That had been the pattern, since Mary, his college sweetheart, had returned his engagement ring. It seemed she loved the idea of a new car more than marrying him, and her daddy had delivered on the deal-a brand new red Corvette.

"What did Blair say?" Ty asked.

Reed pushed the troubling thoughts from his mind.

Why screw a perfectly good day with thoughts of a woman who'd rejected his heart and his ring?

"That she had given our talk consideration and decided I wasn't serious about getting married. It would be best if we ended our relationship."

"Hey, she made it easy for you." Ty picked up his bag and racket.

"She confessed to attending the *Twelve Steps of Dating* seminar. The woman teaching the course had given clues to when someone wasn't really serious. I hit every one of her benchmarks," Reed said.

Ty high-fived him.

"Blair said, 'I know you don't want to get married.'" He paused. "What could I say? She's right. I'm not getting married. Ever."

At thirty-two, he was done with *forever after*. When a woman thought a car was more valuable than her relationship with him, then he could use women for what he wanted. Sex. And more sex.

Ty's brown eyes stared at him, curiosity in his gaze. "What now? We've wrapped up your project and spent a month resting. You have no girlfriend. What's next?"

The familiar zing of excitement gripped his chest, and he couldn't wait to get started back doing what he loved. He smiled at Ty, anxious to see his reaction. "Yesterday, Graham gave us a new project."

"What dictator are we taking down?"

"I have to thank Blair for giving the idea to Graham."

"Blair? The girlfriend?"

"Yes, our next documentary is on a relationship coach."

Ty's groan echoed over the empty court, and he raised his fist in the air and took a pretend swing. "Crap."

"Hang on, man. It gets better," Reed said laughing at his camera-man's antics. "I did some research. It seems anyone can hang out a shingle saying she's a relationship coach. You acquire a special certificate then start a coaching practice. Some are therapists, but most are just ordinary individuals who think they know what's best for people."

For the first time ever, he'd turned Graham down when he'd told Reed about the documentary. At first he'd thought this wasn't his style of film, but then when he learned what Ms. Morgan was doing and how much she was charging, he'd known he had to expose the beautiful schemer. And when Graham had promised Reed his choice of subjects for the next film, he'd jumped on board ready for the adventure.

Ty's forehead wrinkled. "And we're going to do what?"

"We're going to expose relationship coaches as frauds. And we're starting with Lacey Morgan," Reed said. After meeting the charming charlatan, Ms. Morgan, his reluctance had changed into excitement, especially since Graham had promised to give Reed free rein on the next film.

"Does Ms. Morgan know you're about to take her down?"

Reed smiled, feeling like the big bad wolf about to take down Little Red Riding Hood. "I'm meeting with her next week."

"Do you think she'll agree to let us film her? Not many people want to watch their business butchered on the big screen."

Reed laughed, unable to keep the excitement of showing Ms. Morgan for the crook she was out of his voice. "I'm pitching it as a film to highlight the services relationship coaches provide. How they are helping couples find each other in a world where discovering the right person can be difficult."

Motivation flowed through his veins like a fine wine,

making him drunk with anticipation.

"And after we film her, you'll add in the testaments about how relationship coaches harm people…how there are no regulations or specifications…how anyone can do this." Ty nodded.

"Bingo. And believe me, this chick will rock the film. She is one hot babe."

"Man, you and I both know your relationship with Blair would never have lasted," Ty said, stating the obvious.

"True. But Ms. Morgan's seminar also ended Graham's relationship. And he's pissed."

Ty shook his head. "Great! Not one, but two rejected males. For the good of men everywhere, this woman's going down!"

Graham Turner, owner of Graham Productions, was not someone you wanted to provoke into putting a target on your back. *The Twelve Steps of Dating* had ended at step one for him. And he'd been madder than a kamikaze wasp. His sting was lightning fast on target, and brutal!

"You think? And we have Blair to thank for leading me to Lacey Morgan-relationship expert, who thinks choosing the right person is all it takes to have a solid relationship."

"Hot women and dating," Ty said with a smile. "It could only be better if they were wearing a bikini."

A little charm should convince Lacey to sign a release form.

Suddenly eager to get started, Reed took a deep breath to quell the rapid beating of his heart. They couldn't begin soon enough to exposé this woman.

"I think we need to drink to our next documentary Lacey Morgan. Relationship coach."

Chapter Two

The next morning, Lacey stood in front of her favorite restaurant, waiting for her sister, Kerri. The wind blew Lacey's hair into her face, and she shoved the long blonde strands behind her ear.

At seven-thirty sharp, a phone call had shattered her dreams and roused her from bed. Kerri had insisted Lacey meet her for lunch. Lacey had agreed with the hope of spending the rest of the weekend alone with Dean after she picked him up this afternoon.

Now, she stood tapping her foot impatiently as she waited outside the door of their favorite salad bar. After a busy week spent indoors, the warm May sun caressed her face like a lover's hand.

She glanced across the parking lot and watched her mother hurrying towards her. At fifty-five years of age, Brenda Morgan-Spencer still appeared a knockout with bottle blonde-hair and a trim figure. Doing yoga kept her slim, and she'd always been an eccentric dresser, preferring the more outlandish styles that looked like leftovers from the sixties.

Kerri hadn't mentioned their mother joining them for lunch. Unease tickled like a spider creeping along Lacey's spine.

"Hi, Mom," Lacey said, as her mother reached her. She gave her a quick hug and kiss on the cheek. "I didn't know you were coming. Kerri called and said it was urgent I meet her here for lunch. Do you know what this is about?"

"She told me the same thing. She didn't sound upset."

"She already knows what medical school she's attending," Lacey said. "Something else must be going on."

"Yes." Her mother frowned in that I-don't-understand-you- girls-way. "She spent sixteen years of her life in school. I don't know why she's going for another eight of medical school. I keep wishing one of you girls will get married and give me grandbabies."

Inwardly, Lacey's female parts shuddered, and went into hiding. Being the oldest, she'd heard this rant so many times that the word *babies* made her body go into lock down.

"I'm sure whatever Kerri has to say must be important or she wouldn't have called so early this morning," Lacey responded, changing the subject away from babies.

"Two grown children and neither of them married," her mother lamented. "Maybe my next husband will have grandbabies." She stopped and gave Lacey a questioning glance. "Is that something I can put on my profile? Can I ask for a man with grandchildren?"

Lacey bit her lip to keep her jaw from gaping open like the Grand Canyon. She stared at her mother for a moment and then pretended ignorance. "Your profile?"

Fortunately, her mother spotted Kerri.

"Oh, look! There she is," she said ignoring Lacey's question. "She looks happy. Maybe it's more good news."

Lacey watched as Kerri's long blonde hair swayed against her lean body as she jogged toward them. Her appearance was more of a high school girl than someone about to enter medical school.

"Hi, ya'll," her sister drawled, giving them each a hug. "Let's get a table."

Inside, the waiter sat them at their favorite corner booth away from the main crowd. After they placed their drink order, Lacey and her mother turned expectantly to Kerri.

"What's the news that couldn't wait?" Lacey asked. "You're valedictorian?"

Kerri lifted her left hand. A dazzling rock graced her ring finger.

Lacey sat there starring at the diamond, her lungs no longer seeking air, her blood no longer flowing, her body no longer feeling.

Their mother squealed in excitement, while Lacey resisted the urge to plug her ears with her fingers as her body shuddered, her eyes blinded by the sparkling gem.

"My baby girl is getting married," Brenda gushed.

Their mother leaped to her feet, threw her arms around Kerri and yanked her sister close. Shock held Lacey prisoner, keeping her butt super glued to the chair.

Lacey sat like a rock in a disconnected haze, her chest tighter than if she were held in a wrestler's grip. After a moment only the murmur of voices and the clink of dishes and muted voices echoed around them as her mother and sister turned and sent her scathing glances.

"Lacey?" her mother asked. "Aren't you happy for your sister?"

In two weeks, her sister would graduate from college, but the required dedication to medical school dictated Kerri was too young to rush into an institution they had sworn they would never get divorced from.

"Of course, I am. I'm just stunned. You were going to wait until you were out of medical school," she said trying to snap out of this daze that held her in its grip.

As children, they'd made a blood oath they would not live the life of their mother and have multiple marriages. Together, they had suffered the agonies of one step-father after another, step-brothers and sisters, people who were families one moment and enemies the next. They'd made a solemn oath to marry only once.

Kerri blushed, and her blue eyes danced with happiness. "We don't want to wait. I'm still going to medical school, but I can't imagine my life without Matt. He's perfect for me and he makes me very happy."

"How long have you guys dated? You just started mentioning him to me," Lacey said. Worry settled in her stomach like a stone plunging to the bottom of the pond.

Kerri smiled and patted her sister on the hand. "Four months. Long enough for me to know we belong together."

Her mother nodded, silently siding with Kerri. "Yes, I've always known with each of my husband's that he was perfect for me."

Lacey spewed the water she'd just sipped from her glass onto the table. Picking up her napkin she quickly wiped the water away. "If they were so perfect, why did three of your marriages end in divorce?"

Her mother's face glowered with disapproval. "They were perfect at the time. I can't help it if two cheated and one loved the bottle more than me. My poor Billy and Sam died. When you find true love, it's obvious. You might look a little harder for the emotion."

Lacey's whole body tensed, and she reminded her mother of an important fact. "I have a boyfriend."

"Yes, I know. You've had him now for a year, and that's the problem. I see a boyfriend, not a lover. There are no sparks flying between you, and I don't see a ring on your left hand."

"That's not fair!" Lacey said, her voice rising above the clink of dishes.

Kerri drew the conversation back to her. "Excuse me. This is my engagement announcement."

"I'm sorry, Kerri," Lacey said. "I just wasn't expecting you to reveal you were engaged today."

Her sister pleaded, "Try to act a little more excited."

"Do you remember that blood oath we promised as kids?" Lacey gazed at her sister, willing her to remember the challenges of their youth. The reasons why they'd sworn to marry only once.

"Yes," her sister said, not looking at their mother.

"What oath?" Brenda demanded.

They ignored her.

"Do you love him enough to spend the rest of your life

with just him?" Lacey asked, needing to hear her sister say the words.

"Yes, I believe I do. Lacey, he takes care of me. He's thoughtful and kind. He's everything I've wanted in a man and because of him, I strive to be a better person."

A heartfelt sigh escaped Lacey and she realized at this time, it would be futile to try to talk sense into her sister.

"Will someone please tell me what oath you two are talking about?" her mother repeated, her voice rising in agitation.

Her sister shook her head to warn Lacey to refrain.

But oh no, Lacey couldn't hold back. She persevered to be honest and upfront with her mother. Forging ahead toward the edge of the maternal cliff, she took the plunge.

"When you were on husband number three, Billy, I believe, Kerri and I made a pact that we would only marry once, so our kids would never experience step-families." Lacey figured in less than thirty seconds a volcanic eruption would explode from her mother's mouth.

"You just couldn't keep quiet, could you," her sister said softly to Lacey.

Their mother's face flamed a scarlet color, and Lacey knew she'd just ruined her sister's engagement lunch. When would she learn to keep her mouth shut?

"Tell me how you kids had it so bad?" her mother demanded, her voice shrill over the clank of dishes.

Kerri shook her head. "We made the pact the night that Billy's kids smeared dog poop all over the clean clothes in our drawers. Remember that little incident?"

A frown flitted across her mother's tense face, and she sighed with an air of acceptance. "His kids were little monsters," she said. She straightened her shoulders into a rigid motherly stance. "That was years ago, Lacey, and if Kerri is happy and thinks that Matt is the one for her, she should embrace this moment. You're the one who is almost thirty and hasn't even had a great love affair that I know of."

"Dean and I are perfectly happy," Lacey said softly, trying to downplay her mother's response. Who needed great love affairs? She preferred honesty and stability, neither of which she'd witnessed in her mother's relationships.

Her mother rolled her eyes in that insolent way of hers that made Lacey crazy.

"Except Dean's about as interesting as cardboard, and if he's anything like that in bed, then no wonder you're still single."

"Mother!" Lacey said her voice indignant. "Just because I don't jump into relationships like I change my underwear does not make me a bad person."

Her mother's chest swelled like a Thanksgiving turkey. "I want you to know that I do not choose the men I fall in love with. There is a burst of instantaneous attraction that leads me to marriage. It's called passion. You should try it sometime."

"I'm a relationship coach. I help people like you make conscious decisions about dating the right person and finding the right mate, instead of being led by their emotions or impulse."

Who needed great love affairs? You needed honesty and stability, none of which she'd witnessed as a child in her mother's relationships.

"You can't pick and choose who you're going to fall in love with," her mother replied hastily.

"Then you have no need for my matchmaking services."

Her mother opened her mouth to respond, when Kerri snapped her fingers.

"Excuse me!" her sister said, her voice rising. "Would anyone care to know how he proposed to me or about our future plans?"

Lacey and her mother sent each other one last glare before they pivoted to Kerri.

"Sorry, honey. How did he propose?" her mother asked calmly.

Lacey went through her mental process of deep, slow breaths, exhaling her anger. Good breaths in, ugliness out. It would do no good to fight with her mother. This argument was an ongoing one, and no matter what, this issue never got resolved.

Kerri's eyes misted, and she glanced at her ring. "Yesterday, after my final exam, he picked me up from school. We went out to the lake and sat enjoying the spring sunshine. Suddenly, a jet boat came by bearing a banner that said, 'Marry me, Kerri, Matt.'" She wiped her eyes. "I sat there stunned, until they came around a second time honking their horn. Then I lunged for Matt and said 'yes. Oh God, yes.'"

"Oh, honey, how romantic," her mother said, her voice once again that soothing, sweet, give you diabetes, make you want to grit your teeth tone.

"He's a great guy, Lacey. I love him."

Lacey smiled and wondered when she could get Kerri alone to try to talk her out of this insanity.

Lacey glanced at her mother and her sister. Yes, she wanted a great love, but she never wanted to inflict her children with multiple marriages. And her family seemed to be cursed with this affliction.

~

Lacey dropped by the office to find her hardworking friend toiling away on a Saturday. She slumped in a chair across from Amanda, defeated.

"My baby sister is engaged," Lacey announced, shaking her head. Anxiety squeezed her heart, and wrung it out like the spin cycle on the washer.

Amanda looked up from her computer monitor. "Do you like the guy?"

"He's okay. I've met him a couple of times and he seems nice enough. It's just they have so much to do before they're ready for marriage. Graduation, medical school, her internship, not to mention all the hours she'll be studying or working." She paused, the situation so unexpected, she still found it hard to believe. "Kerri says Matt will support them while she goes to school, but just graduating, he'll be lucky to make forty thousand a year."

Kerri had a promising future as a doctor. She didn't need marriage at this important juncture in her life.

"What does Matt do?"

"Accountant. He's studying for his CPA license and hopes to do corporate tax accounting." Lacey couldn't stop thinking this was a mistake. A mistake they'd both lived through before.

"There has to be some money in that."

"But not right away," Lacey said. She wanted to somehow stop or at least postpone this wedding. "Kerri should stay focused and finish medical school. And I had to listen to all this crap from my mother that Matt and Kerri are destined to be together."

Memories of her childhood flooded her, a new step-father, moving, changing schools, the fights, the drama. "She had the nerve to tell me that Morgan women need men who bring out passion in them. I have never heard so much nonsense in my life." Tears stung behind her lids and she refused to let them fall. "And she wonders why I became a relationship coach. So, other small children will not have to watch their parents marry time and again and have enough step-brothers and sisters to form a baseball team."

Amanda laughed a nervous kind of twitter. "It's also

what makes you good at your job. I'm sure you learned about human behavior from all those siblings." She shrugged. "Besides, passion is not a bad thing."

"At the right time, with the right man-when you're ready. Your life should not be ruled by men, emotions, passion, sex, or hormones. I've preached to my sister, telling her to set her goals in life and go for them." She sighed, the sound weighted with sadness, loud in the small office. "You're more qualified than my sister to get married right now. Your life is settled, but she's still on the journey to becoming a doctor."

"It will work out Lacey. You know how engagements often end before the wedding."

"Yeah I know." Amanda was right. She knew that, but she loved Kerri, and didn't want to see her sister hurt.

"Yet, I envy your sister. She's found a man she is willing to marry. I just can't seem to find the right man," Amanda confessed.

"You said things were going well with Jason." Lacey was surprised that her friend seemed to have doubts. Had she been so wrapped up in her own drama not to notice her friend's relationship had hit the skids?

"The guy meets all my criteria. We've been dating for three months. We've had sex. Everything seems perfect," Amanda said, yet there was something in her voice that wasn't quite convincing.

"Then why did you say that?"

Her shoulders moved up in a quick shrug. "I don't know. I guess I'm afraid," Amanda admitted. "Sometimes I don't think he's as into me as I would like."

"Keep your focus on the goals you've set, and if Jason's the right one, you'll soon know. When it's time, he'll propose," Lacey advised, worried about her friend's doubts.

"Yeah, I know. He's supposed to pick me up here in

about five minutes. You don't mind if I go off and leave you?"

"Hey, it's Saturday. You're not supposed to be working. I just needed someone to commiserate with, and I came looking for you," Lacey said, reality once again returning with the weirdness that was her family.

Amanda smiled. "I wanted to make sure everything was ready for this week."

Lacey shook her head, knowing Amanda took her position in the company seriously, and trusted her to handle all the publicity. "No, you would have been here, even if we didn't have such a busy week."

"I get a lot done over the weekend. And this week is important to Mate Incorporated."

"Yes, it could be interesting." So much was at stake this week and in the midst of a busy work week, Dean was coming home, and now she had to deal with Kerri's engagement.

Jason stuck his head around the corner of Amanda's office. "Hey, you ready to go?"

"Yeah, just a second. Let me shut down my computer."

"Hi, Lacey. How are you?"

Lacey gazed at Jason, his auburn hair reflecting tints of gold and red, a quiet, geeky kind of guy, who appeared to have a silly side to him, and she worried he would break Amanda's heart. "I'm working too hard and now I get to help plan a wedding."

"You're getting married?" he asked, his eyes widening in a surprised stunned look.

"Oh, no. It's my sister, Kerri. She graduates college in two weeks, and she's getting married in July. A rushed wedding." One she hoped to postpone for at least four years.

His lips turned up in a cocky boy grin that most women would have loved, but had no effect on her. "Aren't women good at organizing those kinds of things?"

"You sound sexist, but yes, I know I could get this wedding together. The problem is, I hope I can help her realize the value of waiting."

"Lacey, you know family members are the hardest to convince," Amanda warned and walked to Jason's side.

"Yes, but this is my baby sister."

Jason wrapped his arm around Amanda. They were a striking couple with his six foot frame and red hair and her short, five foot frame and shoulder length mahogany hair with blonde streaks. Amanda had met him at one of their seminars and so far the relationship rocked along right on track. If only he could outgrow his silliness just a bit and Amanda could loosen up, there was a chance the couple would make it. Lacey hoped for the best for her friend.

"We're leaving," he said. "I've got a night of surprises planned."

Amanda glanced at him and smiled in appreciation.

Oh yeah, they were doing great. Amanda's worries were concerning, but they were only three months into the relationship. "You guys have fun tonight."

"How much longer are you going to stay?" Amanda asked.

"I'm leaving now. I have two hours to get ready before I pick up Dean at the airport. You two aren't the only ones who are planning a night of surprises." Anticipation, excitement and desire raced through Lacey like the Indie 500, speeding her pulse rate, leaving her breathless with excitement.

Amanda and Jason gazed at each other and grinned. "See you Monday."

"You too. Bye, Jason."

"Bye, Lacey. Send me an invitation to the wedding."

"There's not going to be a wedding," she yelled after him as they walked out the door.

Lacey refused to let Kerri make the biggest mistake of her life. And she refused to let her ruin her welcome home night with Dean.

~

A buzz of warmth and excitement zipped along Lacey's spine sending shivers of anticipation through her, as she watched Dean stroll toward her at the luggage carousel. A grin the size of Texas graced her face and consumed her heart. No, he wasn't dashingly handsome, sophisticated or grizzly-bear manly. Most people considered him a nerd, yet he was a gentle man with a nice smile and a beautiful heart. At six two, he stood above the other passengers with his short dark hair and deep chocolate eyes that gleamed when he saw her. A small smile flitted across his chiseled face.

Rockets didn't go off when she saw him, but he made her happy. They both knew what they wanted in life and were on the journey together to achieve their dreams.

"Hi," he said. His voice deep and strong. "I missed you."

Dean drew her into his arms and hugged her close. He gave her a brief kiss on the lips. Tremors didn't overcome her and the earth didn't move, but the touch of his lips felt nice. A sweet kiss that she hoped promised more for later tonight.

"How was your flight?" she asked.

A girl beside him jumped into the arms of a man standing at the baggage carousel. She squealed with excitement, and then they engaged in a kiss that must have included tonsil swabbing.

Dean frowned at the public display of affection and shook his head. Lacey knew from experience he wasn't into PDA.

"Long," he responded. They stood watching the

carousel go round, the thump, thump, thump of luggage as one after another hit the belt. "It took forever to go through customs in Atlanta."

"Your trip was successful? Did you find the plants you were searching for?"

His face looked tired, his eyes bloodshot. A month had passed, and she needed some reassurance from him that nothing had changed between them.

Yes, her thoughts were irrational, but her mother's voice echoed in her head, and her sister's engagement had rocked her self-confidence. She wasn't wrong. Her whole life revolved around relationships that were sane, rational, and worked. Hers worked.

"Yes, we found what we needed. I think I've got a deal where we can harvest these plants for the company. The landowner is all grins at the offer we made him. I think management will be pleased with our results."

"Great, so you won't be returning to the rainforest anytime soon?" she asked, hoping they would have some time together. She'd missed him. She wanted some normalcy in their relationship. She wanted him home by her side. She wanted to wake up beside him in the morning.

"I wish, but until all the details are worked out, I'll be traveling back and forth between here and Sao Paulo."

A rock of disappointment sank onto her chest. She took a deep breath trying to shove the emotion away. "Oh honey, I just hate it when we're apart."

He smiled. "Yeah, I missed you too, but if I get this deal completed, then my bonus this year should be enough that I can buy that new Mercedes I've been looking at."

A Mercedes. Dean didn't mention marriage or a nice vacation or even a house, but rather a car. "That'll be nice."

What could she say? It was his bonus, and they weren't married.

His bag came around the carousel, and he grabbed it.

"Let's go. I'd like to eat some American food and hit the bed early tonight."

"I thought we'd go to that restaurant out on the lake, and then we could go back to my apartment and relax in the hot tub."

He placed his arm around her. "Love the idea of the restaurant at the lake, but I think I'm going to pass on the hot tub. I'd really like to sleep in my own bed tonight. I'm exhausted."

Another rock of disappointment landed on Lacey's chest almost knocking the breath from her lungs. Her mother's voice reverberated through her head. After being separated for a month, the lure of his own bed and a good night's rest was more tempting than sex?

"How's the relationship business?" he finally asked.

She snuggled into his side, needing to feel his body against hers. It seemed like forever since they'd experienced sex, and she craved his touch. She wasn't a needy woman, but right after her family luncheon, she required the reassurance that Dean was perfect for her.

Her mother's dysfunctional hypothesis about love, passion, and marriage had planted seeds of doubt in Lacey's mind, even though she struggled against such nonsense.

"Good. I had a man approach me about doing a documentary about my business. I'm waiting to learn more about his films before I make a decision. And one of my clients set me up with a television producer. I have an appointment with him this week about a possible television show. "

"Honey, that's great. That's been your dream all along."

"Yes, I'd love to have my own talk show." Both of them had great careers, were over-achievers, and wanted the same things in life. They were perfect for each other.

Weren't they?

"You get the television show, and when I get my bonus, we'll go to Italy," he said, his voice warm, promising, and so convincing she wondered about her doubts.

She turned and gazed at him. "Really?"

"Of course. We could spend a week traveling the countryside. It'd be fun."

According to Dean, they were unofficially engaged, though he'd not presented her with a ring or even gotten down on his knee. It was just a matter of time and Italy would be the ideal honeymoon.

They slid into her Toyota Prius, and he glanced around, his expression one of disdain. "You know, when we move in together, you should really see about getting a different car."

"Why? I like my car," she asked perplexed.

"It's not the right image for a successful television personality."

Lacey shook her head and smiled at him. God, she'd missed his pompous goal setting. "I have to get the show first."

"You will. It's what you're working towards. You'll achieve your goals," he assured her. "It's one of the things I love about you. Your determination."

Warm fluttery butterflies flew through her midsection, spreading their heat and reminding her of why Dean was so perfect for her.

"What kind of car does a successful talk show hostess drive?"

"You need a Lexus or a BMW."

"I don't know. I like my Prius. It gives me a warm fuzzy feeling like I'm doing something good for the environment."

He shrugged and gave a little sneer, his voice condescending. "It just doesn't have the right image. When you're on TV, image is everything, sweetheart."

"When I get the show, I'll consider it," she said, wishing he wasn't quite so materialistic.

"How is the apartment hunting going? You know I want a place where we can entertain," he said.

"I know, but we also need to be close to DFW."

He sighed. "Yes, I know, or we'd be searching Highland Park."

Neither of them made enough money to live in the most exclusive suburb of Dallas. "I have three properties ready for us to see. We just need to compare our schedules for the next week and decide when we can look at them."

"I'm good until Wednesday, and then I have to fly to New York for a meeting."

"Oh, I was hoping we'd get to spend more time together," she said with a sigh of disappointment.

"Yeah, me too. But I should return on Friday."

Lacey drove into the restaurant parking lot at Grapevine Lake. They got out of the car and walked toward the door.

Dean reached over and slid his finger along her cheekbone. "Let's eat, and then you can take me home and tuck me in for the night. Maybe we can have breakfast tomorrow morning and spend the day together."

She glanced at him, wondering why she'd spent so much time prepping for this date. She'd shaved, lathered on lotion and misted perfume in all the right places, anticipating a night of satisfying sex.

Lacey shot him a sly smile. "What if instead of tucking you in, I stay the night and we spend some time in between the sheets together?"

He glanced at her and grinned. "I love it when you talk dirty to me."

For a moment, she thought maybe the date could be saved, but he quickly dashed that idea.

"Frankly, I'm worn out. I'd like to sleep alone in my

bed. Maybe we can catch up on the sexual side of things tomorrow. Tonight I'm just too bushed."

What could she say? Business trips were exhausting. She wanted him to covet tearing her clothes off as much as she desired stripping him naked.

Lacey sighed, her chest tight with unshed tears. It was as if her mother were standing there handing her the bitter pill of being with Dean. Her voice echoed in her mind. *That relationship is about as exciting as a Funeral Director and an accountant at a medical convention. You'd see more action at the bowling alley.*

Never would she confess to her mother or her sister that when Dean returned after a month apart, she'd taken him home to his apartment with no sex. To them, it would only confirm that this relationship lacked passion.

And there was passion. Wasn't there? So why did this feel wrong?

Another pleasure-filled evening spent with BOB-her battery operated boyfriend-awaited her.

Chapter Three

On Monday, as the film credits rolled Lacey sat stunned, her brain reeling, her stomach churning from the power of Reed Hunter's work. The man had deftly showed the bankers cheating the American Government during the bank collapse. Shocked by the man's talent, she turned to Amanda. "He's a great filmmaker."

Amanda stretched in her chair and yawned. "Reed Hunter films things that are controversial, and puts an edge on the subject matter. I never thought about financial reform that way. Now I'm ready to fire my banker and my broker."

Lacey couldn't help but frown as she popped the CD out of the DVD player. Her mind churned in a thousand directions, challenging, searching, and suspecting everything about Reed Hunter's motives. "Why does Mr. Hunter want to film relationship coaches? We teach people how to find the right person. Why is he interested in doing a project on people, rather than corporations or morality?"

Amanda shrugged her shoulders like even a simpleton knew the answer. "We help people look realistically at love. We don't solve world peace."

"For some people, we are tampering with destiny," Lacey said, still considering why Mr. Hunter wanted to film her business.

"A divorce destiny maybe. What do you think? Should we do this documentary?" Amanda asked.

Lacey sank onto the couch, her mind still in that mental warp exploring all the possible reasons why he would do a film about her business.

"I can't make a decision yet. I need to know how Mr. Hunter's going to portray us. If he's here to ridicule what we do, then no, he can find some other sucker to film."

"Dang, I was looking forward to spending several

months of staring dreamily at him. He's not hard on the eyes." She stood and stretched, raising her arms above her head.

"You're in a committed relationship," Lacey reminded her friend. Yes, looking at Reed Hunter was anything but hard on the eyes.

"That doesn't mean I can't enjoy the scenery."

"Hot, sexy, with a six-pack that begs me to take a drink. Mr. Hunter is well aware of his attraction to the ladies," Lacey said, a tingly flush of heat dancing along her nerves. She was in a committed relationship.

Amanda laughed, her hazel eyes shining with a mischievous sparkle that matched her smile. "Yeah, I knew you'd pick up on that right away. And speaking of committed relationships, you're in one as well."

"Men like him are dangerous. I can look at them all day, but that doesn't mean I want to sample the merchandise," Lacey replied, thinking of her mother and the men that had traipsed through their lives.

"How did your date with Dean go? Did you guys catch up?"

Lacey put her fingers to the bridge of her nose and shook her head, still trying to understand what had happened the other night. "Dean caught up on his sleep. We went to dinner, and then he went home alone to rest. We had plans for Sunday, but an emergency came up and he flew to New York."

Every time she thought of their date, her chest tightened and her mother's voice vibrated through her head. *No passion.* Dean's career was important, but what about the two of them?

"I'm sorry. Jason and I went to dinner, then to the baseball game. He loves the Rangers." Amanda twisted a pencil in her hand and shook her head. "I reminded him how much I dislike baseball. To which he responded, '*But it's the Rangers playing the Yankees.*' Later, he redeemed himself by giving me the best damn sex I've ever experienced."

Lacey sighed all her pent-up frustration rolling through her like a locomotive. Thirty long days had passed since she and Dean had actually spent time in a bed together. Between his job and her job, it seemed that either they were too tired or one of them was out of town.

"An orgasm sounds wonderful. I wish my weekend had sex in it. We've got to find some time to spend together this week. Of course, Dean did promise me if I got this TV show we would go to Italy."

"Hey, that would be fun."

"Yeah, but there's no guarantee for a television show," Lacey said, trying to keep her case of nerves under control. She wanted this show more than her next breath. More than Dean.

Wow! Where had that thought come from?

"Do you have the proposal ready?"

"Mailed him a DVD of my group and individual sessions and sent a proposal along with the DVD of what the show would entail over a week ago."

"And your appointment is the day after tomorrow?" Amanda asked, her eyes drawn together, her expression serious.

"Yes. Let's hope that either TLC or the Oxygen channel will consider a couple of test shows." Lacey's heart and soul and brains had been a part of the proposal she'd personally delivered. If only one channel would deem interest in her dream.

"When do you meet with Reed Hunter again?" Amanda asked.

She rubbed the back of her neck and sighed her heart dancing the carumbai in her chest. "He's on the schedule for tomorrow. Seriously, I may turn him down. There's no point in taking a chance on how he's going to portray us if we get the television show."

"Agreed. After watching his filmmaking style, I want to be certain he's not going to make us look as bad as those bankers. He really showed them as greedy bastards."

Lacey nodded and stood, smoothing imaginary wrinkles out of her skirt. "I get enough grief from my mother. It would confirm for her that…that love is not a choice, but a chance meeting of two people's souls on the highway of life."

Amanda laughed. "Gag me! My soul keeps finding the wrong men."

"Yes, well, my perfect match has left town again. I just hope he gets back before I have to leave next week." No time for the two of them. No time for sex. No time to spend with Lacey. So far his homecoming had been less than stellar.

"And if he doesn't?"

"Then it will be another two weeks before we get time with each other. Two long, lonely weeks."

In addition to the month they'd already spent apart. Her stomach clenched and her body shivered. Why did he seem so distant?

~

Reed walked into the offices of Mate Incorporated. Beige and blue overstuffed chairs and paintings meant to soothe visitors graced the hunter-blue walls. He felt as if he'd walked into a doctor's office-a love doctor who cheated people out of their money.

"Can I help you?" the receptionist asked.

"I have an appointment with Lacey Morgan," Reed said, realizing the receptionist probably thought he was a new client. Like he'd ever use a dating service. Women were easy to find- toss them a smile, buy them a drink, and ask questions about their life. Just a little personal attention, and they were yours.

He smiled, wondering how many men actually came into her business.

"Your name?" she asked, looking up at him with a professional disinterested expression on her face.

"Reed Hunter."

The young, blonde woman picked up the phone and called Lacey. "Mr. Hunter is here to see you." She waited a minute. "Okay, I'll show him the way."

"Please follow me to the conference room where Lacey will join us in five minutes. Right this way." The receptionist led him down a hall. "Can I get you something to drink?"

"No, thanks. How long have you worked here?" he asked turning on the charm. Getting one of the employees to give him dirt would be like hitting gold.

"Lacey is my sister."

The charm came to a screeching halt as his blood froze and he shelved any ideas of coercing information from an employee for now.

"I help out in the afternoons after classes."

"Attending college?" Reed asked. Until now, he hadn't seen the resemblance between the two women and he wondered how much information he could obtain from the sister.

"Yes. I graduate this weekend."

"After you graduate, do you plan on working here full-time?" he casually asked hoping that if they accepted his proposal, he could befriend the young woman and eventually he would become her confidante.

"Oh, no. I'm getting married and going to medical school," she told him, her smile making her face glow.

"Marriage and medical school. That's a full load." He paused, considering what she'd just told him. "Did you meet your fiancé through Mate Incorporated?"

"We met in college. We're both about to graduate."

"How did your sister became a relationship coach?" he asked, wondering how much she would tell.

"Lacey saw a need that ordinary counseling wasn't addressing, and she's built a business around helping people. She's quite successful."

"You're getting married without going through her coaching? Why not?" he asked, digging deeper, trying to find out why an employee, her sister, had not gone through her relationship practice.

"Are you a new client?" she asked, her brows gathering.

Reed couldn't help but smile. "No."

She took a moment to assess him as they walked down the hall. "I wasn't looking for a relationship. It found me. Lacey is great at finding someone for her clients, but me, I found my fiancé at college."

"When's the big day?"

"June. Right before I go to medical school."

"Being married and going to medical school…won't that be difficult?" he asked as they entered a large conference room.

"We think we can handle marriage and school."

"What does your sister think?" He watched the conflicting emotions cross her face and realized he'd found a subject that he'd like to explore.

Lacey walked through the doorway and frowned at her sister. "Thanks, Kerri. I think the phone's ringing."

Kerri ducked her head and exited. Tension seemed to vibrate in the air between the two women. And Reed knew he needed to see if he could arrange time to talk with Kerri more.

"She's a sweet girl. I didn't see the resemblance at first."

"Thank you. Kerri works part-time for me while she goes to school." Lacey pointed to a chair. "Please be seated."

She sat across from him. "Amanda will join us momentarily."

"Did you get the DVDs?"

"Yes. We watched them together. You're a good filmmaker," she said her voice sincere. "But the film we watched and from what I've learned about you, you usually do exposé types of films. Why the sudden interest in relationship coaches."

He shrugged. "When you do so many exposés in a row, you begin to think the whole human race is nothing but jerks. I needed something lighter. A film that would leave my audience feeling good."

He cringed inside, thinking maybe that last line was a little over the top.

A tingle of warning seemed to vibrate through him. Her demeanor seemed more subdued as if she'd already made her decision and it wasn't in his favor.

"What do you know about relationship coaches?" she asked.

"I've been doing some research. It's a growing new field. You're not counselors. There are no requirements for a degree in psychology or psychotherapy. You help people recognize what is wrong in their relationships. You help them to realize what they want in a partner."

"You've done your research," Lacey said her brows drew together in a contemplative expression. "Tell me. What's your slant with this film?"

Reed choose his words carefully, knowing that whatever he said here would later come back to haunt him.

"I'm going to focus on how you help couples find each other. How you help individuals realize what they expect or want in a relationship. We'll show some couples who have met during the process. I want to show the different aspects of your business and how everything you do is centered on the relationship."

Amanda stepped into the room and sat. She smiled at Reed, her expression a business mask. He'd been unable to read from either Lacey's or Amanda's facial clues if they were going to consent to him filming Mate Incorporated.

"What would you need from us?" Lacey asked.

"I need complete access to you. We would film your seminars. I'd have a camera-man trailing you at all times," Reed said.

She leaned back to study him, and Reed knew she was tempted, but something held her back. He needed to erase the doubts and concerns he could see in her body language and hear in her voice.

Her brows drew together, and her blue eyes gave him an intense look as if she were searching deep within him. "How will I know what you're filming is going to be a positive representation of us? How do I know you're not going to reveal us as matchmakers who are only in this for the money and not in it for helping people?"

Reed took a deep breath and pushed away the guilt that gnawed at his stomach lining. He hated lying, even though it was sometimes necessary in order for him to get the footage he required for a film. Lying went against his principles and left him feeling slimy. "You don't. You'll have to trust me. I'll let you see the final product before I send it out to theaters."

"But if I want to change anything, will I be allowed to make any final cuts or changes?"

Gullible wasn't one of her traits. Appearing intelligent and accurate at reading people, Lacey Morgan was indeed thorough. He gained a new respect for her.

"You're free to make any suggestions, but I'll have the final editorial say in what the film will show. After all, it will have my name on it, and Graham Productions is producing the documentary."

She took her pencil and doodled on the paper in front of her, considering his words, and finally raised her gaze to his. "Reed, do you have a girlfriend or a significant person in your life?"

Reed squirmed in his chair, wondering about this new line of questioning. "Not right this moment."

"What kind of person are you looking for?"

He shrugged, not really wanting to answer her questions. "What does it matter? I'm not a client."

She smiled, her blue eyes penetrating, yet a soft expression on her face. "It helps me to understand you, your personal prejudices and what kind of slant you might put on the film."

The way she watched him made him uncomfortable. He knew he had to respond or lose the chance to film her. "I want someone who realizes that my life is my work. I want someone who understands when I'm gone for two to three months at a time filming a documentary. I want someone who is there for me when I need her," he said, surprised by how easy it was to tell her what he wanted in a woman, although he never intended to find this mystery person.

Lacey considered him for a long moment. "As long as someone is taking care of you, then the relationship fulfills all your needs. But what about the other person's needs? What if your girlfriend wants you home to spend time with her? What about marriage and kids?"

"I have no plans on getting married, and I don't want kids."

"Well, you're clear about that," she said. "Do you believe in relationship coaching?"

The question was slipped in amongst the personal questions, and he knew this was the decision-maker. He swallowed and tried to keep his facial expression unreadable, but knew he'd failed when she raised her brows at him. "I think it may work for people who need it, but I know what I want in a relationship. So I'm not a good candidate."

"Yes, I think you know exactly what you want in a relationship." She sighed and pushed back the strand of hair that had fallen in her face. "I appreciate your offer of doing a documentary about my business, but now is not a good time. I think I'm going to have to pass on this opportunity."

Reed sat there dumbfounded and realized she didn't feel comfortable with him. In all his years of doing documentaries, he'd never had anyone turn him down when asked to be the subject.

"You're turning me down because I'm not a good candidate for your business?" he asked, knowing his response had been the deathblow. Even the most egotistical dictators who had known Reed was going to do everything he could to expose them for crimes against humanity, had worked with him, trying to make him believe they were honest people.

"No. It's just not right for me at this time," she said.

He stood, not knowing what to say. Determination filled his lungs and expanded his chest as he rebounded like a basketball player on steroids. He would make this documentary with or without her. But first, he had to play nice. "I'm sorry that's your decision. Could I at least interview you?"

"Not now, but maybe in a couple of weeks."

Reed reached for her hand and wrapped his large palm around hers. He slipped her a business card. "If you change your mind, you can reach me at the number printed on the card."

"Thanks. I appreciate your interest in my business, but I think we need to pass."

A rush of anger charged through him, causing him to freeze like a tin man as he tried to remain cordial. "I'm disappointed. You were the best relationship coach I researched."

"Thank you," Lacey said, standing.

"See you around," he said, and Amanda walked him to the front office door.

Although Lacey thought they were done, Reed would find a way to film this documentary. Her crimes might be minor compared to some people he'd filmed, but her transgressions affected people's emotions. They were personal.

He lifted his chin and walked to the car, dauntless conviction in every step. He would film this documentary. He would not be denied.

~

Lacey wasn't certain if she'd just made the biggest mistake of her life or if she'd done the right thing. The publicity would put her business in the public spotlight, but it felt as if she were taking a leap off a cliff into a dark hole. When Reed told her he wasn't in a relationship, alarms had gone off like sirens in the middle of the night.

Amanda burst through the door, concern reflected from her hazel eyes. "You doubt your decision, don't you?"

"You know me well. He doesn't believe in what we do." Men like Reed Hunter didn't believe in relationship coaches because they didn't think they needed help.

"Maybe. He's also the type of man who is your best client."

"Yes, but only when a girlfriend or wife drags men like him in here kicking and screaming," Lacey said as she pushed back her hair. If she'd read him correctly, he only wanted a girlfriend for sex. And even the most risqué of women grew bored of men who only wanted sex.

"I think you could change him," Amanda said.

"He's not a client. He would be filming us, and I couldn't trust him to show the business in a positive way." Doubt assailed her and she clenched her teeth. What if she'd just made the biggest mistake of her life? What if he would have filmed her business in a positive way? What if he'd trashed her business and she'd lost all of her clients.

She took a deep steadying breath suddenly trusting her gut and knowing she'd made the best possible decision.

Amanda shrugged. "Well, at least we've still got that chance with the television producer."

"I'm nervous about that deal. I want that show badly and it's not good when all my hopes are on one project," Lacey responded, her stomach clenching with nerves at the thought of her own television show. This was her dream, her big career goal.

"Well, I have a new list of cities we're taking the road show to, so that should excite you," Amanda said her expression teasing, her voice trying for excitement.

Lacey gazed at her best friend and groaned. "I'm trying to feel the love. I know its great exposure, but traveling is so tiresome."

"We're scheduled for a week on the road, and then we return home."

"That's not too bad."

"When is Dean returning?"

"His plans changed again. He'll be in tonight. Tomorrow, we're going to take some time off and go look at one of the apartments I've found."

"So, you're going through with moving in together?"

Doubts assailed Lacey, like a hail storm battering a roof in spring. Yet, Dean was her perfect match. The man who fit all her criteria. Recently they'd hit a rough patch and all relationships occasionally had trouble.

"Yeah, he convinced me it's the next step. What about

you and Jason?"

"We're not moving in together. We're enjoying each other's company, and if he asked, I'd say no."

"You haven't discovered he's a sex fiend with a closet full of whips and chains, have you?"

Amanda laughed. "No, that was the last boyfriend. So far, Jason's normal. Have you told your mother yet that you and Dean are moving in together?"

Shudders skittered through Lacey leaving her cold, like the temperature had dropped fifty degrees.

"Are you kidding me? At Kerri's lunch, we snapped at each other. I decided to wait until later. I'm not ready for the lecture on why should he buy the cow, when he's getting the milk for free." Even though she was in her late twenties, she would catch hell from her mother for this decision.

"Because you're not sure you want to buy the bull."

Lacey grimaced at Amanda. "Funny. I'd rather find out before I go down the aisle than after."

"Amen. If the meeting with the producer doesn't go well, are you going to be okay with your decision not to do the documentary?" she questioned.

Lacey squirmed as turmoil ripped through her. Her gut instincts seemed to have gone on vacation. The idea of doing this documentary had been exciting, yet frightening at the same time. Turning Reed down had been gut wrenching. But his last responses to her questions had shown her he didn't believe in what they were doing.

"I don't know. The company is growing, though slower than I had anticipated, and I want Mate Incorporated to be successful. I just think television is our next venue, and we need to do whatever we can to get there. The bottom line is I didn't trust Reed Hunter."

~

"Did she take the deal?" Graham Turner, owner of Graham Productions, asked, sitting behind his big desk, making deals, creating story ideas, and changing or destroying lives.

Reed's stomach plummeted; his lungs no longer sucked air as he sat down across from his boss. He sighed. "No, she turned me down."

"Crap!" Graham said.

"But, I can still film most of it without her. And I'm going to see if I can convince a couple of employees to speak with me on camera. I think we can still do this without her help."

Reed didn't like doing individual, emotional subjects for films. He enjoyed taking down dictators and exposing unfair trade practices.

"I'd rather she was in there helping us, and then we slammed her with the information. But you do what you can. Just put this bitch out of business."

He especially didn't enjoy filming something so malicious toward a woman. Something that if not done properly could create a backlash that could ruin someone's career or make their life a living hell.

"Agreed. And the next film, I can choose any subject I want."

"You are in total control of your next film," Graham promised him.

How could he turn down the opportunity to pick and choose his next documentary subject?

"Ruin her, Reed. I lost Juliet because of this woman. Make the bitch suffer."

Chapter Four

Reed glanced at his production schedule. He'd been refining it for several weeks. Now with Lacey Morgan out of the picture, he was revising it once again. Still he intended to show the folly of using a "Coach" for anything other than sports. There were life coaches, spiritual coaches, wellness coaches, career coaches, you name it and they were out there. But what credentials did these people have?

Ty stuck his head in the office. "Hey man, how's it coming?"

"Almost done. We're still going for the same approach. I want to show how these people are making large sums of money on innocent people. It's a sham," he said with vigor. Plus, it had cost him a girlfriend and more importantly his boss a girlfriend. Damn, he missed sex. "How did the meeting go?"

Though Ty was the cameraman, they worked together, and when Reed couldn't get to a meeting, Ty would step in and take over. They had a great business relationship and worked everything out between them. Except the editing. Reed did all the post-production work. This kept their costs down and their profits higher.

"I didn't have time to listen to Graham's Christmas list of what he wanted in the film."

"It's lengthy."

"Knowing Graham, I'm sure it is."

"Are you okay with changing the focus?" Ty asked.

What choice did Reed have? He may not be able to film Lacey's corporation, but if he had enough interviews with dissatisfied members, then he would say she refused an on-camera interview to tell her side.

"I'm flexible. But I'm still going to show 'Mate Incorporated' with its leader Lacey Morgan. Two disgruntled members have agreed to on-camera interviews, and I'm hoping an employee will come forward."

An uncomfortable moment of silence stretched between them, alerting Reed that something bothered his friend.

"In the past, you were more interested in showing the world something you thought was morally wrong. But what's the harm in what Lacey's doing?" Ty asked. "Yeah, your girlfriend dumped you because of Lacey, but her reasons were legit."

For a moment, Reed was stunned, and he fairly exploded. "Why is a relationship coach telling women how to choose a partner? She has a certificate. Big whoop! A piece of paper, not a degree in psychotherapy."

Ty rubbed his chin and frowned. "I don't think what she's doing is all that wrong. There are a lot of dating services that offer the same or even less than her company, and they don't give you any guidelines on choosing the right person."

Ty stepped into his office, and Reed whirled in his chair to face him. It wasn't often they disagreed.

"Good because I'm going to compare this 'coach' crap to a dating service and show how what she offers is a glorified dating service where you pay more. And dating services, who needs them?"

Ty glanced away and shrugged, his face relaxed. "Fair enough. But I have a buddy who met his wife on one of those on-line companies."

Reed rolled his eyes. What kind of man used a dating service? "I consider those places man-bait shops. They provide the hook, the bait, and the reel. Your friend was a sucker. He got caught."

"He's happy," Ty said, leaning against the door frame. "He's married and getting sex every night. That's more than us."

"He's trapped."

Ty shook his head. "Sometimes I think being trapped has its advantages."

"You just need to get laid," Reed said, laughing at his cameraman.

"Definitely," Ty said with a sigh and changed the subject. "When do we begin production?"

"I'm working on the shooting schedule now. Our first meeting with the crew should happen next week. And then we begin."

Reed wanted to get this film completed, so he could begin a documentary he had longed to do for several years. He longed to shoot a film comparing European and American tax structures.

"This is our fifth documentary together," Ty said, his voice raising, "and I've been excited about working on all of them, but this time, I have a bad vibe, man. I don't know. I hope this project doesn't blow up in our faces."

There was only one thing about Ty that got on Reed's nerves. His bad vibes. Every film had a vibe, and at the beginning, they were always catastrophic. Every film he was certain would be their last film. Every film would be a disaster.

"You're always nervous in the beginning. Remember when we were shooting that dictator in Africa? You were so afraid you threw up three times before we even got on the plane."

Ty's brows raised, his eyes widened. "Hell, yes, I was afraid. If he didn't like you, you'd face a firing squad. I kept envisioning my brains splattered on the ground."

Reed shook his head. "And when we went to Russia to film the sex slave trade, I thought you were going to skip town on me before we finished."

Throwing up his hands, Ty said, "When some guy threatens to cut us up into fish bait, it kind of freaked me out."

"You get freaked out every single time before we start shooting. You should be thankful this time we're staying here in the good ole USA and not traveling to some third world country," Reed said, blowing off his friend's concerns.

Filming Mate Incorporated would be the easiest documentary he'd produced.

"Ruining someone's life in my own neighborhood means nothing?" Ty asked, his voice rising. "What if they have a father or brother who doesn't appreciate our talent? I don't mean to sound negative…"

Reed gritted his teeth, tension ricocheting like a tennis ball inside his body, bouncing off his organs. The urge to grab Ty's camera and film him, just so he could play back this nonsense after they were finished, consumed him. "Then shut-up. We start production in a week, and we're going to show how relationship coaches are nothing more than high-priced dating clubs."

"Dating clubs have some great looking women."

Reed gazed over at his cameraman, not certain he understood what Ty was trying to tell him. "Have you tried a dating club?"

Ty nodded. "My date was a smoking hot babe that never returned my phone calls."

Reed stared at Ty in surprise. "Really?"

"Yeah, I also tried online dating. But it sucked."

"Then find girls the old fashioned way. Go to a bar!"

~

Lacey glanced around the exterior office of Chimney Rock Productions nervously while she tried to appear interested in a gossip magazine. She couldn't tell you who graced the cover.

She had worn her best looking cream slacks with a peach tailored shirt and cream heels. The shirt accentuated her slender figure and made her complexion glow. Amanda had said she looked professional this morning.

Pictures of the different productions Stan Whitaker had been involved with hung on the walls. He'd done everything from comedy to reality TV. Nerves whirred in her stomach like a blender on high. Someday her show could be displayed on that wall.

"Ms. Morgan, Mr. Whitaker is ready for you," his secretary said, waiting to escort her to his office.

Lacey stood, her knees quaking, her stomach whirring, her heart jumping like she'd run a red light. Her body reflected DEFCON 1 on the anxiety front.

She smiled and followed the secretary, focusing on deep, calm, steadying breaths. She'd prepared a kick-ass proposal, and now the show was in fate's hands.

Entering his office, she spotted a picture of her client Linda Whitaker, sitting on his desk. Because of Lacey's work, Linda had met Stan, and the two of them had married over a year ago. So in a roundabout way, Stan was a product of her coaching.

As he talked on the phone, he motioned for her to sit down. "Listen, I have to go, but I need those numbers faxed to me today before five o'clock." He paused to listen to the other person. "Okay, thanks."

He hung up the phone, stood and walked around the desk to grasp her hand. "Hello, I'm Stan Whitaker."

"Nice to meet you, Stan."

"Linda told me all about how you worked with her to find the right guy and look how that turned out. We're celebrating anniversary number two next month in Hawaii."

"Congratulations."

"Thanks, I'm a lucky guy."

"Linda was one of my brightest clients. She learned quickly."

Enough of the chit-chat, she wanted to rush him to the nitty-gritty. She wanted to know what he thought of her proposal. Did she have a chance at a television program of her own?

He walked around his desk and returned to his chair. "Tell me about your business."

"I've been a relationship coach for five years. Currently, I have about twenty-five people I'm working with. I give one to two lectures a week on dating. In my matchmaking division, I have over three hundred clients searching for a mate. Last year was our best year ever, even in a down economy."

His face was blank of emotion, and all her training of reading people failed her.

Then he sat back and gave her a smile, his brown eyes gazing at her. "Impressive. I went over your proposal, and I must admit I'm intrigued. Your show idea is sound."

Lacey's heart did a little mambo dance of excitement, and her knees joined in the steps, shaking. She pressed them together. "Great."

"I took the liberty of showing your proposal and DVD to several networks I work closely with, and they expressed interest. We even discussed a pilot program to see the audience reaction."

He took a deep breath, and she sensed a "but" coming.

"They liked the idea, but they didn't recognize your name or the name of your business. They kept asking about your credentials. How long had you been in practice, etc? In this economic climate, no one is willing to take a chance on an unknown," he said, his voice all business as he placed his hands on top of the desk and clasped them together.

She frowned, her excitement plummeting like an elevator in free fall. "But my practice is growing. I thought the show would make me well-known and increase my business.”

Aargh, how could she become well-known without working even harder? This would mean more seminars, more traveling, and more time spent working one-on-one with couples. Seven days a week appeared to be her future.

“Yes, it would, but they want you to have a certain amount of fame, name recognition, before they spend several hundreds of thousands of dollars producing a television show.”

Lacey wanted this so bad she would have put up her own money for the production, if she had enough.

“How can I increase my notoriety enough to make them want to do this show?” Lacey asked, wanting him to confirm what she already knew.

“Your bio says you’re doing seminars in multiple cities,” Stan said.

“Yes,” she replied, grasping at ideas like a cat in a fish bowl. Her chest tight with disappointment.

“You’ve got to grow your audience in every city. Maybe even expand the number of cities in which you hold seminars.”

Like a lightning bolt, Reed Hunter’s face appeared in her mind. “What if I told you I have a filmmaker interested in doing a documentary on relationship coaches and wants to film my business?”

“Who?”

“Have you ever heard of Reed Hunter?”

She watched the name recognition appear on his face and sighed, knowing she’d made a huge blunder.

“God, yes. He’s done several documentaries for PBS, and his last one, the collapse of the financial system, got him nominated for a film award.”

“I turned him down,” she said. Stupid, stupid, stupid, she thought, despair wrenching her insides into a pretzel.

Stan’s eyes widened.

"I wasn't certain about the angle he intended to show my business. It wouldn't be good if he destroyed my business. And I wanted to use my time on this show, not on a documentary." The words poured from her mouth like a flash flood.

"Can you contact Mr. Hunter and tell him you've changed your mind? I can almost guarantee I'll have a network interested in buying the show once they find out about the documentary."

Oh God, to go crawling back to that egotistical good-looking man who didn't believe in what she was doing, but thought he could convince her of his credence.

"How long do documentaries take to film?"

"It can depend, but usually a couple of months, and then a month is spent on editing and final film production. His documentary could be in theaters or purchased by one of the networks no later than six months down the road."

Six months down the road, she could either have her business booming or looking for a place to hide, from Mr. Hunter's exposé. What choice did she have? She had an opportunity that could be good, or it could be incredibly bad.

"In the meantime, I'll go back to the networks and tell them you have a documentary on your business coming out. This could be their last chance at this show." He smiled. "I think we'll get an offer."

All her uncertainties rushed through her, seizing her lungs, her heart, her brain in a painful grip. She could lose everything.

"But what if it's not good? I mean if he trashes my business, then no network is going to want me," she said, her fear rising like an elevator racing to the top floor.

Stan took a deep breath. "Yes, that wouldn't be good. Sometimes you have to take a chance to get what you want. You have to decide if you're willing to let this man film your business and possibly get a network show, or film your business and possibly be ruined. It's your decision."

Great! Even he realized she was taking a huge risk.

"And you think if I do this documentary, you can get me that television show I'm wanting?"

Stan smiled at her and nodded reassuringly. "The network liked the idea of your show; they just want someone with better name recognition. If you're in a documentary that has worldwide distribution, you and your business will be stars."

Lacey bit her lip. Part of her wanted to jump up and down, and part of her was screaming, you're risking everything. But sometimes to achieve your dreams, you had to take big risks.

She took a deep breath and released it slowly. "I'll contact Reed and hope and pray he still wants to use my business."

No risk, no pain, no gain. She would either have a successful business or be looking for a job in six months. Like a gambler in Vegas, she was rolling the dice.

"Yes, do that right away. If he says no, call me and let me know."

"Hopefully, he's still interested. It hasn't been that long. You'll approach the networks once I find out Reed is willing to film my business?"

"Yes. We could have a deal by the time the documentary is finished filming."

Lacey grinned, her heart fluttering inside her chest. God, she hoped she was making the right decision. "I can't believe this is really happening. My dream could be coming true. This should make my business flourish."

He laughed and stood, letting her know their interview was over. She rose her knees still knocking, but not from nerves. This time it was from excitement.

"Oh, I think you're going to be surprised at how this

will affect your business. You may need to consider adding more staff."

Walking her to the door, he said, "Call me after you talk to Reed and get the documentary finalized. That's the key to making this happen."

~

Lacey rode down the elevator, her mouth turned up in a grin that must have been blinding to the people around her. Sure, she was afraid Reed had found another relationship coach, but they were so close to achieving her dream. He couldn't have found someone else. She would throw herself at his feet and beg if that's what it took to be part of his film.

Barely concealed restraint kept her from yanking her cell phone out and calling Amanda. Excitement danced like it was Carnival season in Brazil along her nerve endings, making her legs want to break out in a dance in the parking garage. She forced herself to remain calm until she reached her car.

She ran to her car, jumped in, and slammed the door shut. She released the scream of excitement bottled inside. People around her must have thought she was nuts, but who cared. She was close to realizing her dream.

Finally, she pressed the Bluetooth in her car.

"Hello," Amanda said.

"Are you ready for television?"

"Oh, my God, he's going to do the show?"

"Well, not yet, but we're close. The problem we have is name recognition. When I mentioned we'd had the offer of a documentary, Stan reacted like a thousand watts had zapped him. Once the networks learn a documentary will be coming out about us in four to six months, he thinks we'll have a deal."

"But you turned that down," Amanda said,

disappointment vibrating loud and clear through the car.

"Yes, I did. His card is in my top desk drawer. Call him and tell him I need to meet with him immediately. Today, tonight, tomorrow, just as soon as possible."

"What if he's found someone else?"

"What if he hasn't?" Lacey responded, trying to remain upbeat and optimistic. "Call him. Now."

"I'm on it, boss."

The phone line went dead.

Lacey grinned as she drove to her next appointment. She needed to research documentaries. She didn't want to be a complete idiot when it came to what Reed would be doing, besides following her around and filming her. Now she needed to choose which of her clients she thought would work well with the camera crew.

But first she had to cinch the deal with Reed.

~

Reed's cell phone rang, and he glanced down at the number, Mate Incorporated. He let the call go to voice mail, wondering what they wanted. The scene sequence for the documentary was completed. So far he'd found two disgruntled clients of Lacey's company. He'd lined up a psychotherapist to talk about the differences between coaches and therapy. Dr. Lewin had repeated there was no accreditation or even a governing body to regulate relationship coaches. Anyone could hang out a shingle with promises they would help you find the person of your dreams.

Filming Lacey's business would have been easier, the film would have been better, but he'd find a way to get what he needed.

His phone beeped, letting him know there was a message. Reed dialed his voice messages and heard Lacey's assistant ask him to call her. Lacey wanted to schedule another meeting with him.

Reed smiled. Two could play this cat and mouse game. He glanced at his watch. It was ten. This morning he had errands to run, and later this afternoon, his high school filmmaking club met. Lacey Morgan would just have to wait.

~

Lacey tried her best to show interest in the apartment she and Dean were being shown. A nice three-bedroom with a study, fireplace, twenty-five hundred square feet, in one of the nicest areas. The apartment even had a garage for one of their automobiles.

The agent switched on the lights as she walked through the apartment. "This is our largest apartment. We have washer/dryer hookups and, if you don't own your own, we have a rental company that offers them to you at twenty-five dollars a month. Our leases are twelve months and require a credit check, insurance, and one month's deposit."

"What do you think, honey?" Dean asked her as they strolled through the sprawling apartment.

She glanced at her watch. Six hours had passed, and Reed had yet to return her or Amanda's calls.

Dean frowned at her. "Lacey, honey, are you with me? Do you like it?"

"It's nice. The rooms are the right size, I like the kitchen, but this is the first one we've seen. I think we should look at several apartments before we decide."

He shook his head, obviously disappointed, and smiled at the apartment complex rental agent. "Thanks for your time. We'll let you know."

"No problem. Here's my card."

They walked back to his Jeep. "I really liked that apartment. It had everything we're wanting."

"It's the first one we've seen. We may come back to it, or there could be one we like better that we've yet to see."

"But what if this one is rented by then?"

"There will be others."

She realized he was on the verge of being mad. "Do you want to go back and sign the lease? Are you ready to take that step?"

He frowned. "I guess not. You seem distracted today."

Like he'd never been distracted? How many times had she waited for him? Missed him? Well, he could just damn well be understanding of her today.

She sighed. This waiting was getting to her, and if she wasn't careful, she'd take it out on Dean.

"I'm sorry. I told you I'm waiting to hear back from Reed Hunter about the documentary. Everything depends on getting this film." Lacey bit her lip. "I should have just done the damn thing."

"Why did you turn it down?" he asked perplexed.

Now, he wanted to second-guess her. Now, when he hadn't been here when she was wrestling with the idea.

"I…I don't know. I wasn't certain how he would depict my business. I knew I had this meeting with the television director, so I went with my gut. Now, I'm regretting my decision."

"What's changed? Do you know any more about this documentary?" Dean asked.

"What's changed is that I need his documentary to get my television show. He's not the type of man who appreciates what I do. For all I know, he could show my business as a simple dating service, taking people's money and playing with their emotions."

So much was riding on this documentary, and it was all out of her control. All she could do was speak to Reed and try to get a feel for him once again.

"But you're going to take the chance because of the

television show."

"Probably."

"And if he is doing a documentary about you as a scheming, money-making, date shop, what then? Have you got a back-up plan?"

The possibility of someone smearing the business she'd built from nothing was unthinkable, and her chest tightened in fear. Nothing could be worse. She'd experienced people who didn't believe in her business. But usually after meeting her, hearing her success stories, and the results of her system, they admitted she changed lives. She helped people find mates that had meaningful partnerships. She put people together for life.

Frustration nipped at her like a dog biting her ankles, and she all but snapped at Dean. "I don't know. I have no back-up plan. I'd want to help Mr. Hunter make the best documentary ever as long as it has a positive message about my company."

Dean glanced over at her. "You're taking a big chance, aren't you?"

She must be making Dean miserable, but she couldn't help herself. Everything was so unsettled. Once she talked to Reed and could put this anxiety behind her, she'd be fine. But everything hinged on a man she'd known a week.

"Yes." She glanced over at him, suddenly feeling remorseful for her crankiness. "I'm sorry if I haven't been very attentive or even excited about looking at this apartment today. You deserve my full attention. We're about to embark on a new life together, and I should be focused on you."

He pulled the Jeep out into traffic on the freeway, and then gazed at her. "That's what I love about you. Even when you're at your worst, you realize the problem and accept your part. You make me feel good."

She smiled at him. "You're welcome. Now where are

you taking me for dinner? I'm starved, and I promise to think only of us."

"How about the—"

Her ring tone started playing, and she grabbed her cell phone from her purse. "Hello."

"Reed Hunter."

Immediately, she felt a sense of relief. Finally, he was calling, and she could make some decisions. "Hello, Mr. Hunter. How are you this afternoon?"

"I'm well, thank you. Your marketing director, Amanda, called and said you wanted to meet again. Can I ask what this is about?"

"Mr. Hunter, I've reconsidered. I'd like to discuss the possibility of doing your documentary. But before I make my decision, there are some things we need to discuss."

"How about dinner tonight?"

Lacey glanced at Dean. His forehead drew together in a frown. God, she wanted to go, but how could she go off and leave Dean? Yet, how could she wait another day without knowing or making a decision?

Dean mouthed at her, obviously hearing their conversation. "It's okay. Go if you need to."

"What time?"

"How about seven thirty?"

Lacey glanced at her watch and realized that would give her two hours to get ready and get to the restaurant. "Where?"

"I'll meet you at Brucelli's."

"I'll see you at seven thirty," she said almost giggly with relief. Either way, at least a decision would soon be made.

"I'll be there," he said and disconnected.

Lacey glanced at Dean, a smile on her face. "Thanks, honey, I really appreciate this. I promise you once I get this settled, we'll find that apartment, and soon we'll be

across his handsome face.

Relationships, women, dating—none of these topics appeared to bring about any expressions of excitement or even enthusiasm. Reed seemed distant at the mention of marriage or girlfriends.

Lacey smiled. "Yes, it is a restaurant that specializes in romance."

More like seduction, but she would never tell him that.

"They also have outstanding food," he reiterated.

"You said you used to bring your girlfriend here."

"We're no longer together."

"I'm sorry to hear that."

He shrugged. "No sweat."

A careless attitude that made her wonder what brought about the couple's demise. He'd either been hurt really bad or simply hid his feelings very well.

"What about yourself? Are you currently in a relationship? Married?" he asked.

"I'm in a committed relationship, but I've never married. I decided years ago to wait until I was certain before I walked down the aisle."

Reed leaned toward her, his brows drawn together, and he gazed at her intently. "How can you be certain about someone? You could think he's perfect for you and wake up one day and realize you hate the guy."

She nodded. "True, but by knowing exactly what you want and searching for someone who meets your qualifications, your chances of appearing in divorce court are much less. There's no certainty about anything in this life, but I like to at least make my odds a little better."

The waitress appeared and poured their wine. While Reed ordered, Lacey tried to figure out the man. Obviously intelligent, he'd never married. Good-looking, and yet he was alone. Reed appeared nonchalant about women in general, yet he clearly wasn't gay. Why would a man like

Reed want to make a documentary about a relationship coach?

He didn't seem to believe in love or relationships.

She sipped the cool chardonnay, the flavor bursting in her mouth. "Tell me again why you're making this documentary?"

"I like to tell real life stories about what is going on in the world. I want to show injustices. I want to show people who are helping one another. I want to give people a view of the world they don't see in their ordinary lives."

From what she could discern about his personality, he didn't seem to believe in love or relationships.

"Sounds impressive."

"Why did you become a relationship coach?" he asked.

She sat back, wondering how much she should tell him. "My mother married five times before I left for college. My sister and I moved constantly, and we had multiple step-brothers and sisters. Turmoil was the norm between the kids, and even between some of my step-fathers and us. I decided I wanted to help people find the right person and keep other children from suffering what we'd experienced."

Reed chuckled. "I'm sorry. I'm not laughing because of what you just told me. I'm laughing because the thought of you in a house filled with chaos doesn't fit. You're so calm, cool, and collected. What you're telling me is difficult for me to picture."

Lacey shook her head and frowned. "It wasn't pleasant. One of my step-sisters stole my clothes whenever she visited for the weekend. I didn't dare mention my favorite shirt, or it disappeared. In fact, I often told her I loved a shirt when I actually loathed it. The shirt disappeared, making me happy."

"Didn't you tell your mother what was going on?" he asked, an incredulous look on his face.

She shook her head and frowned at him. "At first, my sister and I tried to tell her, but mother was trying to win over my step-sister, Becky, who hated all of us, so there was never any punishment." Lacey gazed at him and wondered how many relationships he'd experienced. How many women's hearts he'd broken or how many times he'd been dumped. "Tell me more about this documentary."

"I brought along the production schedule. I thought maybe you'd like to see it. It shows who I'm going to interview and how I'm going to compare dating services to your business," he said, pulling some folded papers out of his jacket.

"Okay, but I have a matchmaking service," she said, wanting to make sure he understood the difference.

"Yes, I know, but I want to compare how you match couples to how the dating service matches couples."

She gazed at him as he handed her the schedule. "Some services put your picture on the website and say 'go for it.' There is no thought to if the two of you have anything in common or not. There are a couple of dating companies who use personality tests to match you."

"Then there are the free websites," he said.

Music played softly in the background as he gazed at her intently. She refused to acknowledge he was damn good looking or the little hitch in her breathing he seemed to create.

"You get what you pay for. You don't have any idea who you're meeting. It could be a serial killer, rapist, or a cult member looking for a new wife."

He appeared to contemplate her remarks. "Tell me what makes your service different from other dating services?"

"All of my clients are required to have a criminal background check, personality tests, and self-evaluation. Clients must attend at least one of my dating seminars and fill out a complete and thorough application, disclosing what they're looking for in a mate," she said, taking a sip of her wine.

Reed raised his brows. "That's a lot of personal information."

"Kept strictly confidential."

"Do you turn some people away?" he asked.

"All the time. We only help people who are serious about finding a mate. And if you're looking for or needing therapy, that's not my expertise." She glanced over the production schedule and noted with interest that he had penciled in several of her seminars. On paper, the impression appeared favorable, but she couldn't quite get a feel for how he intended to portray her.

"This looks acceptable. But my career, my business, is hinging on how you film this documentary. Do you believe in relationship coaches?" she asked him, needing to know.

"Finding women has never been a problem for me."

She couldn't stop the chuckle that bubbled forth. No, women would gravitate to Mr. Hunter. His looks, his smile, his flirtatious manner, so why was he alone?

"You didn't answer my question."

He sat back and stared at her, while the music played in the background. Did she really have any choice, but to accept his offer? She needed his documentary in order to impress upon the studios that she was ready for television. Yet, she hesitated, needing to know how he felt about her business.

"I'm not convinced your service is necessary for some people."

A smile slipped into place as she lifted her wine glass to her lips. She'd dealt with men like him before. They came in, determined to show they didn't need her, and after several sessions, were eager and excited to see the changes in their dating experiences.

"Why are you doing a documentary on relationship

coaches and dating services if you don't believe in them?"

Reed leaned into the table. "It doesn't matter what I think. My job is to film you and let the viewers decide for themselves if what you're doing helps people. As long as you have nothing to hide, you should look great."

Lacey angled toward him, wanting him to understand how what he did with the film could affect her. "Can I depend on you to represent me fairly without letting your personal prejudice show?"

Reed sat back and smiled at her. His green eyes darkened, and he took a deep breath. "I understand your concern. But I'm a journalist. I make documentaries. Ty films and I do the editing. All I can promise you is that what I film is what the audience will see. It's up to them to make their decision as to whether or not the service you provide is legitimate and satisfying for the people you work with."

Anxiety gripped Lacey, wringing her insides, until she felt nauseous. She would place the business she'd spent years building into this man's hands in order to reach the next level. A level she had not confided to him.

For some reason, she didn't want to tell him about the television show. That card she'd keep close to her chest. Right now, he didn't have to know she needed him more than he needed her. Eventually, she would tell him, but not yet, not now. Not until he'd earned her trust.

"Tell me why you've never married?" she asked, staring at the way his eyes reflected the candlelight, looking for anything that would help her understand him more.

Her television show as the result of his documentary could only help him, as well. And while he kept insisting the final edit would be the result of the camera, she knew better than to believe that. How could he edit film without his personal prejudices slipping into the editing process?

Reed's brows rose at her question. He leaned back to study her. "What has that got to do with my documentary?"

"I'm trying to understand you and your world view."

He laughed, his green eyes widened. "My world view?"

"Yes. The more I know you, the better I'll see what kind of film you'll make."

He shook his head at her. "Psychology major?"

"No, though I did take a lot of psych classes."

Raising the wine glass to his lips, he sipped and watched her, studying her like an ant under a microscope. Finally, he set the glass down. "Many of my college friends have had a big wedding only to realize two kids later that this is not what they wanted," he responded, his brows drew together, his gaze dark as he shook his head. "It's not fair to the kids. You know that better than anyone."

"Don't you think you would pick the right person or that you could do a relationship better than your college friends?"

"Maybe. But once I was engaged to a woman, and she chose a car over me. Since then, I've never found a woman who kept me interested enough that I was willing to take another chance. My career is my relationship, and we're doing just fine."

"A car," Lacey said.

"Yes, a red Corvette. Her father said if she would dump me, he'd buy her a car." He shrugged, and she knew he tried to act like it meant nothing, but he failed. Could this be the reason he seemed closed off, not open to love?

"So you gave up on love."

He stared at her. "I'm way better than a red Corvette. She chose the car. I haven't found a woman who has made me regret my decision to give up on marriage."

Reed didn't acknowledge that he'd given up on love, but she could see it in his posture, in the tone of his voice, that he no longer believed in love.

"What about kids?"

"I like kids, but I don't want my children shuttled back and forth between two homes and two parents, having to deal with step-parents or brothers and sisters. You of all people should understand where I'm coming from."

She nodded.

He pinched off a piece of bread and raised it to his lips. "Until the day comes when I find a woman I can't live without, I'm careful there are no accidental pregnancies."

His career was his life, and until he believed in love once again, no woman would complete him. But what were his career goals?

"You've won an IDA award?" she asked, trying to avert her eyes from the way he licked his lips after eating the oil-dipped bread.

Reed smiled. "Yes, my film on the Russian sex trade won an IDA award. Now my film on financial reform is up for an IDA award."

"Congratulations."

"But my last film about the underground sex trade in Russia and France disturbed me. I exposed how girls are often forced into brothels or sold by their parents. Despicable business, but the film garnered huge attention, and the studio made a nice profit."

She shuddered. "That sounds grim compared to what you're doing now."

"Yes, I needed something fun and not so dark. Even filmmakers suffer from burn-out," he said, with a smile.

His face lit up when he spoke about his films, and his voice became animated with emotion and excitement. Lacey couldn't help but think this documentary would be a perfect opportunity to show the world the joys and the heartbreaks of her business in a sensitive way people would understand. Yet, she would have to prove to him she offered a valuable service to people. She would have to show him love was a valuable emotion.

"What is your biggest career goal?" she asked.

"An Oscar," he said immediately. "I want to win the big award that all filmmakers covet."

Many people had been disbelievers when they started her program, and when they finished, many of them shouted her praises. She would have to show Reed Hunter how her twelve step program mated people for life. She would have to show him love mattered most of all.

Once he started filming her, she was certain he'd see the value of a relationship coach.

Their food arrived, and as she savored the first bite, the violinists strolled up to their table and began to play a sad, romantic ballad. She wanted to roll her eyes at them, but instead, she concentrated on her manicotti. The cheese was excellent, and the music was irritating. Did they really think that crap worked on women?

The trio ambled to the next table, and Reed gazed at her in surprise. "I thought you would like this restaurant."

He must have seen the eye roll. "Why? Because it's romantic?" she asked.

"Well, yes. You're in the romance business. I knew we were meeting for a business dinner, but I thought this type of restaurant would appeal to you." He held his fork in mid-air, his green eyes wide with surprise.

Lacey sighed and wanted to scream with frustration at how people assumed so much about her business and relationships in general. "My business is tough on romance. I'm not in it for hearts and flowers. I find people partners who are compatible. Who share the same interests and goals and complement each other," she said, letting her frustration come through in the pointed way she finished each sentence. "As for the sparks or passion, as my mother likes to call it, if the desire is there, fantastic. If not, as long as they are satisfied with one another, it doesn't matter."

Reed sat back and began to laugh, staring at her in surprise. "I admit I'm shocked. This is not what I expected from you."

"Why? The divorce rate in this country is almost fifty percent. If we as individuals concentrated more on the person and less on the passion, then the divorce rate would decline."

"But the passion is what draws us together," he said, leaning toward her until they were inches apart. "Passion is what makes a man pursue a woman."

"Not intelligence, compatibility, or even looks?" she asked him, leaning forward herself, until they were right up in each other's faces.

"That's the icing on the cake," he said, his voice whisper-soft.

For a moment, she felt breathless as she stared into his gaze. His heated stare left her body warm, her pulse tingling, and she leaned back in the booth to escape the restless sensation. Oh, this man could charm his way into a woman's bed before she remembered to say no. Lacey would have to be very aware of his charismatic appeal.

"That means it's okay for us to just hop into bed with one another, regardless of the fact we have nothing in common?"

"Yes!" His response was enthusiastic and loud enough that people around them turned to stare.

Most definitely, he was all about the passion and not about the romance and the monogamy.

"I totally disagree. When I sleep with someone, there has to be a connection. But I need a kinship of the mind and the soul, not just of the body," she said, her voice rising in pitch.

"God, I wish my camera was on you now. I wish I was filming the passion for your business that I see on your face right now. Very interesting," he said. His voice breathless, his gaze intense.

Lacey stopped and stared at him, surprised at this side of him. They'd disagreed about this subject, and yet, he recognized her excitement about relationships. She knew she loved her job, but she'd never thought about how it came across to other people-her emotions exposed on her face, the dedication to teach people to dig further, before they acted on urges that affected them for a lifetime.

With sudden clarity, she knew everything was going to be all right. Reed Hunter's responses to her questions seemed honest and forthright. Even telling her he didn't believe in her line of work.

She had to trust him to show her profession as one she loved, one that she was passionate about. A professional love he could capture with his camera lens.

"Mr. Hunter, I'm going to trust you to show my enthusiasm for my job in this film. I'm going to trust you with my life, my business."

Reed raised his wine glass, and she raised hers. "To a great documentary."

"To a film that'll win you an Oscar and grow my business," she said, certain she'd made the right decision.

~

Reed hit the speed dial number on his phone.

Graham answered on the third ring, his voice groggy like he'd been sleeping.

"It's a go!"

His voice immediately changed. "She said yes."

"We're hitting the road with her next week, and she's going to give me a list of clients who agree to be filmed."

Adrenaline pumped through Reed's veins like a speed junkie. He could hardly wait to start filming Lacey Morgan. Tonight at dinner, the animation on her face had revealed her passion as she spoke about relationships.

Expressions like those were the kind he strived to show in his films, even when he didn't agree with the subject.

Such dedication he recognized because he felt that way about filmmaking. And every time he saw it in someone else, it surprised him.

"Way to go, Reed. I can't wait to see how you hang this bitch," Graham said. "I'm sleeping alone tonight because of her."

Reed felt a moment of unease. Something that he'd never felt before when he worked with Graham. They'd always been in complete harmony, and they would be this time, as well.

"Well, you won't be sleeping alone for long. I'm sure once Juliet sees what we discover about Mate Incorporated, she'll come running back."

Reed couldn't understand why Graham didn't want to move on. He couldn't understand Graham's single-mindedness to go after Lacey. They'd both been dumped, but Reed was wise enough to know that eventually Blair would have given up and left him.

"I trolled her website this evening. I answered the questionnaire about true love and even considered signing up to find someone who meets my needs," Graham confessed.

"Geez, are you nuts!"

"It's just I really like the idea of finding my true love and mating for life."

Reed laughed, knowing he'd been had. "Funny, you had me going there for a moment. I believed you were falling for this crap."

Graham chuckled in the phone. "Just testing you."

For what? Did he not believe that Reed wanted to reveal this charlatan as much as he did?

Well, to be honest, when he'd first met Lacey, he'd agreed her business was shady, but after dinner tonight, he thought she believed in what she did. Even if it was outrageous. "So did I pass?"

"With flying colors," Graham said. "Now bring me a documentary that reveals this bitch."

"Will do," Reed said.

"I expect a report on how it's going in about three weeks."

"Sure thing, boss. Hope you sleep better knowing it won't be long until Juliet is back."

"God, I hope so."

~

Lacey had set the lunch up with her sister a week ago, ostensibly to talk about the wedding plans and ask her what she wanted Lacey to handle.

She waved to Kerri, and noticed she carried a big canvas bag. Her sister was a bigger planner than herself, and that canvas bag could only spell trouble.

"Hey, girl." She stood and hugged her sister. "What's in the bag?"

"Wedding magazines, brochures. I need your help in a huge way. Do you realize the wedding is two months away?"

Lacey hoped to convince Kerri she was making the biggest mistake of her life. She wasn't any more ready for marriage than she'd been ready to go away to college at eighteen, opting instead for junior college.

College with training wheels and now she was experiencing her first serious relationship with training wheels. Kerri wasn't ready for the big bike of marriage.

"Yes, are you sure we'll have time to put one together by then?"

"No choice, we have to. I've been accepted to the University Of Tennessee Health Sciences Center, and we're moving two days after the wedding. Wedding, honeymoon night, pack the car, and drive off the next. Life's going to get crazy!"

Lacey glanced at her younger sister's flushed cheeks, bright gaze, and the obvious tension around her mouth. She grabbed her hand. "You're not pregnant, are you?"

Her sister laid down the menu and gazed at her in complete shock. "Of course not."

From her frosty tone, Lacey knew she'd just made a huge blunder. "Look, I'm not being critical. I would love you regardless if you were pregnant. The way you two are rushing things, I thought maybe there was a reason."

"Rushing things?" her sister replied, her expression incredulous.

God, could Lacey botch this any worse? "You graduate college next week. Getting married in two months and starting medical school a week later, I'd say you're on the fast track to killing yourself."

"And you think I should wait?" her sister said in that tone Lacey recognized from when they were kids and meant Kerri was pissed.

"I don't want you to make a mistake like Mom."

"I'm not our mother. Matt makes me happy. I go to bed wanting to be with him. I wake up wanting to be with him and only him. He makes me think about things in different ways. He's kind and considerate. He takes care of me and loves me even when I'm an angry, PMS-raging, hormonal bitch. He wants to be with me, and only me, and I want to grow old with him." She took a deep breath, and Lacey sensed Kerri's anger simmering around them.

How did you make someone see reason when the person they loved took care of them when they were a PMS-raging, hormonal bitch?

"If you don't want to be a part of the wedding, let me know now, and I will find someone else. You've always been there with me, and I thought you would be again, but maybe not."

Lacey felt like an ogre. She couldn't have been any uglier than if she'd turned green. "I love you, but I'm afraid for you."

"Why? Matt takes better care of me than Mother ever did."

"I don't want to see you hurt." Lacey reached out and grabbed her sister's hand. "I want to be involved in your wedding. Just remember, if you change your mind or you have second thoughts, it's never too late to back out."

"I'm not going to back out. I'm committed to Matt. I'm wearing his engagement ring. The wedding ceremony will legalize what I feel for him."

Lacey sighed, knowing she'd lost this skirmish, but not the war. She was still determined to help her sister realize she wasn't ready for marriage. "Okay, what's the plan?"

"We need to schedule a day to go shopping for a wedding dress. Mom wants to go along."

"She's not very happy with me right now."

"Yes, you two fight worse than any two alley cats I've ever heard. Talk about a real downer sometimes. Could you please try to get along with her and make it a fun time when we go shopping?" Kerri asked.

Lacey went on the defensive. "I'll do my best, but you have to admit, she causes a lot of the problems between us."

Kerri's eyes bored into Lacey. "Yes, she does, but sometimes Lacey, I think she's right. While Dean may be the perfect guy on paper, I don't sense you not being able to live without him or that he makes you happy."

Stunned to hear her sister say she thought their mother was right, Lacey sat back and stared at her. Did she not understand that giving in to your emotions left you vulnerable?

"Dean and I are doing fine. I haven't told you because

this is yours and Matt's time, but we're moving in together. We've been looking for an apartment. I planned to tell you the day you announced your engagement, but felt that the day was yours."

"You're moving in together?" Her sister's eyes widened with shock, and she shook her head. "You know what mother thinks about living together. Please, please, I don't want to listen to the two of you fight while shopping for my dress."

Lacey shrugged, not looking forward to the conversation with her mother. "Okay, I'll put this off for as long as I can, but Dean is pressuring me for us to find a place and move in."

"If he loves you, why doesn't he just marry you?" Kerri asked, her eyes flashing *duh*.

"Neither of us is ready for marriage just yet," Lacey responded in her calm, rational tone.

"Yet you're ready to commit to live together?"

"Yes."

"Maybe the reason you're not ready to commit to marriage is because you're not certain he's the one," Kerri said, her expression so much like their mother's that Lacey had to do a double-take.

"I'm testing everything before I agree to walk down the aisle. I only want to do this once."

Kerri leaned toward her sister. Her eyes were warm, her brows raised, and her expression one of sincerity. "Lacey, I only want to do it once as well, but with Matt, I knew within weeks he was the one."

The news that she'd known so soon that she wanted to marry Matt stunned Lacey. Was Kerri becoming their mother? Fear for her sister crackled along her nerve endings, shooting through her like lightning. The very idea frightened her. "I hope like hell you're right."

"I know I am. But I wonder about you. I wonder

sometimes if you know what real love feels like. I worry about you, Lacey."

Chapter Six

Jason released a relaxed sigh and rolled onto his back. Amanda curled around him, slipping her arm across his naked chest. Her breathing slowly returned to normal, as her world righted itself.

"Hmmm, God, Amanda, nothing beats great sex."

She smiled and pressed her breasts against his ribs. "Pretty amazing." The air conditioner caressed her sweat glistened skin, as a chill danced over her body, and she pulled the sheet around them, entwining her legs with his.

With her finger, she drew a lazy circle eight around his nipples, amazed at the texture of his smooth skin interspersed with soft hair. She loved cuddling after sex, talking and luxuriating in the sensations.

Jason stretched across the bed to the nightstand and found the television remote. He pointed it at the TV on the wall and hit the on button. Quickly, he scanned the channels until he found a baseball game.

Stunned, she gazed at him in horror. *What the hell did he think he was doing?*

"Great, we haven't missed much. The Yankees play tonight. I've got to watch the game." He pulled his arm from around her, causing Amanda to fall flat onto the mattress. He straightened the pillows and sat up.

Anger rose like a tiger inside her, and she all but roared. "Well, I guess we're through with intimacy for the night."

Dark eyes gazed at her, and he raised his brows questioning. "You had an orgasm, didn't you?"

She threw the sheet back, stood, and walked into the bathroom. "Intimacy," she called over her shoulder as she entered the bathroom. "You know, where two people connect both emotionally and physically after sex."

Shutting the door, she took a quick shower. Hot steam soothed her hurt emotions. Did she expect too much? What happened to time spent cuddling after they'd experienced mind-blowing sex?

She toweled off and spread lotion on her legs. Okay, so maybe she'd overreacted a little. She needed to step back and look at things realistically. Life was not like in the movies. Life was not a fairy tale where Prince Charming swept you off your feet, gave you oral sex, and promised he'd love you forever.

She yanked on her nightgown, brushed her damp hair, and entered the bedroom. Jason lay in bed, engrossed in the baseball game on the television. Suddenly, she wanted her bed back. She wanted her room back; she even wanted her life back. But he planned on spending the night. Right now, she was ready for him to leave.

Amanda sank onto the bed and gazed at him. Was he the one she wanted to spend the rest of her life with?

A commercial for Viagra came on, and he pulled her against him and kissed her.

He released her lips and gazed into her eyes. "Honey," he drawled, "you know the Yankees are my favorite team."

"Yes, I know," she said. "I had hoped to spend more time focused on you, here in my bed."

What man turned down attention in the bedroom?

"You were great, and we spent all the time we needed to on sex."

For a moment, Amanda stared in stunned disbelief. He thought they had spent enough time on each other. Ten minutes of foreplay, twenty minutes of sex and one minute of cuddling. Not quite wham-bam-thank-you-ma'am, but certainly not the night of intimacy she'd anticipated.

The commercial ended and the game came back on. His eyes were glued to the television as he said, "Hey honey, could you get me some water and maybe bring a bag of chips. All that sex made me hungry."

She stood, and he patted her on the butt. She wondered if she were in a time warp and they'd been married for twenty years, instead of just dating for three months. Yet, she liked Jason and until tonight, hoped that, over time, her feelings would morph into love.

"Please tell me you're not going to eat chips in bed," she said, heading towards the kitchen.

Love took time and right now, her only emotion was irritation. She'd never experienced someone turning on the television right after they'd had sex.

"Yeah, and bring that new salsa you bought."

Lacey preached choosing the right mate, searching until you found someone who shared your interests, your goals, your dreams, but did Jason really meet that criteria?

She took a bowl of salsa and the chips into the bedroom. He took them from her and patted a place on the bed.

"Come on, Hon. Sit here and watch the game with me."

She gazed at him and wondered what marriage would be like with him. Jason was good-looking, had a great job, had set life goals and shared her vision of wanting one good marriage. But…

He patted the bed again and smiled at her. "Please, it's lonely here without you."

The voltage of that smile lit a thousand watts inside her and sparked an ember within her. He was a typical sports obsessed guy. She should cut him some slack.

She crawled in bed beside him, taking care not to spill his salsa. He placed a chip between her lips, and she savored it. He leaned over and kissed her, his mouth moving over hers slowly, fanning that small ember into a spark.

"Hmmm…sweet and salty," he said.

A roar erupted from the television as the crowd

screamed their approval. His head yanked ninety degrees as he threw up his hands. "Oh no, the Red Sox hit a home run. Shit, now they've tied it up."

Once again, his attention was diverted to the television. Amanda picked up her book from the nightstand. If this was what marriage would be like, was she certain she couldn't live without Jason?

~

Reed stood beside Ty, as he filmed Lacey in the San Antonio Hilton Hotel ballroom preaching the gospel of dating. The first day of shooting, and so far there hadn't been many glitches. A lost camera they'd located, not enough copies of the release form for the audience and the lighting. The hotel ballroom's lights sucked, and he'd rented several lamps to place on the stage, hoping Lacey knew enough not to stand near them.

Lacey ambled across the raised dais, giving her segment called "Dating is More Than A One-Night Stand".

"People, I'm not passing moral judgment. But banging Bubba at two a.m. is an act of loneliness, unless you have an emotional connection with him. And the next morning, you look over at him and think *what the hell was I thinking?*"

Inside, Reed was laughing. He'd experienced this from the male perspective. But his ah-ha moment was when the woman refused to leave the next morning. He wanted her gone, and she wanted to move in. *Not good.*

Silence filled the auditorium as she paused, letting her message resonate with her audience. "Dating is the process of getting to know the person. Finding out whether or not you have shared interests besides loneliness. In my matchmaking service, we ask our clients not to have sex for at least ten dates."

Yeah, right. Nowadays it was sex on the first date if

you were lucky, but always by the third date.

The audience groaned. "Yes, I know ten dates seem like forever. It's more than the three date average. But if you've made it to ten dates, you've already decided whether or not you like the other person and whether or not this relationship has a chance of success. If our couples want to wait longer, that's even better. But ten dates are usually over a month to two month time frame. Does everyone do what we ask and wait that long? I don't know. Our policy is not to grill our clients on their sex life."

Again, the audience laughed.

"Sex is an intimate act between two people who are expressing love or at least that they care about one another. If you don't know the person, how can it be anything but physical? And if that's what you want, then go for it. But I'm trying to help you find the one person you want to spend the rest of your life with. When you have sex too early in the relationship, it can get awkward and stress the budding relationship."

Reed kept waiting for her to talk about the physical side, the way sometimes you just want to rip someone's clothes off and go for it. But she didn't talk about that all-consuming passion. Had she never experienced it? No, someone with her background must have experienced passion so great that all you could think about was getting that person into bed.

"Let's go back to our friend Bubba. It's two a.m. You're lonely. It's late. You've had a couple of drinks, and he's whispering into your ear as you dance across the floor. Your defenses are weak. It feels good to be in his arms." She paused and walked across the podium.

Facing the audience, she raised her hand and her voice, like she was giving a sermon. "What are you doing there? Why aren't you home in bed? I'm not saying don't go out partying or dancing. I'm saying go home before you reach that vulnerable time of night when all you feel is your loneliness. If Bubba is interested in you, he'll wait."

Reed no longer went out to dancing bars. He hung out at sports bars, and the women were just as easy there as they were at the dance halls. Now he was pickier; he got to know them before he even asked them out on a date.

She paused, letting the audience absorb the information. "Let me say that again. If Bubba is interested in you, he will wait."

Reed watched the audience and could see from their expressions that some clearly understood her message. Others, especially the men, frowned as if they knew the number of women who would be turning them down had just increased.

"Again, I'm not passing moral judgment. You can bang everyone within six counties if you want, and that's your business. What I'm saying is if you want to find someone to spend the rest of your life with, why aren't you exploring that person? It's all about getting to know someone. It's all about finding that one person who will balance you, help you grow as an individual, and share the same values. Permanent relationships are built on good foundations, just like a home."

She paused, and Reed watched as Ty glanced over at him and grinned. He shook his head and rolled his eyes. Reed couldn't help but laugh. Everything Lacey said made sense, but he'd be damned if he'd use any of her techniques. He wasn't interested in a forever after. Not any longer.

"So let's make sure everyone understands what dating is." She took a sip of water. "Dating is him-or-her, picking you up and taking you to do something that you both enjoy. Or it can be simply sitting at dinner and getting to know one another. But how can you find out what the other person likes if you just do them?" She walked across the stage.

"Before you walk down that aisle, why not date this person and use this time to explore whether you have the same tastes, the same values, the same desires? You don't have to like everything identical. In fact, it's good if the other person helps you to experience new things, but you at least need to have the same values."

Lacey faced the audience, her features were animated, her hands gestured, and voice preached. "Throw sex into the first or second date and you don't know who you're sleeping with. I'm not saying sex is bad. I'm saying if you want a permanent relationship that lasts your entire life, you need to do your research.

The audience laughed.

"I'm serious. Put on your Sherlock Holmes hat and investigate that person and if you think this is someone you could spend the rest of your life with, if you think this person is someone you want to know more intimately, go out and have the best damn sex of your life with them. Burn the sheets up. But realize sex always changes the relationship. It makes it intimate. And that's not a bad thing when the relationship is ready."

Surely, these people weren't buying into this crap. Surely, they weren't going to change the way they looked at dating. Were they? He gazed out at the audience and noticed people were paying attention. They were listening to Lacey.

She stared out at her audience. "Okay, we've had enough seriousness for a while; let's take a ten minute break."

Ty laid down his camera. "We're getting some great stuff."

"Yeah, let's see if we can get someone to talk on camera."

Reed walked up to a man in his mid-thirties who sat

 Sylvia McDaniel

staring reflectively off into space. "Excuse me, sir. Could I ask you some questions on camera?"

"Sure."

"What do you think of today's seminar? Has it been everything you've expected?"

The man smiled. "It's been more. She's made me think of relationships in a new way. I need to do better at getting to know a woman and what makes her happy."

Reed stopped, stunned. That wasn't the answer he'd expected. The man must be lying. He'd try a different tact. "Do you think this will change the way you date?"

"Most definitely. I've already signed up for her matchmaking service, and I can't wait to go out on my first date."

"What do you think of Ms. Morgan? Do you think she's presented this seminar in a professional manner? You do realize that relationship coaches are not doctors and don't even have a Master's degree."

That question would get him the footage he needed. The shocked expression, where the man would admit he didn't know and probably even walk out.

"What does a degree matter if she's teaching you something that will help you for the rest of your life? I'm not looking for therapy. My relationships kept ending, and now I realize that was a symptom of me not really knowing these woman. I hope to do better in the future."

Well, crap. Time to find a new source.

"Thank you for your time, sir."

Reed walked over to a blank wall, and Ty pointed the camera at him. "Some relationship coaches have a certificate from a training center, but they are not therapists. There is no therapy involved, only someone helping you figure out the problems in the relationship and your role in those problems."

Reed made a cutting motion with his hand and let the

mic drop. "I know this is the first day of shooting, but right now, I don't think I've found the angle I want to pursue."

"I'm telling you, man, I don't have a good feeling about this one."

"Yeah, I know you keep telling me. Relax, it's the first day. It will get better."

It had to get better, or Graham would have Reed's hide. Find the dirt on this woman or find another job. He didn't doubt for a moment Graham would fire him if he didn't like the film Reed produced.

"This woman is good. Even I was beginning to wonder if I might need to rethink my dating habits."

Reed gazed at his friend and cameraman. "Come on, you're kidding me."

"No, I'm not. I don't go to bars and hook up with women. In my past relationships, I've always looked out for my best interests and didn't give a shit about what the woman thought. Maybe that's why I can't keep a girlfriend."

Reed shook his head. They still had weeks of filming. They would find something on the clever Ms. Morgan. "I understand, but do you want a permanent relationship?"

"No."

"Then, who the hell cares what you do? Be upfront with the woman and have sex. As long as she knows you're not interested in forever, just enjoy the moment," Reed said. Was his cameraman being indoctrinated with this psychobabble? How jacked was that?

Ty nodded. "Yeah, you're probably right. But why is it starting to sound wrong?"

~

Lacey stretched her neck, releasing the tension in her tight muscles. Her back ached from the long day of being on her feet.

Reed walked up and watched her. "Tight neck?"

"Yeah, after being on stage all day, I'm tense."

He placed his hands on her shoulders and began to massage them.

"God, that feels good." His hands were strong and warm, his fingers working magic on her shoulders and neck. She sighed and knew she should stop him, but the pleasure was too great.

"Thank you," he replied, his voice near her ear, his breath tickling the back of her neck.

"Did you get some good film today?" she asked, trying not to think about the way his hands were making her feel.

"Yes, we did. We even got a few people to talk on camera."

"They gave me raving reviews, right?"

"Yes, they did. We talked to two men and two women. One person said this was the second time she'd taken this seminar, and this time she'd brought her girlfriends."

Lacey felt a little tension seep out of her, relieved her clients were saying good things on camera about her. "Great!"

"I don't know if men will think that way. I'm sure there are bars all over Texas where the Bubbas of this world are going home alone," he said, his voice sliding like warm butter down her spine.

She laughed, the tension leaving her body under the ministrations of his fingers. "Good. We'll be helping lower the STD epidemic."

"Where to now?" Reed asked.

She wanted to close her eyes and let him continue to make her feel so relaxed. "Back to Dallas, where I have a full day of client sessions, a church singles meeting, and my Friday night mixer. Plus, I have to go apartment looking."

"You're moving?"

"Yes, my boyfriend and I are moving in together."

Reed's hands felt heavenly, but the thought of Dean made her stop and think about what she was doing. Another man's hands giving her pleasure would not be appropriate for an engaged or married woman. She stepped out of Reed's reach.

"Thanks that feels better," she said and reached up to rub the back of her neck, where his hands had left her skin warm and tingly. His ministrations had felt heavenly, and she'd had to force herself to move away from the heated touch of his hands.

"Known each other long?" he asked, leaning against the wall, his arms and ankles crossed as his emerald eyes perused her leisurely.

"Yes, we've been dating for almost a year. We decided to take it to the next step." There was something about his gaze that left her strangely aware of him as a man, and she had the urge to run.

"And you waited ten dates before you had sex?" he asked, his eyes dancing with merriment.

She laughed. "I don't think that's any of your business, but yes, we did wait at least ten dates."

"God, he must be a candidate for sainthood."

She smiled, remembering how Dean had kept pressuring her, but she'd held steadfast. "No, we agreed to wait." She put her notes in her briefcase. "Found a new girlfriend yet?"

He shook his head, his lips curling into a grin. "No, I'm still currently without."

"When you decide you want to change that, let me know, and I'll set you up."

"No, thanks. Women in your business are looking for permanent. I've yet to meet anyone who would change my mind on staying happily single."

"That's a shame. Married men live longer."

"Well, I'm hardly an old guy."

"No, but you will be someday." Yes, she knew exactly what type of man he was. He didn't believe in what she did for a living, but if she ever had a chance to work her magic with him, by the time she was done, he'd be a great candidate for marriage.

"Thank you, Ms. Morgan. I will take that under advisement. Right now, I'm the type of guy you probably hate. My women know right up front it's all about sex. When we're done, we're done. No commitments, no permanency, no sharing an apartment, not even a drawer in my house."

Lacey grinned, remembering previous clients like Reed. "Oh, I don't hate guys like you. I enjoy seeing them change and grow into men who women can appreciate."

"But I have no intention of changing."

"That's what they all say," she said, turning to leave. "Wait, we need to set up a time to do a one-on-one interview with you."

She waved her hand at him. "You'll have to check with Amanda. She keeps my schedule."

Chapter Seven

Lacey lay beside Dean in the big queen-size bed, cuddling against his naked skin. The earthy smell of musk surrounded her, and she breathed deeply of the soothing scent. She ran her fingers over the strong width of his chest. Finally, they had managed to squeeze some time for each other into their busy schedules.

When they lived together, this wouldn't be such a problem. Yet, there were still so many decisions they needed to make before they could combine their households. "Whose furniture will we use in the new apartment?"

He gazed at her and kissed the top of her head as he shifted in the bed and wrapped his arms around her. "Honey, I was going to talk to you about this. You know I love your apartment, but it's girly."

"I'm a girl."

"I know; it's one of the things I love about you," he said, his lips soft against her forehead.

"I'm open to change. Our new place should be a merger of our tastes," Lacey said.

"I agree."

Lacey wondered how they would combine their apartments, their furniture, including his ugly football chair. "While we're talking about furniture, I have a problem with your recliner."

Beneath the sheet, she rubbed her foot against his leg and then entwined her leg with his, trying to make him feel loved, even though she hated that old chair.

"What's wrong with my recliner? It's comfortable," Dean asked, gazing at her like she'd halted world peace.

"I'm sure in the 90s it was very comfortable, but blue is no longer a fashionable color," she said, letting her fingers trail down his chest.

"I don't care if it's avocado green as long as it fits my butt well. That's my football-watching chair."

"And it's butt ugly."

"I planned on putting it where guests couldn't see it. I thought maybe the office," he said, his expression hopeful.

She smiled at him. "We'll be sharing an office."

Dean was quiet for a moment, and a crease formed across his forehead. "This isn't going to be easy."

"We could always sell our furniture and buy new," she volunteered.

"Yeah, but that's such a huge expense, and I'd hoped we could save some money moving in together."

"Speaking of finances, we've not discussed how we're going to pay for everything," she said, gazing up at him.

"I assumed we'd split the expenses."

"I agree, but living together, our credit could affect each other. Is your credit good?"

A long pause interrupted the flow of conversation, and Lacey felt a trickle of unease skitter down her spine.

"My credit isn't bad; it's just not great. During college, I ran up some bills, and when I graduated, I owed over twenty thousand dollars."

"Ouch! I hope you had a great time in college," she said, her mind racing with this new insight into Dean. He was so meticulous she'd never imagined his credit could be a problem.

He shrugged. "I wish I could say I did, but frankly I don't know how the balance became so high."

"College was several years ago. How much do you still owe on the card?"

A long silence was his response, and Lacey knew she'd just discovered something new about her soon-to-be fiancé. Could Dean be hiding his financial situation for a reason?

Finally, he said, "I owe twenty-one thousand on my credit card."

Stunned, Lacey lay there, her mind reeling like a spin-top out of control, her breath freezing like she'd gotten locked in a cold storage unit. Twenty-one thousand dollars in debt? The cost of a new car and she'd had no idea. She remembered the expensive dinners they'd shared, the luxurious weekend getaways, the sleek car he drove, and the top of the line clothes he wore. Dean's millionaire looks could grace the cover of GQ magazine. She'd known he wasn't worth millions, but she had no idea he was so deeply in debt.

He sighed, his face void of any expression as his eyes carefully studied her. "That's why I thought moving in together would save us both some money."

"I thought we were moving in because we loved each other and wanted to be together," she said. Discomfort squeezed her chest like a bra two sizes too small.

"Of course," he said, his voice satiny smooth and full of reassurance.

"How much money do you have in savings?" she asked, needing to know if he was prepared for an emergency.

"That's kind of a personal question," he said, his forehead drawn together, his eyes sparking with irritation.

Lacey took a calming breath and ran her fingers across his chest. "Yes, it is. We're about to start sharing our life together. I need to know what I'm getting myself into."

His body tensed. "A couple of thousand."

"So, if you're in an automobile accident, you have just enough to purchase a new car. What about a job loss? Do you think that two thousand is going to get you to your next job?"

He withdrew from her, sat up, and threw back the sheet. "It's tough out on your own and paying all the bills. Sure, I make good money, but I work hard and a guy deserves to have some fun occasionally."

She shrugged and wondered at the way she could see him pulling away from her. "I'm not saying you don't, but do you have the money for a down payment on the apartment?"

"Don't worry about it. I'll have the money," he said, his voice clipped as he crawled out of bed.

She dropped the subject, seeing how tense and angry he was becoming.

"We're scheduled to meet two property managers on Saturday," Lacey said, observing his retreat.

"Yes," he replied, as he pulled on his pants. "I've already blocked out time on my schedule for us to meet with them."

"I thought you'd come over Friday night, and we could spend Saturday together."

He glanced at his watch, not responding to her suggestion.

"Is there someplace you have to go?" she asked, her irritation growing by the second. He couldn't run away every time they got into a disagreement or hit a bump on the road of life. If he did, they would never make it as a couple.

"No, I should get home. Tomorrow is a work day."

"Yes, I know. What about Friday night?"

His face became a blank mask, his eyes cold and dark. "Let me see how the rest of the week goes. I may have to work late."

She rose from the bed, grabbed her robe, and pulled it around her naked body. Whenever they hit a subject that was sensitive, Dean shut her out and walked away. "If something is bothering you, we need to talk about it. As a couple, we're going to have issues come up we'll need to discuss."

He yanked his shirt on and buttoned it, averting his face from her. "I know. Tonight, when you mentioned getting rid of my favorite chair, it made me realize moving in with you will be different."

She softened her voice and said, "And when you mentioned your money problems, that reminded me I may not know everything about you I should."

He gazed at her, his lips turned up in a slight smile as he wrapped an arm around her waist. "Okay, so we've got some things we need to discuss. But not now. It's late, and I'm tired."

She walked him to the door, knowing once again, he'd put her off. It was a concerning pattern of Dean's and one she needed to think about. "Let's talk about them Friday night."

"Sure."

At the door, he kissed her goodnight. "Later, Cupcake."

"Goodnight. Be careful going home."

She shut the door behind him and flipped the lock. Why did she feel like his reluctant admission of financial issues was a dark cloud looming over their happy future? When they'd discussed moving in together, she'd never dreamed of this problem. What else did she not know about Dean?

~

Reed watched Ty film the session in process. They were getting some great film, but he'd yet to find that one piece of footage that exposed this gig as a fraud. But he was a patient man and sooner or later, it would come through.

A pleasant flowery smell tweaked his nose, and he couldn't help but wonder where she'd put that drop of scent that intrigued him. He'd love to search that smell out on her body.

"James, last week I gave you an assignment. Do you remember?"

Sitting across from Lacey, the client, a thirtyish meek

man, squirmed in his chair. "Yes, you told me to contact one girl online, one girl via the dating group, and one at the Friday night get-together. You told me to make at least one date." James glanced away, unable to meet her gaze.

"Did you do that?"

The man sat tense and didn't respond. Reed could see why the man had trouble getting dates. Extremely shy and unsure of himself, at the first sign of rejection, he probably ran.

"If you don't do the assignments I give you, then you're wasting my time and yours. My job is to help you make a connection with a woman. We set a time limit on how long I was to help you with the promise that if you didn't do your part, I could withdraw from the contract at any time. Do you remember that commitment contract I had you sign?" Lacey said like she was dealing with an errant school kid.

"Yes." His eyes traveled to the ceiling, then down to the floor.

"Did you connect with at least three women?" Lacey asked her voice firm.

"It was a busy week, and the first girl I asked told me no."

Yep, he'd run at that first rejection with his tail between his legs. Reed had been there in high school, and thank God, he'd overcome that fright. It was paralyzing.

"How did that make you feel?" she asked.

"Like hell," he said, licking his lips nervously. "I mean I'm trying, but when I get turned down, I think no one likes me."

"It's a numbers game, James. It's all about reaching out to the right people. We discussed the fact you could get turned down, and you might even be rejected after a couple of dates."

"Yes, I know, but this one hurt," he said, his voice soft.

"Why was this one so different?"

Who was he kidding? All rejection hurt, and until you learned to blow it off and walk on, it could demoralize you.

With a frown, he glanced at the camera. "They're taping all of this?"

"Do you want me to tell them to go away?"

James thought about it for a moment. "No."

"What made this rejection hurt more?"

"Because I met her at your seminar. I thought she'd understand and say yes. I thought she was pretty."

Lacey leaned back and studied him for a moment. "There are no guarantees even at my seminars or the Friday night get-togethers. There are no guarantees anywhere."

He nodded. "I know, but I was disappointed."

When you were rejected, you had to learn not to take it personally. Sometimes you won, and sometimes you were shot down before you even got in the game. The cure was to move on until you found a yes.

"You were rejected by one girl. What about the other two girls? Did you contact two others?"

"Well, I went to the Friday night social, and I didn't see anyone I wanted to meet."

"What did you do? At these socials, they play games, they talk and eat dinner. Did you participate in the games and speak with people over a meal?"

"I…I went in and stood around and then I left."

He needed a few yeses under his belt, and then he would feel the confidence women loved and gravitated towards.

"So, you left the social without speaking to anyone?" Lacey confirmed.

"Yes."

"Did you contact anyone online?"

"No, I looked around, but I didn't contact anyone."

The hum of the camera filled the room. Tension

gripped Reed and he hoped his future film audience, as he waited to see how Lacey would deal with her client.

"James," she said softly, her voice firm. "I'm not here to do the work for you. This is the second time I've given you an assignment I don't think you've put your full effort into. You're paying me a lot of money to help you get into the dating pool, and you're not making much of an effort to help yourself."

"It's hard," he whined.

Damn straight it was hard, but this was a life lesson the man should have learned in high school…at the latest college. *Grow a spine, man.*

"I understand it's difficult. But, I don't have time to waste on someone who is not serious about what we're doing. You fail another assignment, and we're done. Do you understand?"

"Yes. I want to date, but I don't know how."

"I'm trying to teach you, but I can't do the work for you." She paused a moment and stared at him like a mother reprimanding a child. "Are we clear?"

"Okay. What is my next assignment?"

"You are to go to the Friday night special and meet three women. When I say meet them, I need to know their names. Out of the three, I want you to ask one on for a date. You are to play the games and dine with the group. I also want you to bring me emails showing you've contacted two women online."

He took a deep breath. "Women aren't attracted to me."

Women were attracted to men who were in control and were confident. This poor soul didn't have the confidence, and Reed wanted to grab him by the shirt collar and say, "Buck up man. You can do this."

Lacey gazed at James and shook her head, her voice turned consoling. "James, you're an attractive man. But you're shy. Women like a man who is confident and has a take-charge kind of attitude. I want you to go into that social Friday night tall, with your shoulders pulled back. Smile at every woman you meet and say hello. A smile will get a woman's attention almost every time. I know this isn't easy for you, but you came to me wanting to change."

"Okay," he said and started to rise.

"James?"

"Yes," he asked, standing before her.

"How are you going into that room Friday night?

He pulled his shoulders back and smiled at her.

"Perfect. You're a good-looking man, and a woman would be lucky to be with you. Now go out there and conquer the world. I know you can do it."

Reed drew his shoulders back, smiled and resisted the urge to beat on his chest. He wanted to go out and conquer the world, and he knew what a crock this business was.

Lacey stood. "You worked hard today. Give me a hug."

James gave her a quick hug and walked out the door, giving the camera a quick, shy glance.

Lacey sank into a chair and seemed to melt. She made some quick notes in the computer and turned to Reed.

She was good, damn good, and this man did need some confidence to meet women. Reed wanted to go to a bar, smile at all the women he met, and try out her techniques. And he knew he'd be successful because he'd used those techniques before.

"Did you get what you needed?"

Reed sat down across from her and gave her his best come-and-get-it-smile. "That was great. I'm ready to go trolling and try your techniques."

She shot him an exasperated glance, clearly not affected by his moves. "Please, promise me you will not make him look like a fool. He's a sweet, shy man who needs confidence and some help in learning how to date."

Reed shook his head. "I'm not here to make your

clients look like fools. I'm here to show how your business works. But that was good, and you were right."

A twinge of guilt poked him at the lie he'd just told. He reminded himself he was doing it to help people see how relationship coaches were not legitimate. Yet, what she'd done with James didn't really show that. In fact, nothing he'd filmed so far showed her doing anything, but being helpful.

"My next client does not want to be filmed, so you guys need to disappear."

He sighed, still searching for that one piece of evidence that would show her as a fraud. "Our next shoot with a client is not until tomorrow. I think I'll hang around and talk to some of your staff."

God, she looked gorgeous sitting there. A frown creased her forehead, and he had the most insistent urge to reach over and kiss her full on the lips. He wondered what she'd taste like. He wondered how she'd feel in his arms.

"All right, but don't film any of my clients that come in the door. I don't need anyone to sue me because they were filmed when they didn't sign a release," she warned.

"You worry too much. People love to be on camera."

"No, not everyone loves to be on camera," she said. "And make sure my staff has signed a written release to appear in your documentary."

"Okay."

He shook his head to clear his mind and his body of the image of the two of them wrapped in each other's arms, breathing heavy, bodies glistening with sweat. She was dating someone, and he was making a documentary about her business that would be less than flattering and expose her as a fraud.

Naked thoughts of the two of them didn't belong in his brain, even if his body did like the idea and the reaction.

~

Amanda gazed at the cameraman Ty. He was kind of cute, with his jeans, sandals and t-shirt. He wasn't the kind of guy she was normally attracted to, but then again, the men she seemed to date never worked out, except for Jason. And even with him, there were times she wondered what she was doing.

Ty pointed the camera, and Reed took a seat across from her. She flipped her hair off her shoulder and tried to calm her nerves.

"Action," Ty called.

"Amanda, how long have you known and worked for Lacey Morgan?" Reed asked, his expression all business.

"We went to college together. Five years ago she decided to form Mate Incorporated and asked me to join her as the marketing director." Those had been the days they struggled to make enough money to pay their salaries.

"What do you do for her business?" Reed asked, his professional voice silky smooth.

"I schedule her speaking engagements, try to get us new speaking venues, and do all the promotional materials for the company."

"You attend all her engagements?"

Amanda smiled at him. "Yes, I'm the one behind the scenes, setting everything up, making sure we have all the necessary handouts, the refreshments, selling tapes and videos."

A nervous buzzing began in her stomach. This felt stilted and not at all natural like she'd imagined the interview would go.

"Her business has grown in the last two years."

She crossed her legs and tried to relax, easing her tense shoulders. "Yes, people are tired of dating the same old way or even online. At least, by using our service, we screen who they meet."

"Are there ever any problems? Stalkers? People who dislike each other at first sight?"

The question felt odd, and for a moment, she wondered why he wanted to know. "Every business has problems. As for stalkers, our clientele are thoroughly screened. We've had clients who disliked each other, but the files are marked, and we reevaluate their needs and what they're looking for in a mate."

His face was devoid of emotion, no excitement, no displeasure, just a blank expression, like she was talking to a robot.

"Any angry boyfriends or girlfriends come after Lacey for breaking them up?"

She frowned and wondered at his questions. Why wasn't he asking about the business side of what they did? "Lacey is not the reason behind a couple breaking up. Our clients are taught to look inward and recognize the type of person they're searching for. Our clients make all their own decisions. Lacey only helps them discover more about themselves and what they want. When a person knows what he wants in a mate or companion, then he makes better choices."

Reed glanced down at his notes, like he was searching for a magical question. This interview was stranger than any she'd ever given before. She kept waiting for him to ask how they'd gotten started or how they'd grown the business, but instead he was focused on the negative.

"Even at her speaking engagements, there have never been any angry spouses, boyfriends, girlfriends, looking to get back at Lacey for ending their relationship?" he asked, gazing intently at her like she was withholding information.

Amanda stopped, took a deep breath, and carefully considered her response. She didn't understand why he was focusing on possible problems and not about the business itself. Didn't he want to know how they'd built this business from nothing to being prosperous?

"Never."

He'd asked this same type of question over and over, each time from a new angle like he was trying to confuse her into revealing something terrible. It wasn't going to work. Leaning towards her, he smiled. "Surely, there have been dissatisfied clients."

She shrugged her shoulders. "There are always people you can't help or who refuse to be helped. Our goal is to help the people we can. If we can't help them, we refund their money and wish them well."

"You refund their money?" Reed asked, his eyes wide with surprise.

"Of course," Amanda responded, straightening in her seat. "We want satisfied clients." She enunciated every single word and watched his mouth purse with displeasure.

She liked seeing him a little unsettled. His questions were creating doubts about how he intended to portray their business and that disturbed her. Lacey was her best friend, her business partner and Reed Hunter was crazy if he thought she'd be unprofessional and spill company secrets in this interview.

Reed motioned for Ty to cut the camera. Then he stared at her. "Would you mind if I continued this interview at another time?"

Her mouth opened in surprise as unease gripped her insides like moss to wet concrete. That was it? It was over? "But we haven't talked about the business model or our mission statement. I thought you'd want to discuss those."

Reed smiled at her in a condescending way. "Sure. But let's do it another time."

Ty laid the camera down and began to pack away the equipment. Amanda watched as Reed rose from his chair and began to help the cameraman.

 Sylvia McDaniel

"What about the other employees? Do you want to talk to any of them?"

Reed glanced back at her, his brows raised. "I'll let you know."

Bewildered, Amanda sat there. All the questions he'd asked seemed pointed toward the negative. He didn't seem interested in learning about the positive aspects of their business. Maybe she'd misinterpreted something that wasn't there, but her inner voice warned her maybe things weren't as they appeared.

To have a documentary expose their business in a negative way would be devastating. Lacey needed to know Amanda's suspicions about Reed Hunter.

~

Tired, Lacey rode the elevator down to the parking garage, her briefcase full of notes on clients she needed to match and ideas to research for the television show. There was always something to do, and she usually worked each night at home for several hours.

But she loved her work. She loved helping people find the connection that lasted a lifetime. She loved helping people get out of a dating rut, especially clients like James, who were shy, loveable, and lonely.

All in all, her life was good. The days of her mother's bohemian lifestyle and being dragged from one home to the next were long gone. Sharing rooms with step-sisters, the ugly break-ups, and packing on the sly were in the past.

Now her life was stable, content and her job fulfilling. Dean and his less than perfect credit score was the only blip on the radar at the moment. They had yet to discuss the matter, and her intuition told her he was putting off the discussion.

Coach Lacey would tell a client to step back and take a serious look at this man. Make certain there were no other hidden surprises lurking before you took that next step. Yet, she felt uncertain. She loved Dean.

The elevator door dinged and opened into the depths of the building, the smell of exhaust fumes smacking her in the face. Her heels clicked across the concrete as she hurried to her Prius.

Two cars down from hers, a man was bent over, deep into the bowels of his mustang engine, cursing. His rear end was round, firm and… Oh, my God.

"Reed?" she asked.

He rose and turned to gaze at her, his face red from being bent over. "Hi."

"Is everything okay?" she asked, seeing the frustration etched on his scowling face.

"My car won't start."

Lacey set her briefcase down, glanced under the hood, and wiggled a few wires.

"Do you know what you're doing?"

Why did men always assume a woman knew nothing about cars? *Big mistake.* "Stepfather number four was a mechanic and insisted my sister and I learn the basics of auto care, in case we ever stalled somewhere," she said, not rising up from examining his engine.

"Oh," he said, surprised.

She rose and glanced at him. "Your problem is pretty easy. You have a dead battery." She pointed to the poles. "See that corrosion? That's acid and you don't have any juice left in it."

"Damn! You can see I haven't spent much time under the hood of a car," he said, peering inside at the ugly white chemical goo. "I could call the auto club, but they'll take forever. I'm expected at Skyline High School in twenty minutes."

"I think you're going to be late." She gazed at him. "Can I give you a ride?" She had no plans tonight other than to work at home, so she didn't mind helping him.

"Would you? That would be a big help. I'll find a ride back from the school afterwards."

"Not at all. My Prius is over here."

"You drive a Prius?"

"Yeah, I love it," she said, as he slammed the hood of his car and manually locked the doors.

"Are you all green and into the environment?" he asked.

People just assumed you were an environmentalist when you drove a hybrid. Though her reasoning was she loved the little car, and its gas mileage.

"I try to do my part. At forty miles to the gallon, it gets me around," she said, opening the car door and climbing in. "How many miles does that Mustang get?"

He shook his head. "Let's not go there. Love the engine, love the sports car image, but gas mileage is not its top priority."

She pressed the on button and put the car in reverse. No sound emitted as she accelerated out of the garage and into traffic. At thirty miles an hour, the gasoline engine kicked in and propelled the car down the road.

With Reed sitting in the passenger seat watching her drive. His warm gaze created a little catch in her breathing. Sensuality oozed from him, and her body responded to the sexual signals, leaving her aware of him as a man.

Yet, she was nearly engaged to another man.

Lacey did a mental reset on her wayward thoughts and glanced at Reed. He smiled at her as if he could read her thoughts and knew she was aware of him as a man. She had to distract him. "Why are you going to the high school?"

"I sponsor a film club. I meet with them twice a month. They show me what they filmed that week. Then we discuss camera angles, lighting, and general overall film making."

"Wow. I'm impressed." And she was. Any man who worked with high school kids had her respect.

"I have one kid who's gone from juvie to filming his neighborhood. I helped him apply for a scholarship into film school. We're waiting to hear if he won."

Reed's enthusiasm for this kid and his class filled the little car. Surprised, she watched him talk animatedly about what they were working on, startled at this unexpected side of him. She liked the way he gave back to the community. "What made you decide to help these kids?"

He shrugged. "I kind of figured I was lucky, and I should pass on some of that luck."

"What do you mean you were lucky?" she asked, glancing over at him, wondering what he meant.

A smile curved his lips, and his green gaze sped up her heart beat. Awareness tingled along her spine, tripping into her midsection and heating other parts of her.

"My background kind of looks like Ozzie and Harriet. Mother and Dad have been married for forty years. I grew up in a decent middle-class suburbia setting. Mom worked, but was waiting at home for us after school. I went to college without working two or three jobs to put me through, and I have no school debt to repay. That kind of life doesn't happen to every American kid. This is my way of paying back the universe for putting me in a good place."

She smiled at him. There was more to Reed Hunter than she'd expected, and she liked that about him.

"What about you? You mentioned step-father number four. What kind of life did you have growing up?"

"I didn't quite have the privileged life you've had. You know about the four step-fathers. I worked my way through college with the help of a scholarship and student loans. But my business is growing, and I'm in a good place now," she said, concentrating on driving and not the masculine scent of Reed that evoked thoughts of tangled sheets and intertwined bodies.

"See, you need to pay something back to the universe for your good luck," he said, leaning close to her. His breath sent a shiver of heated awareness through her, even though the car's air conditioner was working at full blast.

"I guess I've never thought the universe gave me this life. I've always believed I earned it," she responded, refusing to take her eyes off the road and look at him.

Reed's large body, his scent, his touch, his voice enveloped her little Prius. Combine all of that with his warm gaze and she felt trapped in a sensual cocoon that she wanted to explore.

"Either way, it doesn't hurt to help those less fortunate than us. You had the step-father thing going on, so you could probably help a lot of kids who are dealing with that same issue. They need to understand they will get through this and make it on their own."

Finding it difficult to concentrate on what he was saying, she wanted to run her fingers over his full lip and let her hands explore how he felt beneath that shirt.

"Maybe," she said, not committing as they arrived in front of the high school. She put the car in park and turned to gaze at him. "You're different when you're not working on the film."

He grinned at her, his green eyes twinkling with mischief. "You mean I'm a nice guy?"

"Don't get cocky. I mean you're different. The verdict is still out on whether or not you're a nice guy."

"Any time you want to explore the option of finding out if I'm a nice guy or not, let me know," he said, his smile inviting. "I'm available."

"But I'm not," she replied, knowing exactly where his flirtations would lead.

He opened the car door. "Too bad. It could be

interesting."

She laughed. "Or not."

Reed Hunter was the type of man who flirted outrageously, chased insanely, and left his path littered with broken hearts. *Not* her type of man.

"Thanks for helping a stranded guy out," he said, exiting the car.

"You're welcome. See you tomorrow."

"Later," he said and slammed the car door.

Lacey couldn't help but grin as she drove off. Reed Hunter was just as attracted to her as she was to him. A dangerous combination and she couldn't help but wonder if his credit score was above six hundred.

Chapter Eight

Lacey knocked on the door of her mother's apartment, dreading this meeting. Her mother had called and demanded they meet today to discuss Kerri's wedding and her participation as a bridesmaid.

Brenda swung open the door. "Lacey, I'm glad you came."

"Hi, Mom. Of course, I came." Did she think Lacey would shirk her duties as a daughter and not show up?

She walked into the apartment, the cinnamon aroma of something baking luring her in the door. Her mother's eclectic taste of Middle Eastern and Western culture furniture made for an odd mix decorating the living area. Not that Mom had any Middle Eastern ties, she just loved their furniture.

Sinking down onto the couch, Lacey looked around the apartment. "Where's Kerri? I thought she was coming. Aren't we talking about the wedding?"

"This is just between me and you, dear," Brenda said, as she walked into the kitchen and begin to pour iced tea for both of them.

Startled, Lacey realized this parental summons was so Brenda could let Lacey know she didn't approve of her reaction to Kerri's wedding. She sat back, her defense walls rising in anticipation of the upcoming battle.

Brenda glided into the room, her caftan flowing around her. In her hand, she held a plate loaded with cookies. "I made snickerdoodles, just because I knew how much you love them."

Most definitely Lacey was in deep doo-doo. The cookies represented Brenda's way of saying she loved Lacey, yet she was pissed. Baking always confirmed Brenda's anger.

"Thanks, Mom."

Brenda sank down into her chair across from Lacey. "Dear, I wanted to speak to you because Kerri said you haven't called her to discuss the wedding plans. Your sister needs your help."

"We met for lunch a week ago, since then I've been kind of busy. This week, I had three speaking engagements along with taking care of my clients, not to mention the documentary I'm the subject of," Lacey said, defending herself, but also aware of how much she didn't want this wedding to happen.

"Is your work the real reason or don't you want your sister to get married?" Brenda raised her glass of iced tea to her lips, her eyes watching Lacey over the rim of the glass.

As if Lacey were a misbehaved child, her mother was sitting her down to discuss the matter. Growing up, she always started with a discussion and ended with her punishment.

"Both. I've been busy at work, but yes, I think she's making a huge mistake," Lacey admitted, not willing to back down from her original assessment.

"This is your sister's decision. Not yours."

"Why? So, she can ruin her life? Kerri doesn't have time for a husband or even a steady boyfriend."

Lacey yanked a cookie from the plate. "Mom, don't you wish someone would have pointed out to you before you married Ted that he was a drunk? Don't you wish someone would have saved you that heartache?"

"Absolutely not."

"Oh, God." The words slipped from her lips without her thinking. She bit into the cookie, needing something sweet as she pondered the depths of her mother's insanity.

Brenda leaned forward, her brows knit together. "I knew Ted drank when I married him. We had three wonderful years together, before his drinking spiraled out of control."

Aargh, her mother, thought with her emotions, not her brain. "I just don't want Kerri to marry and then realize she's made a mistake."

Brenda leaned back, giving Lacey a penetrating frown while she sipped from her tea. "We're here to support her, not make her decisions for her."

"Okay, I'll call and help her with the wedding, but I don't have to be happy she's marrying," Lacey finally admitted, knowing there would be no rest, until she participated in this wedding disaster.

"Then remove yourself from the wedding party. She should be surrounded by people who are supportive of her on her special day," Brenda said, her eyes darkening as she delicately picked a cookie off the plate.

As Brenda stared, Lacey could feel her anger gripping her insides, making them sizzle like a hot frying pan. She took a bite of the sugar and cinnamon cookie and slowly chewed, savoring each bite, refusing to be swayed by her mother's arguments. Lacey and Kerri had vowed not to be disillusioned by love, and now Kerri was putting love ahead of her future.

"Mom, I love her very much. That's why I keep hoping she'll come to her senses," Lacey said, trying to rationalize with her mother.

Brenda's face tighten into a grimace, as her fingers curled into her palm. "I know I've made a lot of mistakes, but understand, I loved each husband when I married him. I don't know why you girls think the perfect man will keep you from experiencing divorce. My husbands were each perfect when I married them."

"Then what happened, Mom? You can't tell me you accepted their flaws and thought being with them would make your life easier?"

"We all have flaws. Marriage is difficult." With a shake of her head, Brenda sighed and gazed at Lacey, like she was explaining life to a small child. "I want you and Kerri to find a man who brings such happiness to you that, no matter what, you love him and want to be with him."

Brenda was such a romantic, and while Lacey liked the sentiment, it could lead one down a path of disaster. Her mother had taken them down this particular avenue many times, and Lacey no longer wanted to live that way. If she were going to give her heart to a man, then she insisted on a surefooted path that held no major hurdles in the way.

Even a hurdle like a credit report.

The thought stunned her for a moment, and she quickly pushed that revelation out of the way. "I want that experience, Mother, but I want to make sure there are no hidden obstacles standing in my way. I want to know everything about the guy and to be certain we are in complete agreement on how to achieve our goals. I want to know we are compatible that we agree on the important things in life. That we share the same values, and then, we'll fall in love."

"It doesn't happen that way, Lacey. I know you sell this fantasy of finding the perfect mate, but love finds you. You can't match people up and expect it to happen."

Lacey felt her insides twist into a knot. "Are you telling me you don't believe in my matchmaking service?"

"No, I'm telling you that you can do all the arranging you want, but unless chemistry exists between the two of you, it's just not going to happen," Brenda said softly.

"It did with me and Dean," Lacey responded, gripping the chair, resisting the urge to grab another cookie. This conversation needed something sweet, yet her hips didn't.

Her mother frowned. "I don't see it."

"What do you mean you don't see it?"

She shrugged. "There's no passion. There's no chemistry between the two of you. You're like two old friends who kiss."

"Mother!" Lacey said, as her whole body tensed. Anger drove through her faster than a race car. "For your information, Dean has asked me to move in with him. We're apartment hunting."

Brenda raised her brows. "You're going to move in with him without the benefit of a ring? You're just going to give the milk away for free and expect nothing in return?"

Aargh, there was that God awful saying that made a woman into a milk cow. Sorry, she didn't have udders, and she wasn't squirting milk. "That's ridiculous. We're splitting the costs and trying to make sure this will work before we say 'I do'."

"You have the nerve to criticize your sister for getting married? At least a ring is on her finger if something were to happen to Matt or if there are any unplanned pregnancies."

Lacey wanted to scream birth control and condoms kept accidental pregnancies from happening. "And she could be on the same path as you, with multiple marriages in her future," she responded, immediately wishing she could retrieve the words. The tight rein she held on her emotions around her family, loosened and her tongue took on a life of its own.

"Lacey Danielle! At least, I had love with each one of my marriages, even if they didn't last."

Lacey knew when her mother used her middle name, she was furious.

Her mother took a deep breath, her voice restrained. "Dean does not love you. He's using you, but you're too blind to his perfectness."

Lacey threw up her arms. "Explain to me, just how Dean is using me?"

Brenda stood and started to pace the room. "He's all about his career, and you're just another peg on the ladder of success and prestige." She stopped in front of Lacey.

"You're the one who is on the path to multiple marriages because you don't have a clue what falling in love feels like."

Shocked at how confused her mother seemed about love, Lacey sat there unable to move. "Today, a successful career is valued and very important to a man and a woman. How can I be on the path to multiple marriages, when I'm so careful about who I choose? It doesn't make sense, Mother."

Shaking her head, Brenda said, "I don't know how to help you see the mistake you're making." She sank down onto the couch beside Lacey. "I'm not faulting you for being cautious. But without chemistry between the two of you, real love can't exist, and your relationship with the perfect man will end in divorce court."

Lacey picked up her purse. She'd heard enough. "I don't understand why you're happy for Kerri, and you can't be happy for me."

"Because Kerri and Matt have chemistry oozing from them. Love radiates from their glances at one another. Yes, they've chosen a tough road, but they want to be together because they love each other." Brenda took a deep breath. "With or without you, this wedding is going to happen. But you and Dean," she paused to raise her hands in the air, "there's no chemistry. I see two people determined to have hot shot careers and obtain all the material possessions those fancy jobs provide. One day, you'll wake up and realize how cold everything feels."

Hot shot careers! Fancy jobs? Really? An inferno raged through Lacey's body, sizzling from her spine to her toes, leaving an acrid, bitter taste that made her nauseous. Lacey had to get out of here. Her mother challenged everything Lacey believed about relationships. Yet, Brenda couldn't be right because the woman had four failed marriages to prove she knew squat about finding stable, secure love.

"Tell Kerri I'll call her next week about the wedding. I'll do my part and help out."

Brenda watched as Lacey walked to the door. "Lacey, I wouldn't say these things if I didn't love you."

How did you tell your mother she didn't know what in the hell she was talking about? You didn't; you just walked away. "Bye, Mom." Lacey closed the door behind her.

Was she the only sane member in this family who wasn't blinded by this incessant need for love? Why not find a relationship and make sure it was the best thing to do, instead of acting on primal urges?

~

Two days later, Lacey tried to ignore the camera and focused on the clients sitting in her office. The couple were having serious conflict issues, and she didn't have much hope for them.

"David, when you began this relationship with Jennifer, what were your expectations?" Lacey asked.

Twenty-nine-year-old auto mechanic David sat slumped in the chair across from her. He glanced over at the young woman who sat with a Kleenex in her hand.

"I was looking for someone to have fun and hang out with."

Lacey nodded. "Fair enough. Jennifer, what were you looking for when you met David?"

"At that time, I wanted the same thing-someone to have fun with. But we've been dating for three years. I'm twenty-eight years old, and I need something more permanent," she said, dabbing at her eyes.

"I understand, but right now let's concentrate on what brought the two of you together. David, does Jennifer provide the things you wanted when you first searched for a relationship?" Lacey asked.

David shrugged. "Yeah, most of the time."

"Jennifer, does David give what you were searching for when you first met? Are you happy with him?"

She nodded. "Yes."

Lacey frowned and glanced down at her notes. She wasn't getting to the problem. What was holding David back from committing to Jennifer or did he never intend to ask her to marry him? "How long did you know each other before you moved in together?"

"We dated six months, and when my lease was up, it seemed the right time to move in together," Jennifer responded.

"Now you've lived together for two years," Lacey asked.

David nodded. "Yeah."

Lacey leaned in toward David, who sat rigid, trying to appear nonchalant. The man kept a tight rein on his emotions, not letting you see them. "David, what are your goals for the future with Jennifer? Do you ever plan on marrying her and having children?"

David shifted uneasily in his chair. "I don't know. Marriage just seems so permanent, so final."

"Fair enough," Lacey said. "Did you ever discuss marriage and children before you and Jennifer moved in together?"

"I don't remember," he said, glancing away.

Jennifer shot forward in her chair. "You know we did. I would never have moved in with you if I'd known you didn't intend to ask me to marry you. You told me you wanted to wait six months, and then we'd talk."

After Jennifer's outburst, a tense silence permeated the room as Lacey looked from Jennifer to David. "Did you say this, David?"

He swallowed, his Adam's apple moving up and down as he took a deep breath and released it slowly. "Yeah, I said it."

Lacey sat back and considered the kid. David wasn't a bad man; he just had reservations. But Jennifer had waited for over two years for him to propose. How could Lacey help this couple decide if they were meant to be together or separate?

"Do you want to marry Jennifer?" she asked.

In the quiet room, Jennifer began to snivel.

"If you don't want to marry her, I'm sure she would rather learn now than wake up one day and realize you're never going to propose."

Twisting his hands, he glanced over at Jennifer. "It's not that simple. I like living with Jennifer. I like being with her. Why can't things just go on the way they are?"

"Because Jennifer wants a husband and eventually children. Why should she give up her dreams because you aren't willing to commit to her?" Lacey asked quietly.

This problem she'd seen before. Men and sometimes even women just wanted to hang onto what they had and not take that next step. She wondered about Dean. Would she be faced with a similar situation in years to come? Dean told her they were engaged, yet she had no ring.

"Marriage scares the hell out of me," David admitted.

"Okay. How are you going to overcome that fear?" Lacey asked, hoping they were finally going to get somewhere.

"I don't know," David said, looking like he wanted to jump up and run.

"Do you need more time? She's given you two years already. Do you think she's been fair to you? Do you think you could spend the rest of your life with her?"

He glanced down at the floor and then back at Lacey. "Jennifer's been okay; though, lately she nags me. I guess I'm not certain I want to spend the rest of my life with Jennifer."

Soft sobs came from the woman, but Lacey kept her

attention focused on David. "When are you going to know, David?"

"Oh, Jenny, don't cry. You know I love you."

She dabbed her eyes. "Just not enough to make me your wife and have your children."

"I'm not sure. That's all."

Lacey glanced at her watch. "We're running out of time. I have homework for both of you. David, I'm not convinced you want to end this relationship. Your homework is to sit down and make a list of how your life will be different without Jennifer. I also want you to make a list of the things you like about your life with Jennifer. I want you to compare the two lists, and then, I want you to make a third list for me. I want you to write down all the reasons you don't want to marry. Next week, we're going to spend some time looking at your lists. I know this assignment is going to be tough, so dig deep."

David nodded.

"If you don't do these lists, then I think that is a clear indication you aren't serious about overcoming your reluctance to marry Jennifer."

He nodded again and glanced over at Jennifer. "What's her homework?"

Lacey smiled and turned to Jennifer. "I want you to write out a contract. In this contract, I want you to tell David that effective such-and-such date, you will be moving out and getting on with your life. It's time to make a decision for both of you. I'd also like you to make a list of what you like about your life with David. I want the two of you to understand what you have and decide if you're willing to let it go."

She gazed at both of them. "Any questions on the homework this week?"

They shook their heads.

"Okay, you've got a lot of work to do before our next

session. Have a great week, and I'll see you at the same time next week."

"Thanks, Lacey," Jennifer said, and they rose and walked out the door.

Lacey sat back, exhausted. This couple frustrated her with their lack of focus and goals. Two years had passed, and David still didn't know if he wanted to spend forever with Jennifer? Time to commit or say goodbye.

Reed sat down in front of her. "You look tired."

"They drain me. I don't have a good feeling about them. David's holding back, and I can't seem to get through to him. I think he's going to be one of those people who won't realize what he's lost until Jennifer's gone."

Why he refused to commit to Jennifer was baffling. Eventually, she'd get tired and leave.

"You don't think they'll make it?" Reed asked.

"I think if Jennifer stays, she'll regret it because I don't think David will ever commit to her," Lacey said, sadness overwhelming her. She hated it when one of her couples failed. Especially this couple who had met each other through her matchmaking service, but now seemed stuck.

"What's wrong with a man not committing?"

"Nothing, as long as he's up front about how he has no intention of ever asking her to marry him. Don't hold a wedding ring out like a carrot, saying 'in time, this is yours,' and never commit. Two years of Jennifer's life have passed, while she's been invested in a relationship that's stuck. If her life goals are to have children and create a family, then that's not fair to her. You know, if we all just communicated a little better, our lives would be so much easier."

Reed frowned as if he were trying to make sense of what she was saying.

"You think it's better that David tells Jennifer he's willing to marry her, even though he's uncertain?"

Lacey tensed. "Absolutely not. That's a divorce waiting to happen. The real problem is the reasons why he's not willing to commit. Is David being honest about his fear or is he resisting change in their relationship?"

The whirr of the camera reminded her they were still filming; though, she felt like Reed and her were having a private discussion. It seemed as if she were answering a personal question from him.

"You think fear is keeping him from making a commitment to Jennifer?"

Lacey thought about her response, trying to determine how much to say on camera. "A lot of people fear change. Change to the relationship, change in their living arrangements, even change in the woman's body…i.e. pregnancy." She took a deep breath.

By Dean not asking her to marry him and giving her an engagement ring, did this mean he was afraid to marry her?

"I think David needs to decide whether or not he is willing to go to the next step with Jennifer or be prepared to experience the changes his indecision will bring him. If he loves Jennifer the way he says he does, then he'll marry her and continue to work on their relationship."

$\sim$

Reed made the motion to cut the camera. For a moment, he could only reflect about what she'd said. Hadn't his own life experienced a change, not because of his indecision, but because of his unwillingness to go further in the relationship?

Maybe he'd been unwilling to walk down the aisle, but that didn't mean he'd wanted to end the relationship with Blair. She'd wanted a ring on her finger, pronto, and there had been no denying her. Still, he hadn't loved her.

"Shouldn't Jennifer just wait?" he blurted out, knowing they were no longer on the camera, but still curious. "Why such a rush to get married? It seems that's all that women want."

Lacey, who had turned away, swirled around to face him. "Instead of getting married and having the children Jennifer wants, she should give up her dreams and continue on as if her goals are meaningless and let time slip by? The relationship would rock on, until she woke up and realized she was fifty and her opportunity for the family she wanted was gone. How do you think she'd feel about David then?"

Reed squirmed. "Well, couldn't it continue on for another year?"

"She's already given him almost three years of her life. How much more time does he need? David's either in the relationship for good or he's not. It's decision time. Fish or cut bait!"

Reed recoiled, searching inward, wondering what she would have thought of his situation with Blair, but unwilling to confide in her. "What would you tell a couple who have been together six months, and she wants to get married already?"

Lacey shrugged. "Each couple is different. Unique. They have to work through issues before they're ready to walk down the aisle. Some couples do it much sooner than they should."

Reed realized he agreed with her, and yet, he didn't want to concur with her. He wanted to continue to dislike what Lacey did, but watching her work with couples, seeing how she helped people realize their own bad choices hurt them, was beginning to get to him.

Nevertheless, he wanted to continue to believe what she did was evil, charging outrageous fees to vulnerable people who believed this crap.

He wanted to hate Lacey for causing the break-up with Blair; though, he realized he hadn't loved her, and he really only missed the sex she'd provided. Which made him cringe at the selfish man he'd become. What if he'd hurt someone the way David was hurting Jennifer?

Lacey had touched some deeply buried issues from long ago that he'd refused to talk about for years. That one fatal relationship that had closed his mind off to forever. Sure, he'd mentioned he was dumped for a red Corvette, but could Mary have known that neither one of them had been ready for marriage? Could Mary have been the wiser one by taking the out given to her by her father?

They'd been only twenty years old, but still he'd loved her.

Reed stood up to leave. Emotions he'd buried long ago were bubbling toward the surface, like a dormant volcano suddenly active. The need to get far away from Lacey overwhelmed him. He almost wanted to run. "I've got to go. Thanks again for the ride the other day."

"You're welcome." She watched him, her blue eyes narrowing on him, as if she were looking at a slide under a microscope. "I have a question though. What girl broke your heart and made you so gun shy on marriage?"

He grimaced. "That's not open for discussion."

~

Amanda tossed and turned all night, unable to sleep after her interview with Reed. This documentary meant so much to Lacey's dream of television that it had to be good. Great would be even better, but something about the direction of Reed's questions left Amanda uneasy.

His questions had been direct, his tone almost like he'd been searching for anything incriminating to tell the world about Lacey and Mate Inc.-some insider piece of information that would cast dishonesty and mistrust.

Maybe all journalists worked this way. Certainly some reporters behaved like they had no conscience or soul. Yet, he'd specifically told Lacey his film would reflect her business, and the audience could make their own decisions about her. Why had it felt forced?

Amanda went to the interview room and peeked in. Ty was wrapping electrical cords on spools and packing away their lighting equipment.

"Hi," she said, as she walked into the room. "Are you done?"

"For a couple of days. We're heading out on the road with Lacey on Monday. I didn't want to leave our equipment here."

"The next shoot will be in Tyler." Her bags were packed as well, but still, she hadn't known they would be filming.

"Yeah, we're almost packed and ready to go."

"Great," she said, feeling awkward, but needing to ask a few questions. "How have the interviews been?"

"All right," he said, ducking his head.

After that quick, no information response, maybe she should play dumb. "What will the documentary focus on? I mean all Lacey's told me is that you guys would film the way a relationship coach works."

He nodded. His blond bangs fell onto his forehead, lending him a boyish look. "Pretty much."

"Are you getting a good idea of what she does?"

Ty grinned. "Yeah. That couple today, sitting in on how she worked with them, was bitchin'. That poor guy will either be hitched or out on the streets alone."

Amanda recoiled inside, unease flowing like a river through her veins. Lacey would be horrified at his attitude. Is this what the film would show? A couple in the midst of conflict?

"Those clients are dealing with a very sensitive subject that matters a lot to them. They deserve respect."

"Yeah, I know, but it'll be on the film." He laughed.

"Tell me, has your camera caught how wonderful

Lacey is in working with people to achieve their goals? Personally, I think she's the best in the business."

Ty snapped a camera case closed. "She's okay for a head case. That is, if you're into all this psychobabble nonsense."

"Psychobabble nonsense! Whoa, maybe you need to show me what you've filmed so far," Amanda said, fear gripping her chest. "What we do here is very important."

Ty smiled and shrugged. "Hey, I'm just the cameraman. My opinion doesn't matter. Reed's the journalist. He's in charge."

Amanda took a deep breath and gazed at him, trying to discern whether Ty was lying to her.

"But you see what is being filmed."

"And Reed is the editor. I don't know how he will edit this film." He went back to packing his lighting equipment. Then he stood and glanced at her. "All set. I'm going to start loading this stuff in the van."

She walked to the door. "Okay. See you in Tyler."

"Yeah, see you around," he said, carrying his equipment out the door.

As soon as he left the building, she all bur ran straight to Lacey's office and knocked on the door.

"Come in," Lacey called.

Amanda hurried in and saw Lacey was working at the computer.

"Hi," she said. "I'm just making some last minute revisions to my seminar notes."

Amanda sank down in a chair across from her desk. "Lacey, are you certain Reed Hunter is filming you in a positive way? I mean, are you sure this film is not going to show us in a negative light?"

Lacey turned from the computer and stared at Amanda. "He told me this documentary would show how a relationship coach worked, and it would be up to the audience to decide if our company was reputable. How many times have I started with a client who was skeptical about what we do, who in the end believed in us?"

"Most men," Amanda acknowledged. It was true very few men in relationships that needed help came willingly to their office. Even the single men were skeptical when they arrived and only wanted a date, not a lifetime.

"Exactly. I'm not worried. We just continue to do the very best we can for our clients, and the camera will show how we help people."

"God, I hope you're right, Lacey."

Lacey picked up her pencil and tapped it on the desk in a nervous manner. "What choice do I have? If we want the television show, we have to do the documentary. Let's do our best and show the world that Mate, Inc. is a great place to find someone for life."

"I don't know. My interview with Reed seemed like he was digging for dirt on you and the company. I didn't walk away thinking he wanted to show Mate, Inc. and you as the solution to dating problems. And then just now, I was speaking with his cameraman, and either the guy is a complete jerk or they're not making the film we thought they were."

Maybe she was overreacting, but talking to Ty and her interview with Reed hadn't made her feel like they believed in what Lacey was doing.

Lacey grinned and leaned forward toward Amanda. "This is the reason I made you my marketing manager. You're protective of the business and me. You have my back, Amanda, and that means a lot to me."

Amanda smiled. "Thanks, but I'm concerned."

"What did the cameraman say?"

Amanda repeated the conversation she'd just had. When she finished, Lacey shook her head.

"You worry too much. He's an artsy-fartsy cameraman

who looks like he stepped off the pages of *Rolling Stone* magazine. Reed has control of the project and does all the editing. What you're hearing is a cameraman's perspective."

"What about the way Reed asked the questions?" Amanda wanted to know, still uneasy about the documentary.

"He's a journalist. They're supposed to try to trip you up and get you to say something you shouldn't. So far, everything is going fine."

Amanda frowned, but didn't say anything. Her gut instincts were screaming, run for the fire exit, but her boss clearly found her suspicions far-fetched.

"Look, it's past six. I know you've been here since before eight, trying to get everything ready for this trip. Go home. Get some rest, and I'll see you Monday morning."

With a sigh, Amanda stood. Okay, she was tired, and maybe fatigue was clouding her thinking right now. She needed a weekend. She needed Jason, and she needed to have sex. All in that order. "Okay, I'm going. Don't work too late."

Amanda walked out of Lacey's office. Maybe she was a little paranoid, but she would still keep her eyes and ears open. Lacey was her friend, her boss, and she would protect her, at all costs. What Lacey did mattered, and Amanda had her back.

Chapter Nine

Saturday afternoon, Lacey stood in the office of the apartment complex, pacing the floor, waiting for Dean to arrive. She glanced at her watch. A stickler for punctuality, Dean, was thirty minutes late.

They had agreed to meet at three, look at the available apartment, and then go furniture shopping. She'd relented on the idea of furniture, just to keep from having to look at his awful blue recliner, and even agreed to purchase a new living room set, while he paid down some of his bills.

"Do you think he's coming?" the rental agent asked.

"He said he would be here. Let's give him a few more minutes; then you can show me the apartment. I'm sure you have other clients coming."

"All right," the woman said and disappeared back into her office.

Discovering Dean's low credit rating and extensive credit card bills had shocked her. Later, they'd talked, and he'd promised her he would get the balance down on his credit cards. She'd agreed to pay a larger portion of the rent for six months, to help him pay off what he owed.

A Mercedes XL360 turned into the parking lot, and she wondered if this pricey apartment complex was out of their league. The car came closer, and a chill invaded her body, freezing her mind and her vision.

Dean pulled into an available parking spot near her Prius, a grin the size of New York on his face. The car had new tags and the price sticker almost blinded her with sticker shock.

In a trance, she walked outside to meet him.

He put the car in park and hopped out, smiling. "Hey, sweetheart. Sorry, I'm late." Like Vanna White, he stretched his arm out to showcase the car. "What do you think?"

Lacey stood there, while shock waves like small earthquakes rattled her brain. "You're test driving it?"

His forehead creased in a frown. "No, I bought it. They had a great deal on last year's model, so I bought one. I thought with the two of us living together, my bills will be cut in half, and I could now afford the car of my dreams."

The property manager came out the door. "Hi, I'm Sandra, and you must be Dean?"

"Yes," he said, coming around the car and shaking her hand. "We're here to look at the apartment you have available."

She led them through the complex, past an exercise room, pool with a hot tub, and a steam room. She pointed out all the advantages to living at this complex-the gated entrance, the amenities, the status of living at one of their properties. Lacey heard her words, but they didn't seem to penetrate her brain freeze.

She moved like a zombie in a horror film, slow and methodical, her mind echoing with the words, *he'd bought his dream car.*

A Mercedes. An eighty thousand dollar car. Instead of trying to pay off his credit cards and clean up his credit, he'd bought a luxury car. With his credit rating, she was certain he'd gotten a lousy interest rate. The thought of sixteen percent interest on eighty thousand dollars was enough to chain someone to a car payment for years.

"Honey," Dean said, trying to get her attention. "They have a three bedroom available. Would you like to see it or the two bedroom? With three bedrooms, we could have a guest room along with our office."

And who was going to pay the extra rent on a larger apartment, she thought, her stomach knotting like macramé. "No, I think we should just look at the two bedroom."

He frowned, shrugged his shoulders, and told the manager, "Okay, let's see the two bedrooms."

She put the key in the lock and opened the door. Lacey walked into the apartment, as the property manager stepped to the side.

"Our apartments have the top of the line stoves, washers and dryers, as well as marble countertops in the kitchen and the bathrooms. The bathtubs are Jacuzzis, and the showers are large enough they have seats in them with jets in the wall to massage you."

Dean walked around the room and then wandered into the kitchen. "Oh, honey, come see this. They have those new stoves that have the fancy extended vent-a-hood."

Lacey strolled into the kitchen and said, "Hmm."

Excitement just wasn't forthcoming. No matter how hard she tried, all she could think about was that damn car. She couldn't summon even a tiny bit of enthusiasm for the apartment. She walked into the bedroom and glanced at the bathroom, with Dean nipping at her heels like a dog that knew he'd done something wrong.

"This room is so big we might have to buy a larger bedroom suite."

"Yeah," she said, a heavy sense of dread filling her. Warning bells gonged inside her mind like a five-alarm fire bell, causing her head to ache. All she could do was picture that black Mercedes sitting in the parking lot. His insurance would increase. Oil changes and regular maintenance would be overpriced. And gas? How many miles to the gallon did the beast get? A once a week fill of seventy-eighty dollars. Had he even considered the extra costs of this car?

She wandered into the second bedroom. The apartment manager came in and opened the blinds. "This bedroom has its own doorway into the common bath. The last couple who lived here used it as an office. Every room, except for the bathrooms, has a data connection. Our complex has Verizon Fios and Cable in each apartment."

Lacey smiled and tried to muster some enthusiasm. "How much a month is this apartment?"

"This one costs twenty-five hundred a month, and the three bedroom is three thousand a month."

And she'd agreed to pay three fourths of the rent the first six months to help him clean up his finances.

How many clients had she warned away from the situation she now found herself in?

Lacey walked back to the front of the apartment and gazed out the big windows at the view of the maple trees in the courtyard and the Olympic sized pool. From inside, all you heard were the sound of birds chirping and an occasional footstep on the outside stairs. The complex seemed perfect, except for the big ugly black car sitting in the parking lot, gleaming like a beacon of gloom in the hot Texas sun.

She turned from the window to watch Dean examining the kitchen again. He wandered into the separate dining room. "We could have the family Christmas here."

"Yeah, maybe," she responded, sounding as exciting as if she were greeting a bowl of fiber in the morning.

He glanced at her, suddenly taking notice of her mood. "Are you all right?"

"I'm fine," she said.

Dean walked to the door and glanced at her. "What do you think?"

"It's a beautiful apartment."

He smiled, and his eyes gleamed an eagerness not seen since the first time they'd had sex. "Are you ready to sign a lease?"

She shook her head and turned to the apartment manager. "I'd like to think about it. We'll call you."

"Are you sure? They might not have the space much longer," Dean urged her.

"I'm sure." Her voice came out almost growling.

Dean frowned, but walked to the door and opened it for her. She stepped outside into the warm sunshine, yet her blood didn't thaw, and she shivered.

"I'll be here till five." The property manager waved goodbye.

"Okay," Dean responded.

Lacey walked to her Prius, and Dean followed her. "I think we just found the one. I really like it."

"It was nice," she said.

"Honey, what's wrong?"

She wasn't ready to discuss her feelings, but the idea of looking at furniture no longer held any appeal.

"Tell me about the car. I thought you were going to wait."

He grinned, oblivious to her lack of enthusiasm. "I've had a broker keeping an eye out for a deal. He called me late yesterday and set it up for me to drive the car today. It's a great deal, honey. Top of the line, loaded with everything, and they knocked off two thousand dollars."

"Wow, two thousand dollars," she said, unable to keep the sarcasm from her voice. The broker would make that up with the interest on the loan.

Dean didn't notice. "My payments are eight hundred dollars a month for eight years, but what a car. Next time you meet with that producer, you need to drive this car."

Already she hated that car because of what it represented-Dean's lack of judgment.

"I thought you were going to wait until you had your credit cards paid off and your credit cleaned up before you bought another car?"

"Yeah, I was, but how could I turn down such great deal? And I should get my bonus next month. I'll use that to pay off the credit cards. Besides, I'm going to save so much money moving in with you."

If they still moved in together. But she was having doubts. Serious doubts.

"Especially with me paying three fourths of the rent for six months," she said, trying to restrain the sarcasm.

"Just until I get my credit cards paid off," he said. "Hop in and let me take you for a ride."

The thought of getting into that overpriced car nauseated her. She needed to get away. She needed time to think. "Can I get a rain check on tonight? I'm tired, and I'm driving to Tyler tomorrow. I think I need to go home and get some rest. Maybe I overdid this week."

He frowned at her. "You're not coming down with something, are you?"

"I don't know. I just need to get some rest."

He took her by the hand, and she almost shivered. "I was looking forward to spending some time together tonight. Driving around in the car and furniture shopping."

"Yeah, me too," she said. It wasn't a complete lie. Until he'd driven up in that overpriced luxury boat, she'd thought they were back on track. Obviously not.

"I'm going to have a busy week, so I better take care of myself now," she said, knowing she couldn't spend an evening with Dean without losing control of her emotions. They were barely held in check now.

"Okay, I'll drive out to see my parents. You go home and get some rest, and I'll talk to you tomorrow before you leave." He kissed her on the lips, released her hand, and then pulled out his keys. A big grin filled his face. "Watch me when I drive away. I look pretty cool, huh?"

Lacey smiled at him, while inside she was howling with bitter laughter at the absurdity of his comment. "Yes, you do."

She watched him pull away, feeling like she was watching him drive away forever. Was this what she wanted in her life? Was this a precursor of being with someone who couldn't control his urges and spent money he didn't have?

There was no doubt he was interested in appearances. But could he only be interested in his career? Her mother's words echoed in her head, and she wondered if her mother could be right about Dean using her for his career. Was she "the perfect" companion who would help him climb the corporate ladder?

If that were true, could her mother be right about the lack of passion in Lacey's relationship?

~

Lacey stood in front of the audience, giving her seminar. She had presented this lecture so many times, she could recite it backwards, but today felt different. Somehow her confidence seemed to be in the toilet. The excitement she normally felt when she spoke about relationships was right in the crapper with her confidence.

She hit the clicker on the PowerPoint presentation. "Now we're going to talk about communication." She paused and walked across the stage. "How many of you have ever had a problem with communication?"

A ripple of laughter filtered through the audience, and almost everyone held up their hand.

"Do you feel like sometimes you're speaking a different language than your partner? Do you feel like he or she hears you?" She paused for emphasis. "How many of you are busy thinking of your response, rather than really hearing your partner? Don't you think the other person knows you're not really listening? The basis of good communication is good listening."

She let the words sink in and thought of Dean. Even though she was fighting it, she knew her own personal relationship interfered with her performance today, and that frustrated her. As the leader of the seminar, she should be an example. Her relationship should be what her clients strived for, and yet the thought of Dean left her feeling almost slimy. And that couldn't be good.

"A good habit to start is to repeat back to your partner what they've told you. This way they know you heard what was said. In other words, phrase it kind of like this… 'You want me to pay off my credit card debt before I charge anything else.'"

Had he heard her when she said she would pay a bigger percentage of the rent in order to let him pay off his loans? He'd heard the bigger percentage of the rent, but what about his paying off his loans? Had he missed that part?

"Another example, 'When you say I'm overweight, it makes me feel like you don't love me.'" She paused. "See? I owned up to my feelings about what the other person made me feel. I could just as easily have said, 'When you say I'm overweight, it makes me angry.'" She walked across the stage and stopped right in front of the audience. "I didn't scream; I didn't yell. I spoke slowly and precisely, choosing my words with care."

She hit the button, and the PowerPoint slide showed two people screaming at one another. "Do you think they're hearing what the other person is yelling at them? Do you think that name calling and screaming gets through to the other person?

"Studies show that people shut down when you start yelling. You may be screaming the problem to the world, but your partner has shut down, closed his ears, and gone to his happy place." The crowd chuckled.

"Anger is better handled with slow, precise words in a soft, but firm tone. When I say communicate, it doesn't mean exercising your lungs to the point your neighbors two doors down hear you. It means speaking to where the other person knows what's going on with you, and you're clear in your communication about how you feel."

But Dean looked so good on paper. At least, the part she knew he wasn't lying about. The credit issue had come out of the blue, and now she couldn't help but wonder what else she didn't know about him.

Lacey hit the slide button and the words *Deal Breaker* came up on the screen. She wanted to gasp. "Do you know what your deal breakers are?

"A deal breaker is something that will absolutely end the relationship. For some people, its children, alcohol, drugs, cheating, religion, friends, bars, jobs, or even marriage."

It almost seemed like her own presentation was talking to her today. Like she was the client.

"These are things you cannot accept, and you're not willing to change. It's things that, no matter how much you may love the person, you won't accept. Let me give you an example."

She took a deep breath, and her mind went blank with her usual example. She walked across the stage, and all she could visualize was Dean and his damn credit card debt. No matter how she tried. that big black Mercedes rolled into view, and she wanted to scream "what have you done?"

She gave up. "Let's say you and your partner have agreed you're going to pay off all your bills. Then you come home, and when you pull into the driveway, there sits a brand new car. An expensive car. You go in the house, and your spouse or partner tells you the deal was just *'too good to pass up.'* At this point, you have to decide. Is this a deal breaker? Was this a great deal he couldn't pass up or is this a bigger indication of how he will respond to money choices the rest of his life? Does he have issues with money, and instead of you helping to give him some order in life, is he going to drag you down? Will he take your good credit score and trash it, until you share a seat with him in the slow boat to financial ruin?"

She paused, stunned at the words that had just come out of her mouth. They weren't part of the script. She glanced over at Reed, and he smiled at her, while Ty filmed.

God, as they'd taped her, she'd opened a vein in her heart and bled her personal business all over the stage. If she were speaking to a client, she would have told her to cut bait and run. Was she ready to do just that?

Run from the one man she'd thought would be her husband. The man her mother said she had no passion with. The man her sister said was cold.

Was the big black Mercedes a deal breaker?

~

Lacey watched as Reed packed away the camera equipment. She hated to ask him, but Amanda was going to stay at the hotel and take care of the logistics of getting their tapes and books shipped back to the office and pay the hotel. Lacey just wanted to get home. The situation with Dean weighed heavy on her, and she wasn't sure how it would be resolved. Somehow moving in with him no longer held the appeal it once had. She needed to make some decisions.

"Hi," she said, walking up to Reed.

"Hi," he responded as he packed away sound equipment. "What's up?"

"Could I ask you a favor?"

"Sure. What do you need?"

"A ride. Could you drop me off at the office, where I can pick up my car? Amanda needs several more hours, and well, I'm ready to go home." She needed some downtime to examine her feelings, determine if she could continue with Dean.

"No problem. I'm almost finished packing. Ty left in the van. Do you mind riding in my old car?"

"I have a fondness for old cars."

"Great, let's go."

She followed him out the door and crawled into his 70's Mustang. Stunning blue with black interior, it reminded her of an old Steve McQueen movie she'd seen as a kid.

"You got the problem fixed?" she said, buckling up her seat belt.

"Yeah, the alternator went out, which drained the battery. I love old muscle cars. They're kind of a hobby of mine. There's nothing like the sound of a V8 on a clear night."

"I guess. I've never thought of it that way. I just like my little Prius to get me across town and save money on gas. Quiet, too, nothing rumbling."

He pulled out of the hotel parking lot onto the roadway. "Yeah, but you can't pull up to a red light and rev the engine until the person next to you looks over and knows the race is on."

Reed was a such a guys' guy. Ordinary without a pompous need for signs of prestige, yet fun-loving with a serious side.

"How many speeding tickets do you have?"

He glanced over at her, his brows raised. "Tickets? Me?"

"Yeah, racing tickets."

"None so far. Don't jinx me."

She smiled remembering when she'd been a teenager looking for her first car. "I once wanted a Mustang convertible, but I wanted it more for the convertible than the racing engine."

"Most Mustangs are not race cars. Except for the Boss Mustang. Wow, that car has a hot engine. It can outrun a Corvette," he said. The pitch of his voice had risen in that excited tone he used when he spoke about filming.

"My dad would have liked you," she said, surprised at the revelation that stunned her. "He loved muscle cars and owned a Dodge Charger."

"The original?"

"Yeah."

"I'd like to meet your dad."

"I'd like for you to have met him also, but he died when I was ten," Lacey said, the hurt still a dull ache when she thought of her father.

"I'm sorry."

Thinking of her father always made her a little sad. She missed him to this day. "Yeah, he died, and my mother went a little crazy. Not a good way to raise a child."

"That's why your mother has had so many marriages, and you're a relationship coach?" he said, glancing over at her.

"Six months after he died, Mother remarried. After that, it seemed like every few years we had a new step-father along with the children he brought to the marriage."

"I wouldn't have any idea about that kind of life."

"It's not good for children," Lacey said, gazing out the side window. Her mother's voice echoed in her head that Lacey was on the path to multiple marriages, not Kerri.

She pushed the thought away. "What else do you like, Reed Hunter? You like documentaries; you like muscle cars. What else should I know about you?"

He grinned at her. "I'm competitive as hell. Don't play tennis with me, unless you like to lose. I'm a card shark, and I aim to win at everything. Oh, and I like to scuba dive."

"Wow. You like to live on the edge."

Reed shrugged. "I like my life. I used to do really crazy stuff, but now I work and play hard."

Lacey liked Reed. She enjoyed talking to him, and he was always fun. Right now, she needed fun. "And you left out the part about how you don't want a serious relationship."

"No serious relationships. Can you guarantee it won't end in failure?" He shifted gears and the Mustang growled onto the highway.

"There are no guarantees in life. All you can do is make a wise choice and keep working at the relationship." Lacey thought of Dean.

Was she making a wise decision with him? She'd thought so up until these last few weeks, but now she wasn't sure. And when you weren't certain, she advised her clients to take a step back and look carefully at everything.

"You're never going to get serious with someone?"

"Maybe someday, but right now, I'm having fun. I'm in it for the sex."

She laughed. "Spoken like an honest man."

"Haven't you ever been in a relationship just for the sex?"

Lacey thought about the relationships in her past and realized she was so picky there were very few that lasted more than three to five dates. "Nope, can't say I have. I'm more interested in the person's personality and whether or not I enjoy being with them."

He laughed. "Spoken like a woman. You should give it a try sometime."

"And do what? Get my heart broken because all the guy is interested in is having sex and my emotions become involved? I can't do it."

What he was suggesting went against all her principles. She would never just let herself experience sex without being in a relationship.

"No. Keep the emotions out of it. Just experience the passion," he insisted.

"Oh brother, now you sound like my mother."

"How's that?"

Lacey glanced over at Reed, wondering why he was so easy to talk to and why she was divulging this information to him. "It's the word *passion*. She thinks all relationships are based on chemistry and passion."

"And yours is based on what?"

"Mutual goals and interest. What are your relationships based on?"

"Sex. The only mutual goal we have is for us both to reach an orgasm. I usually let her go first," he said with a laugh.

Lacey stared at him in surprise, realizing he was trying to rile her, but she wasn't going to take the bait. "Well, at least you're up front about it. It must be a real trial for you to sit through my seminars and listen to how to have a meaningful relationship."

He grinned. "Not really, but I am shocked at the number of people who attend." He glanced over at her. "You don't look like you would have a problem with passion in your life. Trouble having orgasms?"

She felt her face flame. She could tell he enjoyed this cat and mouse game of trying to aggravate her. She smiled at him. "That is none of your business, but no, I have no problem achieving an orgasm. There is nothing wrong with me sexually. I just…" She stopped and gazed over at him. "Why am I explaining myself to you? You're doing a documentary on me, and I don't need this conversation repeated for everyone in America."

He shrugged. "Worldwide distribution, sweetheart, but this is off the record."

"Still, my sex life is fine. I just don't sleep around," she admitted.

With a quick glance, his eyes conveyed the message men had given women since the beginning of time. "That's a shame. I'd check out the sheets with you anytime."

Lacey felt an unexplained shiver of anticipation go through her. "Sorry, I'm engaged."

Reed sighed. "So I've been told. But I don't see a ring on your finger."

"No, not yet. But still, I'm in a committed relationship. Besides, if that's your 'get me into bed' technique, it's a little brusque." How long was her committed relationship going to last? Especially when Dean brought home high dollar cars they couldn't afford.

He glanced over and with a voice low and throaty said, "Oh, please, tell me you didn't just say that. You've now thrown down the gauntlet for me to show you how competitive I really am."

The way he was looking at her left her breathless, her body buzzing like the low speed on a vibrator. "I take that back. I'm sure whatever technique you use it works very well for you."

The traffic came to a complete halt, and Reed braked hard to bring them to a stop.

"Oh no, this doesn't look good," he said, glancing at his watch.

She sighed. "This could take a while."

He laughed. "Good. That means I can ask you more questions about your sex life."

"I don't think so. My sex life is none of your business."

"Do you want to ask me about mine?"

She glanced over at him; his green eyes sparkled with mischief. This guy was nuts. "No."

"I don't have one right now," he confessed.

She arched her brows. "I find that hard to believe. I thought guys like you just went out to a bar and hooked up with someone."

"Hey, I'm a little pickier than that. I like to find someone I enjoy being with, who wants to have a good time, and knows this isn't permanent."

"And women agree to it?" she asked, thinking how weak some women were when it came to a handsome man with a sharp mind.

"Yeah," he said with a smile.

"And they go along with the fact there's not going to be anything permanent between the two of you?" She watched the frown appear on his face. He had been doing this long enough he'd obviously learned what to expect from women.

"Sometimes I think women think they'll change my mind."

"I just bet they do."

"And then it gets kind of messy when I break it off with them." His hands gripped the steering wheel a little tighter, making the rubber squeak.

"Now I would love to hear some of those stories. I bet they are quite interesting. The female species can be vindictive when they are rejected."

He nodded his head in agreement. "You can say that again. My apartment has been trashed twice. My car keyed. My mattress destroyed and several Facebook pages devoted to what a bastard I am."

"Ouch! I'm not surprised," Lacey said, gazing out at the scenery. "There are very few women who can have sex with a man for long without thinking about marriage and babies. Sorry, but we're just hard-wired that way. We may have the occasional sexual fling, but our goal is to procreate and save the species."

Reed gave her a long look, his gaze was like warm honey on a hot piece of bread. . "That worked for the first couple of thousand years, but I don't think that premise currently holds water."

"No," she insisted. "It's part of our DNA, just like men are hunters. You may not hunt and kill a bear for us to eat, but your basic nature is to be protective and bring home the bacon. It's part of the reason why you're so competitive."

Looking at the car in front of him, he downshifted into second gear. "This is not good." He glanced at his watch again.

"Are you in a hurry?"

"My film class starts in thirty minutes."

"I don't think you're going to have time to drop me off at the office and get to your class. Would it help you if I went to the class with you?" Spending the evening watching Reed teach high school students the art of filmmaking would be interesting. Watching him deal with high school kids could be entertaining.

Dean glanced away from the highway. "Would you mind?"

"No. I was going to go home, feed my cat, and act like all single women."

"How's that?"

"Call my boyfriend."

Chapter Ten

Lacey didn't know what to think as she watched Reed work with the different students. They each had brought in a CD showing five minutes of filming. As the students played their CDs, Reed critiqued what they'd filmed and told them how they could have gotten a better shot with the camera.

She sat in a corner of the room and observed how patient he was with the students and watched the respect on their faces when he praised their work.

"Chad, if you had shot the scene with the sun behind you, the natural light would have highlighted your subjects better. Where did you shoot this film?"

The kid's baggy jeans, sideways ball cap, and t-shirt made him look like he belonged to a street gang. "Downtown Garland. We were hanging out, and I had my camera, so I started filming."

"Good enough. For the final assignment of the year, I want a focused five minute short. Film it like you're telling a story. Think of yourself as a news reporter. Show me the action or the results of whatever you're filming. I'll be looking at how you frame the shots."

"Now, let's look at José's." Reed put the CD into the player.

Lacey stared at how the kid had filmed an elderly couple holding hands as they walked down the street. He'd captured the way the woman glanced at the man and smiled. Birds chirped in the background, competing with the sound of cars and children, while the couple strolled through the park. His film memorialized the elderly pair's devotion for each other on film and warmed her heart.

"Excellent, Jose, excellent," Reed said. "You captured their emotions. The lighting is good, and the audience is with the couple. We're sharing their love as they stroll through the park."

Two squirrels ran in front of the couple, and the camera lens followed them as they chased one another around a tree, until finally one of the animals stopped. The other squirrel leaped onto its back and started humping.

The kids roared with laughter, and even Lacey couldn't help but giggle.

Reed shook his head at the student. "Just when I think you have a great human interest story, you switch to animal lust."

"They jumped in front of the old couple, and I had to see what would happen next," the kid exclaimed, a mischievous smile on his young face.

"Excellent, Jose. Not the humping squirrels, but what you just said. All good filmmakers have to see what is going to happen next. That's what keeps the audience entertained, and their interest focused on your film. The audience must be riveted to the film, or they won't spend their money on your next project."

"It just came naturally," the kid said.

Reed laughed. "Yeah, I see you're a real nature lover."

Warmth seemed to fill her as she watched him work with these young kids. They liked him, and he was eager to teach them what he knew about filmmaking. She'd never expected to see him so eager and open, while he taught.

He stood in front of the students. "When we meet again in two weeks, I want you to present me an outline of what you're going to do for your final shoot. Make it detailed. I want to know you've put some thought into this final project."

Groans filled the classroom.

"Hey, this is a voluntary class. There's a door if you don't want to do the work." He gazed around the room at everyone. "Any questions for next time?"

No one responded. "Okay, I'll see you in two weeks.

Reed sat down at the desk, packing up his notes, while most of the boys scrambled for the door. A few came up to Reed and spoke to him. She couldn't hear what they talked about, but just watching him help these kids from a lower socio-economic high school gave her a new respect for Reed. A first-class filmmaker, he didn't have to spend time helping others, but he obviously enjoyed teaching these boys.

The others left, leaving only Jose. "Mr. Hunter, I thought I was getting some good film."

"Your shooting is excellent. It's your subjects that are lacking." Reed pulled his chair closer to Jose. "Of everyone in this class, you have the best natural talent. You need to prove to me you're serious about making yourself into a filmmaker. I put my name on the line for you when I recommended you to the film school, show me you can produce. I know you have the ability, now prove to me you have the determination."

Reed's pep talk to his student was encouraging, but asking the kid to work harder. And working harder was what it took in today's world.

"I need that scholarship, man. I'll do better," the kid said.

"Good, see you in two weeks."

~

Lacey walked with Reed to the car.

"Sorry, that took longer than I'd planned," he said, as they hurried across the parking lot.

"That's okay."

Reed took her elbow as they went. "Jose's a good kid, but he doesn't have any direction. His parents are not involved in his education. I suspect they're either drug users or alcoholics."

A tingle of awareness rippled through her body at his

touch, and she wondered why her body responded to the feel of his fingers on her elbow.

"Wow. I guess there are worse things than multiple marriages, regarding your parents," she said, not able to fathom having parents on drugs.

"A lot worse. I'm hoping I can get Jose a scholarship into film school."

Lacey gazed at the man before her. There was so much more to him than she'd first believed. A little on the cocky side, but he was an artist, and creative types were carefree individuals who lived life their way. But Reed seemed genuine and caring when he worked with these kids. Anyone who took on a class of high school students in a poor neighborhood had her admiration.

Was Reed more the real deal than Dean?

"Hey, you're zoning on me."

"Sorry, I guess the day is catching up with me. I was thinking about those kids and how tough their world must be, surrounded by gangs and drugs. Makes me appreciate my little corner of the world."

Reed made documentaries that showed different aspects of the world, both good and bad and helped less fortunate kids, while Dean worked for a pharmaceutical company and focused on the next step on the corporate ladder of success. Her role as Dean's wife would be to help him achieve that corporate success. Is that what she really wanted?

"Yeah, they're a tough bunch. If I can help them in some small way, I will, but they have to want to succeed. There are no free rides in life," he said.

Lacey chuckled at Reed's no nonsense approach, but her mind returned to thoughts of Dean. By helping him pay off his credit cards, was she giving him a free ride?

They walked alongside each other, their pace unhurried until they reached his car and climbed in.

"Thanks for coming with me. I know this wasn't what you had planned tonight."

She gazed at Reed, feeling like today had helped her understand him. Even his attempts to rile her over her sex life. "Actually, I enjoyed the evening. It showed me a lot about who you are. Whatever doubts I may have had about you doing a documentary on my business have disappeared. I'm confident you'll do a great job."

~

Three days later, Lacey sat in Dean's new car while he drove them to dinner.

"Is this not the best ride ever? The leather seats are so soft it feels like they just wrap around you," he bragged.

"What did your parents say about the car?" she asked, still not comfortable with the opulent vehicle and wanting to know if anyone besides herself thought he'd dove into a financial pit .

"My mom loved it, but Dad told me I got ripped off. He said I paid too much."

Her thoughts exactly. "That must have been disappointing."

Dean shrugged. "My dad still has the first dollar he ever made. The old man wouldn't know luxury if it bit him in the ass."

They pulled into the drive of the Mansion Hotel and restaurant.

"I thought we weren't going to spend a lot of money?" Lacey said, as they waited in line for the valet.

God almighty! She would have been happy at the local restaurant out on the lake or any number of places that didn't cost two arms, a leg, and your first-born child.

"Oh honey, it's just dinner."

"But it's the Mansion, for God's sake," she said, her voice rising.

"We're celebrating. We've found the right apartment, I bought a new car, and business is going well. We deserve a celebration dinner," he said, reaching over and patting her on the leg in a soothing manner.

Lacey fumed, all her doubts screaming red alert, fear rising up in her chest threatening to choke her. The valet opened the door, and she stepped out, hesitant. What should she do?

Dean came around the car and handed the valet the keys and then took her by the hand as they walked into the restaurant.

At the maître d's desk, Dean said, "Dean Vandenberg, we have reservations for two at eight."

Lacey whipped around to gaze at him in surprise. He'd planned this evening? This wasn't just a momentary decision. Could tonight be the night he asked her to marry him?

An impending sense of entrapment overwhelmed her, and she wanted to run for the door, but her legs had turned to jelly.

But she wanted to marry Dean. Didn't she?

The hostess led them through a doorway and into a small dining room. She placed the napkin in their laps and gave them each a wine list.

"Look around, honey. Do you see anyone famous? Several of the Dallas Cowboys are known for eating here on a regular basis," he said, his gaze searching the opulent restaurant.

Lacey glanced around the room. The crème colored walls and recessed lighting gave the radiated a soft-glow in the elegant restaurant. The paintings on the wall displayed Victorian royalty as the formal waiters moved quietly about the room.

She didn't recognize anyone, and frankly, she didn't care. All she could think about was the expense of this dinner and whether or not Dean planned on proposing. This was the type of restaurant where he could do a grand gesture in front of everyone.

"No, I don't recognize anyone." She buried herself in the wine list. The thought of him asking her to marry him weighed on her. The idea of marriage no longer appealed. In fact, the idea of them living together no longer held any interest.

That realization shocked her. She glanced at Dean. What was she doing?

"Lacey, honey, is that the channel eight sportscaster?"

She really didn't care if it was, but she glanced up and looked across the room. "I don't think so."

"Darn, I really wanted to see someone famous here tonight."

They were moving in together because she wanted to marry him. Handsome, successful, Dean had all the right stats on paper. But he was materialistic, concerned about appearances, and his finances didn't reflect his image. And if she moved in with him, she would be enabling him to continue this reckless financial lifestyle.

The waiter brought the food menus and recited the specials of the evening. Lacey didn't hear a word, as she sat in a stupor, wondering when her feelings had changed. After taking their order, the waiter left, and Lacey couldn't tell you if she'd ordered sawdust.

For the next hour, Dean talked on and on about his project at work. If he noticed she seemed quiet, he never said anything.

After dinner, he insisted on ordering dessert. Over cheesecake, she half-expected him to drop down on one knee and ask her to marry him, but he didn't.

When the meal was finally over, and there was no proposal, she let out a sigh of relief.

"You okay?" he asked, gazing at her. "You've been

quiet tonight."

"I'm fine," she said, realizing just how tense she'd been throughout the dinner.

They brought the check, and she gasped at the three hundred dollar bill.

He pulled out a credit card and she winced. The waiter took it to the back and five minutes later returned. "Pardon me, sir, but there's a problem with your credit card."

Dean looked surprised. "Excuse me."

"It's been declined. Do you have another card or do you wish to pay cash?"

Opening his billfold, Dean thumbed through his cash while Lacey cringed. He turned to her. "Honey, I don't have enough cash. Can you pick up the bill and I'll pay you later?"

Lacey opened her purse, whipped out her credit card, and handed it to the waiter.

Dean smiled and grasped her hand. "I'm sorry honey. I thought I had enough left on that credit card. I guess I didn't."

"Are you telling me your card is maxed out?"

"Yeah, I must have hit the limit."

Lacey said nothing. This would never work. She had to end it, and she had to do it tonight.

The waiter returned her card. "Thank you and please come back."

She all but jumped up from her chair in her eagerness to get out of this restaurant and away from Dean. They walked out of the door of the Mansion, and Dean handed the valet the ticket.

When the car pulled up, the valet opened the door, and she sank down onto the seat. Like sunshine after a storm, relief washed over her, and she sighed a heavy breath.

She'd been stuck with an expensive dinner bill, but she'd escaped a marriage proposal. A dinner bill was a mere pittance for her slow realization that the relationship was doomed. And cheaper than a wedding or even moving in together, only to realize she'd made a serious mistake.

She'd gladly pay the three hundred dollar bill.

"When do you want to sign the lease? I thought we could do it tomorrow if they're open," he said as he drove the car out of the parking lot.

She had to do this now, before they arrived at her apartment. She turned toward him in the seat. "It's over, Dean. I'm through."

He glanced at her, his forehead drawn together in a frown, his eyes searching hers. "Yeah, the meal is over, and now we're going home and having sex."

The image of the two of them together no longer appealed, and she knew with certainty she was doing the right thing by ending this now. "No, I'm breaking up with you. We're not moving in together. We're no longer a couple."

For a moment, he didn't say anything, and then he shook his head. "Come on, honey. I know I stuck you with the check, but I said I'd pay you back."

"It's not the bill. We've dated for over six months, and in the last week, I realized this is not what I want," she said her voice quiet and determined, knowing this break was for the best.

"You're just getting cold feet. We're great together," he insisted.

"No, Dean, we're not."

His hands gripped the steering wheel and twisted it tightly. He glanced at her, his gaze dark and menacing in the mood lighting of the car. "Lacey, this isn't funny. Why are you angry?"

He just didn't get it, and she didn't know if he would ever understand. "I'm not mad. I've realized the relationship is not working for me any longer."

 Sylvia McDaniel

Dean pulled into the parking lot of her apartment and parked the car. He turned off the engine and started to exit.

"I'd like for us to end it right here and now," she said, knowing if she let him into her apartment, she might have trouble getting him to leave.

He halted, his tumultuous gaze turning to her, his expression a mask of pure fury. "Let's go upstairs and discuss this. I'm trying to understand the problem, so I can fix it."

How could he understand the problem between the two of them when he didn't hear what she said? Dean practiced selective hearing and only heard what he wanted.

"Dean, this week I realized we have a communication problem," she said, keeping her voice low and calm.

"We'll work on it," he responded before she could continue.

With a sudden realization, she knew this problem hadn't just occurred tonight. It had been going on for a while, and she had failed to recognize the symptoms. "No, I don't think so. Your car was a deal breaker for me. I had just learned of your credit problems, and then you showed up with this new car. I agreed to pay more than half of our expenses, until you paid everything off, but you went out and acquired more debt. Somehow, I must have failed to communicate to you that being in debt is something I'm not willing to live with."

"We can work this out."

"No, we can't," she said, reaching for the door knob of the car, wanting to get away.

For a moment, he seemed stunned, and then the tightness in his expression increased. "I thought you were happy."

"I thought so, too. But when we started looking at apartments, I began to have doubts," she said. "The car made me realize this wasn't going to work."

"I'm not giving up my car," he said, gripping the steering wheel like he feared the car would magically slip away.

The car was more important than their relationship!

"I would never expect you to," she said, knowing with every fiber of her being she was doing the right thing.

He sighed. "We could go to a counselor and work out our issues."

She cringed inside, realizing this was what she would tell one of her clients. But she didn't want to work on this relationship. She only wanted it over. "I wish I thought that would help us, but for me it's over."

He shook his head. "Damn, you blindsided me."

God, he just didn't get it! Had she been blind these last few months? Tonight, he hadn't said he loved her and would be heartbroken at their break-up. He seemed more worried how she had ruined his plans for the big fancy apartment. Maybe her mother had been right.

She opened the door, knowing the time to end this had long since passed. "I'm sorry, Dean."

He gazed at her, his mouth tight with rage. He turned the key, starting the car. "You know where I'm at if you change your mind and want to talk."

"Goodnight." She shut the door and hurried up the walk to her building, a sense of having shed dead weight making her lighter. Instead of sadness, a sense of calm and rightness filled her as she entered her apartment.

The squeal of tires on pavement pierced the night as a black Mercedes shot out of the parking lot.

~

Amanda sat across from Lacey, munching on a salad while she listened to her friend. When she'd gotten a call from Lacey, she'd expected to find her friend devastated, but instead, she appeared happy, relieved.

"So now, I'm trying to analyze what went wrong. I don't know if I was just blinded by the fact he had so many good qualities or if I never really knew the real Dean. As I look back, I realize how much he didn't hear me. Me, Amanda. I know I was loud and vocal about my desires and what I wanted in life. How could he not hear me?"

Men were difficult and sometimes no matter what, it just didn't work out. Was it going to be that way between her and Jason? "Maybe he didn't want to understand you. If it's something men don't want to acknowledge, they ignore the elephant in the room and hope it won't do too much damage."

Lacey started laughing. "I can't tell you how many times men have said that to me about women. Is this a problem between the sexes or just some relationships? I never thought it would happen to me."

Amanda picked at her salad, thinking it was the fourth time this week she'd eaten leafy greens. She needed something more exciting in her diet and in her life. Men weren't satisfying this urge for something different. "Dean always struck me as sort of selfish, but I thought you could overlook that."

"Yes, I thought so too, but I realized last night when he didn't propose over dinner, I felt relieved, and I knew this wasn't right. I was making a huge mistake."

"You seem happy. When you called me this morning, I thought I'd find you in tears and depressed."

They had a big seminar in Corpus Christi coming up soon, and Amanda had wondered how she was going to keep Lacey all pumped and excited during the program if she was depressed over Dean. But that didn't seem to be a problem.

Lacey leaned forward, her blue eyes sparkling. "It's like a burden has been lifted, and I didn't expect to feel like I'd lost two hundred pounds. The last few weeks, my subconscious has been trying to tell me there was trouble, but I wasn't listening. That's why I couldn't find an apartment for us."

"Have you told your mother yet?" Amanda asked. "I mean she should be happy you're not giving the milk away for free."

"No, we're supposed to go shopping for my sister's wedding dress on Saturday. I'll tell her later and have to listen to her tell me how much she was right and I've finally realized I need passion in my life."

A sinking weight filled Amanda. She wanted to find true love, but sometimes she thought she was going about it the wrong way, even though this was the way Lacey advocated finding the perfect mate.

"I hate that damn word!" she said. "Jason feels passionate about the Yankees. Do you know I had to strip the bed the other night because he'd eaten tortilla chips in it? I refused to sleep in crumbs and salt."

Lacey looked at her. "Are you all right?"

"Sorry, I think I'm PMS-ing today. I could be a dangerous weapon the way I'm feeling," she said, taking a deep breath and doing a 360 degree turn in the conversation. "How do you feel about shopping for a wedding dress for your sister?"

"I've been instructed by my mother to show support for my sister, even though I think she's making the biggest mistake of her life, or be barred from the wedding party."

Amanda rolled her eyes. "Your family is interesting."

Lacey sighed and stared at Amanda, like she wasn't certain Amanda was really okay. "We've talked way too much about my life. How are you and Jason doing?"

Amanda thought about her response and decided now was not the time to talk about her doubts regarding Jason. Her hormones were clouding her thinking, and she needed to wait until her judgment was clearer, so she gave Lacey the facts. "We're doing well. I see him several times a week, and we spend most weekends together."

Always doing what he wanted to do, but that was about to change, and he just didn't know it yet. For their next date, she'd bought tickets to a musical.

"You deserve someone special," Lacey said, her gaze focused on Amanda.

"The verdict is still out on whether or not he's the guy for me. I'm still investigating him," Amanda acknowledged, knowing she wasn't sure.

"Don't rush it, Amanda. I thought Dean was the one and look how that turned out. Make sure Jason's right for you."

"I'm in no hurry," Amanda said, knowing how uncertain she felt about her relationship, but not ready to share that information with her best friend.

Lacey leaned back in her chair and pushed the rest of her salad away. "I think I'm going to focus on getting that television show I want so much, and the way to get that is for me to finish this documentary."

Amanda smiled. "Yes, let's both focus on work. We don't need men to make us happy."

Chapter Eleven

Reed knew he was just looking for an excuse to talk to Lacey, but still he wanted to see her. He knocked on her office door.

"Come in," she called.

He stepped in and saw the phone held to her ear.

"No, Dean. My mind is made up. We're through."

Reed raised his brows at this piece of information.

She frowned. "Now, you're just talking mean. I need to go. Someone is waiting for me here in the office." She rolled her eyes and mouthed the words, "I'm sorry."

Suddenly, she sat straight up in her chair. "If you think making threats will get me back, you're wrong. This conversation is at an end." She started to hang up, then stopped. "Dean, don't call me again."

She hung up, took a deep breath, and stood. Then she began to pace the room, folding her arms across her chest.

"Trouble in paradise?" He couldn't resist asking, while a zing of pleasure at the thought of her alone flashed up his spine.

Her watery gaze brimmed with anger. "Paradise has gone to hell. I'm sorry you had to hear that."

"I heard you use the word *threats*. What kind of threats is he making?" Reed asked, concerned for her safety.

Lacey paused and gazed at Reed, her blue eyes sparkling with unshed tears. "Nothing physical. Dean is not a physical kind of guy. He's threatening my business, my livelihood. He threatened to go to the tabloids and tell them how I'm a relationship cripple. How I can't commit."

Reed started to laugh. "Now, that is funny. From the one time I met him at your office, he seemed very conscious of how others see him. I doubt he's going to want anyone else see he failed at this relationship. In fact, tell him go for it, but you'll tell your side of the story, and it could get ugly."

Lacey laughed softly and wiped a tear from her eye. Reed walked over and gave her a hug. "Don't cry. You'll ruin my image of you as a tough lady who tells people how it is."

She leaned into his chest, and his body flashed heat that had him thinking thoughts of the two of them in bed naked. Not the kind of thoughts he needed right now.

"Thanks, but even tough relationship coaches hate it when they fail at something."

"It's really over between the two of you?" he asked. The scent of jasmine in her hair, the feel of her breasts against his chest ignited his male hormones.

"Yes, I ended it last night," she said.

He leaned back and caught a brief glimpse of a woman hurt and vulnerable. She stepped out of his arms awkwardly, grabbed a tissue, and blew her nose.

"If you ended it, why are you crying?"

She shrugged as though she didn't care, but it wasn't working. "I'm not sad about the relationship. His threats of ruining my business got to me, though. I've spent the last five years building this business and to think one person could ruin it is frightening. This business is my life."

Reed smiled at her, his mind going in ten thousand directions, his conscience reminding him his documentary would spotlight her business in a negative way. If she were crying over Dean's little threat, how would she handle the truckload of misery headed her way?

His stomach knotted, and a pang of guilt rattled him. He reminded himself the audience would draw their own conclusions about her business. But he knew how he regarded her profession. Relationship coaches were nothing more than witch doctors. Or were they?

He refused to consider how this would affect her. "What happened between the two of you? I mean, weren't you about to move in with him?" He studied her closely.

She took a deep breath and gazed at him. "Several things showed me Dean was selfish. Plus, there were some issues that were deal breakers for me."

"Hmm…deal breakers sound serious."

She ignored his comment. "You came here to talk to me about something," she said, returning to her desk and sitting down.

"Oh yeah, I was checking to see what time your flight to Corpus Christi was tomorrow."

"I didn't know you were going," she said, her eyes widening with surprise. "I'm flying out at five thirty tomorrow afternoon."

Coming to her office had only been an excuse to see her today. "I thought maybe we could share a cab to the hotel, but my flight lands at three. That will give us time to set-up for Saturday," he said, his gaze taking in the way her blouse clung to her breasts and how she'd felt in his arms. She was free… He had to stop thinking of her this way.

"When did you decide to go with us?"

"At the last minute, we decided to film one more lecture on the road. We didn't get enough film on the last one and wanted to get some more interviews with attendees."

"Are you guys spending the night?"

"We're flying back Sunday morning."

"Well, I guess I'll see you at the hotel."

He smiled and walked to the door. "See you then."

"Bye," she said and returned to the paperwork on her desk.

Reed stepped out of her office and closed the door. He couldn't keep the grin off his face. The relationship coach was once again an available woman. Her relationship had gone south and for some reason that pleased him.

Yet, his conscience pricked at the thought that he was

the one who she had to worry about ruining her business, not Dean.

~

Saturday afternoon at the conference hotel, Lacey stood in front of the crowd of people and bowed. The day had gone very well, and the audience had been responsive. Amanda said they had a lot of new members for the dating service, and several people had expressed interest in her couples counseling.

Overall, it had been a great day, and now she could relax. She had no plans for the evening. Amanda was going to visit an old friend from college, who lived here, but Lacey had plans to walk down the beach and go to a little restaurant she enjoyed.

She had a good book up in the room and promised herself after the last few days, she deserved some downtime. Some time to herself to regroup and focus on her life goals, to feel the sand between her toes and think about the future.

Two hours later, wearing a new short sundress and strappy sandals, she headed out the hotel door and down the boardwalk to the beach. She loved the wind blowing in her hair, the sound of seagulls, and the pounding of the ocean on the beach. The boardwalk took her over the sand dunes that protected the hotels, and then, there it was, the Gulf of Mexico, sparkling blue, reaching out forever. She stood on the wooden plank and breathed in the fresh salt air, letting the soothing sounds of the ocean wash over her.

"And just where are you going, looking like a goddess in that dress?"

She turned, her body somehow drawn to the sound of his voice. His deep baritone timbers washed over her like a wave from the gulf, the tow tugging at her heart.

Reed stood staring at her, while warmth spread through

her like the setting rays of the sun. "I'm walking down the beach to a restaurant. What are you doing?"

"Going down the beach to a restaurant I love to eat at when I'm here."

"Antonio's?"

"That's the one."

She laughed, feeling giddy at the sight of him. "And who are you meeting there?"

"No one. Who are you meeting?"

"No one."

"Would you care to have dinner with me?" he asked.

A little zing of anticipation zipped through her. Gone were her plans of a quiet dinner alone, but this seemed more interesting. "Yes, I would."

He took her by the elbow, and they moved down the boardwalk to the sandy beach. She stopped and slipped off her sandals and walked in the warm sand, letting the soft grains caress her feet. She went closer to the water and let the surf wash over her ankles.

"I'll never get all the sand off my feet, but I don't care," she said. "The water is cool against the warm sand."

He slipped off his sandals and joined her. "Maybe we should just skip dinner and go swimming in the gulf," he said, glancing around. "We could go naked."

She smiled, the image of the two of them naked in the surf, a pleasant one. "A trip to jail is not what I had in mind for tonight."

A rogue wave, bigger than the others, had her scrambling further up the bank, not looking at where she ran. She watched the water chasing her and ran smack into him. He held her while the water hit the back of her legs, splashing up nearly to her knees.

Laughing, she slipped out of his arms, her heart beating rapidly. "I think we should eat."

She continued walking down the beach, and they

passed families who gathered up their children, sand buckets, and inflatable water toys, trying to get everything together to head for home. The children appeared worn out, their parents sun-burned and exhausted.

God, she wanted this.

She wanted a family with children and a loving husband. She wanted long days building sand castles on the beach and evenings bathing and tucking little ones into bed.

But the man who she could spend forever with had yet to materialize.

Lacey sighed.

"That sigh sounded like it held the weight of the world. You're at the beach. What could be so bad?"

She gazed at him. The wind had blown his dark hair into his emerald eyes, and he brushed it away. She was attracted to this gorgeous man, but something warned her away from him, and she wasn't certain what is was. But tonight, her soul felt empty. "I'm releasing all the tension from the last week."

"Well, you have had a hell of a week."

"Let's not talk about that tonight. How was your week?"

He shook his head. "Not much better than yours. Ty got caught filming some girlfriend half-naked, and after she beat the tar out of him with her purse, I thought I was going to have to get him out of jail. Fortunately, she agreed not to press charges as long as she could have the film."

Lacey started laughing. "Does he do this kind of stuff often?"

"No, and I'm hoping he learned a lesson this time," he said. "Let's see what else went wrong this week. The airport lost a piece of equipment but found it in San Antonio. My mother called to tell me I'd forgotten my father's birthday and gave me hell about it, but other than that, not too bad. I think with this trip, we've gotten all the film we need for your speaking engagements. We're on schedule to wrap this up in four weeks."

"You definitely had a better week than me," she said, taking his hand and running to the restaurant.

When they arrived, Lacey dusted her sandy feet and slipped on her sandals.

The maître d' led them up a flight of stairs to an open patio area that faced the ocean. As she took a seat, she gazed out over the ocean as the sun descended behind the horizon, bathing the sky in golden orange. "God, look at that view."

"I think you like the ocean," he said, leaning toward her.

"Love it. If I were wealthy, I'd own a home right on the water, where I could look out and see the ocean every morning and fall asleep to the sound of the waves at night."

Reed ordered a bottle of white wine, and their waiter poured it into their glasses. Then Reed raised his glass in a toast. "To you owning that oceanfront property someday."

She laughed. "Cheers." She sipped the wine and felt herself relaxing. "Mr. Hunter, where would you like to live?"

"Costa Rica."

She gazed at him in surprise.

"The living is inexpensive, they have a health care system, and the country is in good financial shape. A lot of Americans are retiring there or buying second homes," he said, his gaze warm and lingering.

"You'd move away from America," she asked surprised.

"I'd always be an American, but the world is my work place and I travel quite a bit."

"What about when you get married? Would you live there?"

He gazed at her, a frown on his lips. "Again, I'm never

getting married."

She'd had just enough wine that she wanted to say, really? But refrained herself. How many men had she cured of being unable to commit to the right woman?

"Oh, that's right. I forgot you're the commitment-phobe who's watched everyone around him, except his parents, divorce, and you're not willing to take a chance," she said. Somehow she wanted to dig deeper into his psyche. Most men did not want to live alone.

"Again, I've not met a woman who has impacted my life in such a way to where I would consider changing my marital status," he responded, gazing at her, his eyes twinkling with merriment and warmth. "Now you, on the other hand, have gone the exact opposite way. After having spent the better part of your childhood as a stepsister and watching your mother marry countless times, you are willing to give the institution a chance."

"But only after I spend quality time getting to know that person and I'm certain we could overcome any obstacles life might throw at us."

Tonight, even that seemed impossible. How could you prepare for each and every obstacle? But she wasn't ready to give up on her theory just yet.
"Even an affair?"

"Probably not," Lacey acknowledged. "That's a deal breaker."

"What about a medical condition?"

"For better or worse."

"A job situation?"

"For better or worse."

"What about family members moving in, having to be taken care of, loaned money, etc?" he said, giving her obstacle after imaginary obstacle.

"For better or worse, though the lending money situation would have to be discussed. Honestly, all of it would have to be discussed between the two of us and some guidelines set in place."

He laughed and shook his head at her.

"What's so funny? Couples face those types of situations every day," she said, knowing she and Dean would never have made it. "Even if you live together."

"It's your pragmatic way of looking and dealing with everything. Your setting guidelines comment sounds like a therapist."

"I'm not a therapist. I'm a coach. Big difference. I can tell them what the problem is, but a therapist has to lead them to see the problem. As for being a pragmatist, you're beginning to sound like my mother."

His gaze showed curiosity. "What does your mother say?"

She took a deep breath and felt the wine flow through her blood, warming her, giving her courage. "She said my relationship with Dean had no passion."

Reed laughed.

"It's not funny. I'm trying to be objective and not make the mistakes my mother made. It's my business to help people find partners by being practical, not passionate. Passion seems to get people in trouble."

"But oh, is it ever fun," he said, his gaze lingering on her lips.

Heat smoldered within her, and she resisted the urge to place her hand on his; though, she longed to touch him.

His face was open and relaxed, and then suddenly he frowned. "Have you ever experienced passion?"

"Of course, I have."

"Tell me about it."

"I am not going to talk about my previous sexual situations," she admonished as she wracked her brain for a boy that had made her feel so much she'd lost control.

"Then you've never experienced it," he countered.

"Yes, I have."

"I hear doubt in your voice," he said.

She shook her head. "I'm cautious." Oh God, there was so much doubt. Had she experienced passion before?

"Let's think about this. Have you ever had a one-night stand? Someone you met and there was such chemistry between the two of you that you just wanted to rip their clothes off and do them right that moment?"

He poured her another glass of wine, and she reached for it and drank a large gulp.

The relentless crash of the waves on the beach competed with the soft music of the restaurant.

"You're not answering," he said.

"I'm thinking."

"Well, if you have to think about it, then the answer is no."

She took another gulp of the wine. "Ask me another question about passion. I know I've experienced it, but that question just didn't fit me."

He thought for a moment, his forehead wrinkled in a frown, while his gaze searched her face. "Let's see, from a woman's perspective, it's someone you can't quit thinking about night and day."

"Oh, that's easy. All women have experienced that."

"Okay, how about someone who gives you such mind-blowing orgasms you scream when you come?"

Her glass was to her lips, and she almost spewed white wine as she started laughing. She looked around the room and leaned toward Reed, her voice soft. "This is hardly the place to be talking about orgasms."

"You're not answering the question."

Had she ever had that kind of sexual experience before? She couldn't remember a single time when she'd screamed during an orgasm. "I just don't think that's normal."

"Ah, ha! Your mother is right; you've never

experienced passion. What kind of men do you date?" he asked.

"I date responsible men who don't put sexual prowess first. They want to get to know someone. They want to find out if they are compatible—"

Reed yawned. "B-o-r-r-r-i-n-g."

Not knowing how to respond to him, she gulped her wine. Was everyone right, including her mother? Did she not have any passion? Had she never experienced it before?"

"Okay, you tell me. Have you experienced passion?"

"Many times."

"With women you could have a meaningful relationship with?"

He thought about it for a moment. "No."

She nodded. "See, you can experience passion, but that doesn't mean you can have a compatible relationship with that person."

"I think you can have both. I think you need both to have a really good relationship, but I don't think it's easy to find, and if it doesn't come naturally, then give it up."

She raised her brows at him, thinking that was the most revealing thing he'd said about why he didn't have a permanent relationship. "Are you telling me that none of the women you've dated-that you had passionate sex with-you could have had a relationship with?"

Reed thought about it for a moment. "There were a couple that might have worked out, but at that point in my life, I didn't have the time or energy necessary to give to them. So I blew it off. Do I regret it? No."

"If you met a woman now who you had both passion with and you could have a meaningful relationship with, would you devote the time and energy to that relationship?"

For a moment he was silent as he contemplated her

question, his gaze searching inward as his fingers curled around his glass stem. Finally, he looked at her, his emerald eyes dark. "I don't know. My job consumes me, and I've yet to meet anyone who could take me away from the passion I feel for filming."

She sat back in the chair and gazed at him. Her head felt woozy from all the wine she'd drank, but she couldn't help but enjoy the man. "I understand. I love my work, as well. No one could take me away from my business."

Lacey leaned toward him, and he moved in closer. Her nose teased her with the masculine scent of Reed, and she wanted to lay her face against his neck and breathe. The thought sent the blaze from a smolder to a flame in the very center of her body. She glanced at his full lips and wondered how they'd feel against her own. "Tell me about these one-night stands. Tell me more about this chemistry you feel toward someone enough to jump into bed with them."

He grinned. "I don't kiss and tell."

She laughed and was surprised at how deep her voice sounded. "Darn, I was hoping for some good stories I could tell my clients about how hopping into bed with someone before you know them is not a good idea."

"Well, there was this one night…"

~

Two hours and a bottle of wine later, they began the journey back down the beach to their hotel. Lacey took off her shoes, and this time she went into the water far enough that the hem of her dress became wet from the waves.

Reed watched in awe as she played in the sand and chased baby sand crabs off the beach in the moonlight. He liked this relaxed, playful Lacey. He liked the sound of her laughter, the way she leaned in toward him when she wanted to whisper something she didn't want anyone else to hear, and how she wanted to help people not to suffer from their own bad choices.

She twirled in the water, her dress spinning around her, and he knew she'd had a little more wine than she usually drank. Yet, he loved watching her relax and unwind.

"Reed, come in the water," she called.

God, he wanted to go into the surf, pick her up and carry her to his room and show her some genuine passion. Show her how it felt between two people who couldn't get enough of each other. He wanted to rip the clothes off of her and explore every inch of her naked flesh and feast from her breasts.

Not a good idea. He needed to get her back to her room and then get on that plane tomorrow morning and back to Dallas. Away from this tempting Lacey. "You're getting your dress wet."

She glanced down and saw the wet hem. Then she gazed at him and sank into the water until a wave hit her in the back.

When she rose up out of the water, her dress clung to her, showing almost as much as the airport x-rays. Dear God, all the curves he had tried to ignore, shimmered before him in the moonlight. There was no ignoring them any longer as they were there for everyone to see.

But mainly, they were there for him. And he felt his dick harden at the sight. "I think I better get you back to the hotel," he said, his voice strained as he held back the flood of lust building for this sea nymph.

"Come and get me," she taunted.

She tempted him, and he needed to resist her at all costs. He had to get her back to her room.

He walked out into the water, his pants legs getting soaked and took her by the hand. "I think you've had enough surfing for the night."

She sighed and let him guide her to the shore. A couple

up ahead of them stopped and exchanged a long kiss on the beach.

"Should we tell them to get a room?" she asked, laughing.

"No, why spoil the moment. We're both jealous that they have someone to kiss on the beach tonight."

"Yeah, I'm surprised you were available tonight."

"Why?"

"I just thought a man like you, who experiences so much passion, would have had a date," she said.

"I don't date just anyone. I'm picky." He glanced down at her as they reached the boardwalk.

While she put her sandals on, her dress clung to her, and he tried not to look, but her nipples beamed on high. Lacey was wet from head to toe and more alluring than a fashion model. Over dinner, they had laughed and had fun. If she were his date, he would be well on his way to getting her home and into his bed for the night.

"What floor is your room on?"

But she was business. She was his film, and she would someday possibly hate him. Yet, he was drawn to her and wanted to show her the meaning of passion between two people.

"Second. It faces the ocean. I woke up this morning to the sound of the surf. It was wonderful."

He smiled down at her. They entered the hotel, and he shielded her with his body as they entered the elevator. She shivered from the air conditioning, and he pulled her into his arms to warm her. His body leapt at the feel of her soft womanly curves, leaving him rock hard and wanting.

"I guess surfing in your clothes isn't such a great idea."

"But you had a good time," he said, feeling her back crushed against his chest, his breathing harsh.

"Yeah, I did."

The elevator opened, and she pulled her room key out

of her purse. He followed her down the hall to her room. She slid her key card in, and the door buzzed. She pushed the door open, stepped inside and turned to him.

For a moment, she stared at him, her eyes wide, almost liquid. She took a deep breath and slid her tongue over her lips, gazing at him nervously. "I guess this is good night?"

"Yeah, we've got a busy day tomorrow."

"Thanks for making tonight fun. I had planned on coming back here and reading. I had a great time," she said in a breathless rush.

"Me, too," he said, telling his feet to move.

"See you tomorrow," she said, her blue eyes filled with a heat he tried to ignore.

"Yeah, see you tomorrow." He started to step out into the hallway, when suddenly she launched herself at him. Her lips brushed against his, and he pushed her up against the wall, pinning her inside the hotel room, while his mouth devoured hers, making him so hot, he thought he'd explode any second.

God, how he'd wanted this kiss all night.

Her arms slid around him, and she pushed her hands beneath his shirt, her fingers stroking his skin like a woman searching for hidden treasure.

Her wet body pressed against him, and he could feel every outline of her soft curves, her breasts, her thighs. She smelled of salt water and flowery perfume and tasted of wine and the chocolate dessert they'd shared.

He tried to step out of her embrace, to put some distance between them, yet his feet didn't respond. He had to regain control or be lost. He broke the kiss, and she moaned at the loss of contact.

She opened her blue eyes and gazed at him with enough passion to spark a fire.

Geez, when had it become like this? When had the passion they spoke about become real?

He returned her gaze, his breath coming in gasps. She reached for him, and he stopped her. "Don't touch me, unless you plan on us getting naked in that bed."

She didn't say a word, but pulled him to her, her lips covering his once again. This time he couldn't stop. This time he returned her kiss with an equal one of his own that had his tongue sweeping her mouth, his hands pressing her against his erection. This time he walked her to the bed, his lips never leaving hers.

When they reached the bed, his mouth broke from hers, and he reached for her dress, while she reached for his shirt. In a frenzied haste, they removed each other's clothes and then dropped to the bed.

"Please God, tell me you have a condom?" she said in a breathy rush.

"Yes," he said and pushed her back against the mattress. "But we're going to need more than one."

~

Lacey sighed and reached for him, knowing this was what she needed. She had to have him tonight.

There was no hesitation, as she moved her hands down his warm skin. She wanted to run her hands all over him, and she wanted his hands to touch her. She needed to feel his naked skin against hers. Never before had she felt this urgent need. This sense that she was going to go up in flames at any moment.

Her breathing sounded harsh, but she couldn't get enough air, she couldn't stop her racing heart, she couldn't control this urge for him to be inside her. Joining her, melding her.

His fingers found her center and teased her. "Reed!"

"Oh God, yes," he said as he kissed her, his mouth trailing kisses until he reached her very center.

When his mouth closed over her, she moaned as

pleasure skyrocketed through her. Her fingers found his hair, and she clasped his head. He lifted her hips up until his mouth was firmly planted in her center, and his tongue did the most wicked things to her until her world began to spiral out of control.

Passion built inside her, until she screamed his name. "Reed!"

And he gently bit her, bringing her to a climax unlike anything she'd ever experienced.

Before she could catch her breath, he was tearing open a foil packet and covering his penis in the protective shield. He gazed down at her, his fingers once again teasing her, until she finally grabbed his buttocks and pulled him into her.

He smiled down at her. "You are a greedy wench."

She smiled at him. "Only with you," she said as the spirals of desire reignited. She guided him with her hands on his buttocks as they found each other's rhythm. His mouth covered hers in a kiss that left her gasping for breath.

He lifted her hips, until they were pounding away at each other, the rhythm building inside her until she felt that she would explode.

And then suddenly he gasped, and she let herself go once again as the world tilted around her.

When he rolled off of her onto the bed, she lay there, slowing coming back to earth, wondering why she'd never before experienced anything like this with a man. Why had Reed been the only man to make her world explode around her?

If this was passion, God help her.

Chapter Twelve

Sunlight filtered through the open curtains, splashing across her face. Lacey opened her eyes and stretched…and realized she was naked. Startled, the memory of the night before crashed over her like a rogue wave, shattering the peaceful morning causing her chest to tense.

She glanced over and saw Reed had left. No note graced his pillow. Nothing to show he'd been here most of the night and had given her the most mind-blowing sexual experience of her life. The things he'd done to her had her blushing at the memory of the two of them, their bodies locked together. The sounds she'd uttered, shrieking his name as orgasm after orgasm rocked through her body.

What now? Where did they go from here? How did you walk up to a man you'd spent hours with, screaming in passion?

Good morning? How are you? How did you sleep last night? Was it as good for you as it was for me? Can we do it again sometime?

Yet, she'd gone against her own advice. Broken every rule in her program…and loved every minute.

She couldn't call this a relationship. It'd just been the best sexual experience of her life, and they weren't even dating.

A quick glance at the clock said it was time to get moving. Hopefully, she'd have time to grab a quick bite to eat with Amanda. Throwing off the covers, she jumped out of bed.

An hour later, Lacey sat in a booth in the noisy restaurant in front of a very sleepy Amanda. The clank of silverware and dishes filled the room as the waitresses hurried from one table to the next, taking orders and filling coffee cups.

"I could have slept for another thirty minutes," Amanda

groaned.

"You look hung over," Lacey said, noting the pallor of her friend's complexion.

"You look way too cheerful. What's up?"

"Aren't I always this cheerful?"

Amanda paused and then replied, "Yeah, you're a morning person. But what's going on. Your radiant beam is on high, and you seem even happier than normal. In fact, you're blinding me. Can you turn down the sunshine just a little bit?"

"Very funny. Something happened last night." How did she tell her friend she'd had the most mind-blowing sexual experience of her life?

"Oh, yeah? How much Botox did you have injected to get that permanent grin?"

"No Botox. I had dinner with Reed and then, well…let's just say I didn't do my normal safe routine when I go out with someone," Lacey said unable to keep from smiling.

"He's not a date. He's business."

Unease skittered down Lacey's spine. But she had to tell someone and Amanda was her best friend. "I think maybe for the first time in my life I experienced passion."

Amanda sat back, her eyes widening as understanding dawned. "Are you telling me you slept with Reed?"

"It just sort of happened."

Amanda threw up her hands. "Oh, come on. You tell your clients that it never *just sort of happens,* and now you're telling me that's what happened? Did your brain have a momentary lapse last night and forget your years of training?"

Lacey shrugged, still unable to get the smile off of her face. She couldn't help herself; it'd been great. "I know. I threw out my 'dating rules and regulations' and just went for it. In fact, I don't think technically you could call last night a date."

"Oh, Lacey," her friend moaned. "What have you done? Tell me everything."

Lacey spent the next ten minutes giving Amanda the PG-rated version of the night before, while her mind replayed the X-rated version.

"Why Reed?" Amanda asked. "You weren't sure you could trust him to make the documentary, and now you're sleeping with him. Have you lost your mind?"

"I know. But he's an interesting man. We had so much fun at dinner last night. I like him. When we were saying good night at my hotel room, I kissed him. I initiated the sex, and then, wham, he took it from there. And oh, what a ride."

Looking back maybe it hadn't been her wisest decision, but the night had been fantastic. This morning she'd never felt better.

Amanda shook her head, clearly unhappy with Lacey.

"I couldn't get his clothes off fast enough," Lacey said, watching her friend. "For the first time in my life, I think I experienced passion."

"You can't do this."

Lacey frowned. "Why not?"

"Think about your business. You've just complicated the situation with Reed. He's filming you telling people to get to know the person before sex, and you're boinking him?"

"I know Reed."

"Yeah, and I know my mailman, but that doesn't mean I'm going to screw him."

The glow that had sustained Lacey all morning dimmed. "I know. I don't know where we go from here. Part of me is all aglow from the experience, and the other part is screaming, 'have you lost your mind.'"

"As the marketing manager of your company, I'm

thinking of how this could affect the business. You need to do some damage control and quick. Think about it. He could tell everyone in this documentary that you don't follow your own advice," Amanda said in a voice that made Lacey realize the full impact of what she'd done.

Lacey bit her lip. It was true. She hadn't followed her own advice last night. She'd done something she warned her clients against. She'd had spontaneous sex.

"If you'd picked up some Joe Schmoe down at the bar, it would have been better than sleeping with Reed," Amanda exclaimed.

"I don't have one-night stands or pick up men in bars."

"Well, it sounds like you had a one-nighter." Amanda cocked a brow at her. "Unless you think you're a couple now?"

"No," she said the word as the sunshine washed away all the great feelings left from the night before and reality stared her in the face.

"Honey, you just slept with the wrong man," Amanda said quietly. "You made a mistake."

"Damn, but it felt so good."

"What is your motto? 'Run the feelings by the head and do a gut check on the way.'"

"God, I hate it when you repeat what I've said to my clients."

"This could become a publicity nightmare. Focus on the goal, which is the television show. Not a boinking session with the man filming you," Amanda admonished.

Lacey sighed. "Maybe the break-up with Dean sent me over the edge."

"Maybe. Or maybe you're attracted to Reed."

God, she had enough pure animal attraction to him to keep her pheromones on high alert.

Amanda watched her. "Now is not the time to be lured in by his charm."

Lacey didn't even question her fascination with Reed. The temptation had been there all along. Only now, she knew she liked Reed. And last night had strengthened her interest for him.

"I know." Lacey sighed, the happy, sunshiny feelings slipping away. "So, how do I respond to him now?"

"I think you need to sit down and tell him you were vulnerable because of your break-up with Dean. With the wine, the sea and your vulnerability, you let down your guard."

Lacey couldn't help, but laugh. She hadn't let down her guard. It was buried so deep within her conscious she didn't know where it was hidden. It had yet to come out of hiding.

"Okay, I'll have the talk with him once we get back to Dallas."

"God, Lacey, I leave you alone for one night and you go all crazy on me," Amanda said.

Lacey smiled. It had been the best kind of crazy she'd ever experienced. Maybe there was something to being a little *loco*. "I've never experienced crazy quite like that before."

Amanda frowned. "No. He's off limits. Stay away from him."

~

The next day Reed sat at a Dallas sports bar with Ty, drinking a beer and eating a hamburger. They'd just finished their weekly game of tennis and were about to head over to Reed's house to look at the dailies.

The night with Lacey had been incredible. They had spent the night tantalizing each other into one orgasm after another. And today, she'd intruded into his mind, his thoughts constantly turning to the time they'd spent together.

To his shock, he genuinely liked Lacey and had resisted the urge to call her all day. He couldn't wait to see her again.

The TV over the bar showed the Red Sox batter had just hit a home run, and the crowd moaned as the Texas Rangers fell behind three to two. Reed's eyes were focused on the television, when he heard the voice.

He tensed.

"Reed, oh my God, it's so good to see you," Blair cooed.

She stood before him, looking hot, her blonde hair shorter than the last time he'd seen her. She gazed at him with those crystal blue eyes and pouty mouth, which now just seemed whiney. Memories of the two of them flooded him, but unlike before, he wasn't interested.

"Hi, Blair."

Scene after scene played in his mind of the two of them arguing. Remembering made him queasy. All the reasons why he was doing the documentary on Lacey stared him in the face. Yet, he felt no sense of loss or even excitement at seeing her.

"I'm here with some friends. You look really well," she said, moving closer to him.

"Thanks. Life is good."

"You know, I'm free the rest of the afternoon. We could go back to your place..."

Reed almost choked on his food. The woman who wanted a ring on her finger in the next five minutes, who'd attended one of Lacey's seminars and moved out, now wanted him to take her home with him?

He recognized her move. She wanted sex. "Sorry, I'm busy working on a documentary. Ty and I just stopped by to get a bite to eat, and then we're off to work," Reed said, not interested in picking up where they'd left off.

She cocked her head, studying him intently. A slow

grin spread across her face. "You've got a girlfriend, don't you?"

Her comment took him back.

He shook his head and stared at her in shock. Did he have a bite mark or something on his neck that he'd forgotten about?

"You have that satisfied air about you that you always had after sex."

"I just played tennis. Does that count?" he countered.

She laughed. "No." She paused. "We were good together."

"Blair, I'm still the same guy who refuses to put that ring on your finger. You're the one who went to that relationship seminar and decided to end us. I've moved on and maybe you should, too," he said, wishing she'd go away.

"Yes, I did. But dating is frustrating." She sighed and gazed at him, a quizzical expression on her face. "You never turn down sex." She gave him a knowing smile as she pursed her red painted lips. "I hope it works out for you. Whoever she is, I hope she realizes you're never going to marry her."

Before Reed could respond, she walked back to her friends. Damn! He'd gotten off focus. He'd put his penis ahead of the film. He'd even thought about toning down what he'd filmed so far to make sure Lacey looked good.

His chest froze, ceasing his breath. What the hell was he doing?

He turned his gaze back to Ty, who sat staring at him, his hamburger halfway to his mouth. Waiting.

"She's right. You never turn down tail." He frowned. "Where were you last night? You were going to meet me in the bar."

Reed took a deep breath. He couldn't let what happened last night affect him. It was just another one-night stand, wasn't it? But why did it feel different? "Okay, I screwed Lacey last night, and she had a damn good time."

"Bullshit! Without her going through the relationship steps?" Ty questioned.

"Believe me, we didn't do a lot of talking," Reed said, wishing Ty wasn't so observant and Reed could have kept this information to himself.

"Wow. You skipped steps one through nine and went straight to step ten."

Reed laughed, the sound strained. "Yeah, I guess we did skip a few of the steps. Let's just say a good time was had by all."

"This could blow the documentary out of the water. All you have to do is tell the world that Relationship Coach, Lacey Morgan, doesn't follow her own advice."

Queasiness gripped Reed at the thought of using what they'd done last night against Lacey. He laid his hamburger down, no longer hungry. "Yeah, I could."

"Are you going to?"

He glanced up at Ty and smiled. "No. And lose out on rocking hot sex? Later, in the final editing stages, I'll mention Lacey Morgan doesn't always follow her own rules, but right now, I'm going to sit back and enjoy what the good coach has to offer."

Ty shook his head. "You are one lucky son of a bitch."

A tight grin spread across Reed's face. "Maybe so, but we have a documentary to complete on how Relationship Coaches are frauds. What happened between me and Ms. Morgan doesn't change the focus of my film." He glanced over at Blair, who sat chatting with her friends. "Nothing has changed. We're getting close to the end of the filming. Let's focus on the goal."

Ty raised his beer. "To the Relationship Coach."

Reed smiled. "The Relationship Coach."

~

Lacey pulled into the parking lot of Dresses for Less and saw her mother and sister standing there, impatient frowns on their faces.

She parked the car and approached them. "Sorry, I'm late. I overslept."

Her mother's gaze raked her. "Sleeping in with Dean?"

"No, Mother," Lacey said, determined not to get into a fight with her mother today.

"Let's go try on wedding dresses," Kerri said, opening the door.

Lacey followed them into the shop where hundreds of white gowns filled over half the store. The other section was devoted to bridesmaids and mother of the bride gowns.

"Wow," Lacey said. "This place is really big."

Kerri smiled. "Okay, let's get started. We need a sales consultant."

They began at the front of the store where some of the mannequins had samples of the more popular dresses.

There were long ones, short ones, halter, bare-shouldered, long sleeves, full skirts, slim empire skirts, lots and lots of strapless, and anything else you could think of.

Kerri found a consultant, and soon the woman had them ensconced in the fitting area with a rack of over twenty dresses for Kerri to try on. She went into the dressing room while Lacey and her mother sank into some chairs in the outer dressing area that was surrounded by mirrors.

"You've got to quit trying to hold up this wedding. They're getting married, and there's nothing you can do about it," her mother said, frowning at Lacey.

Kerri came out of the dressing room and turned before them in the room. "What do you think?"

"It's okay. Keep trying on," Lacey said.

"Yes, we need to see the others."

Kerri went back into the room, and Lacey turned on her mother.

"I'm no longer trying to stop her from getting married. It's her life and if she wants to marry him, that's fine. I'm not trying to be difficult; my life has just been crazy the last few days."

Her mother made a harrumphing sound, and Lacey glared at her. "I'm sure that searching for an apartment with Dean has kept you very busy."

Kerri came out of the dressing room. Her gaze flickered between the two of them. "Is everything all right?"

"It's perfect," Lacey said, trying so hard to keep the focus on Kerri, knowing if she said she'd broken up with Dean, the focus would turn to her. "I really like that dress. It fits your body type and makes you look very slim."

"Keep trying on," her mother responded, and Kerri returned to the changing area.

"Now is not a good time for us to talk about Dean," Lacey snapped, not wanting to tell them she'd broken up with Dean.

"As far as I'm concerned, there never is a good time to talk about that man," her mother said in a loud voice that made Lacey wince.

Kerri came out of the dressing room. "What do you think of this one?"

Her mother gushed. "I really like that style, dear. You look like a princess."

"All wrong for you," Lacey decried. "You need a more form-fitting style."

Her sister frowned at the two of them. "Okay, we've still got at least seven more."

When Kerri disappeared, Lacey spun on her mother. "I wasn't going to tell you—"

"Hey, can one of you come in here? I'm stuck."

Her mother stood and strode toward the dressing room.

She helped Kerri into the gown and then returned to her chair.

When Kerri came out a few minutes later, Lacey looked at the dress as her sister spun around. "I like it."

"Not right for you," her mother said. "Keep trying on."

"It's modern, not old-fashioned," Lacey said, realizing her mother would disagree with every dress she liked.

"There's nothing wrong with something a little old-fashioned. But then, I guess you consider marriage to be out-of-date," her mother snapped.

"What? I do not. I just don't want to be married more than once!" Lacey took a deep breath more determined than ever to keep the dialogue between them civil and not ruin Kerri's day.

"And you think I wanted five marriages?"

"Probably not."

"You think it was easy after your father died. You think that raising you girls alone, working a low-paying job, and paying the bills was easy? I made mistakes, but I always tried to do my best by you kids. I can't help it if men turn out to be jerks or alcoholics or even worse," her mother ranted, while Lacey stood back, determined not to argue.

A sob came from behind them, and Lacey and her mother whirled around. Kerri stood there crying.

"Oh, Kerri, I'm sorry," Lacey said, knowing she would probably take the blame for this fiasco. She went towards her sister, who held up her hand to stop her.

"We're supposed to be having fun. I'm marrying the man I love. We're picking out my wedding dress, and the two of you are making this a miserable trip." She sniffed. "I'm going to go in and try on another dress, and when I come back out here, we better start having fun, or I'm going home." She went into the dressing room and slammed the door.

Lacey sighed. "Mom, we have to do this for Kerri. It's

not fair to her."

Her mother frowned. "You're right. But you hurt me when you say things like that. I didn't want to marry multiple times."

"I know. And later I'll be happy to tell you I think you were right about something in my life, but not now. Kerri deserves to have fun today, so we have got to do this for her."

"I was right about something?" her mother said, her forehead wrinkled with surprise.

"Yes, but drop it for now. Let's find Kerri a wedding dress," Lacey responded. God, she was trying; she really was trying to keep the focus on Kerri and her happy day.

Her sister came out of the room in a strapless dress that had a fitted bodice full of bead work and fell into an A-line skirt. The dress was stunning on Kerri, and she looked absolutely beautiful.

Lacey and her mother gazed at Kerri and then at each other. Tears welled up in their eyes, and they wrapped their arms around each other's waists. Together, they stared at Kerri and smiled. "That's the one."

Kerri smiled at the two of them. "I thought so, too."

She came into their arms, and the three women stood there and hugged while tears flowed. Finally, Lacey said, "Oh, you look so beautiful, and I know that Matt is going to be a great husband for you."

Kerri sniffed. "You do? I mean you think I'm doing the right thing?"

"If he makes you happy and you love him, then I think you two should make it official."

"Thanks, Lacey, to hear you say that means a lot to me." She stepped away and looked at the back of the dress in the three-way mirror. "Do you think Dean would be a groomsman? I mean you and him are probably going to be married someday. I just thought it might be a nice touch to include him in the wedding."

Lacey smiled. "That's very nice of you to consider him, but we're no longer dating."

Chapter Thirteen

Amanda held onto Jason's hand as they walked up the drive to her family reunion. "I'm so glad you came with me," she said, staring into his brown eyes. "All of my cousins are married. I stick out 'alone and available' at the family picnic. Everyone else is showing off their kids, grandkids, and then there's me."

He shrugged, his body tensing. "I'm not going to know any of these people." He had been less than thrilled when she'd told him their date destination today.

"You'll know me," she said, giving his hand a squeeze.

"They're not going to have a lot of strange food, are they?"

"No, only the sacrificial goat on the altar of the barbeque."

He glanced at her, his forehead drew together in a frown. "I don't like weird food."

"What's weird to you may be normal to everyone else," she said, realizing he was a real whiner when they weren't doing something he wanted to do. "It's a barbeque. Hot dogs, hamburgers, and the usual condiments. Plus, all the homemade ice cream you can eat."

"Now, that sounds good."

"And my parents will be here."

There was a long silence as they continued walking up the driveway. Did he not want to meet her family?

"You know by bringing me, everyone is going to assume we're serious," he said, gazing at her.

Surprised at his comment, she glanced at him. A frown sat on his face like he'd just learned the Rangers had lost.

"Yes, and if we aren't seriously dating, what are we doing?"

"I mean they're going to think we're getting married."

If things worked out between them, wouldn't they

eventually get married?

"Usually a period of dating leads to the couple pledging their undying support of one another in front of a minister and committing the rest of their lives together. I'm not ready to commit myself to you, but we are dating. Right?"

He let out a sigh and shook his head at her. "You always break it down to the basics." Jason opened the gate to the backyard, and they entered the family zone.

"Hi," Amanda's cousin Mary cried as she ran to hug her. "I'm so glad you came. And you must be Jason."

"Nice to meet you," he replied.

"Later, I'll grab you and tell you all kinds of horrifying family stories about Amanda."

Jason laughed.

Amanda frowned at her. "We're not going to bore him to tears with stories of our misbegotten youth."

"Catch me later, Jason. I'll fill you in on all the gory details," Mary teased.

Amanda spotted her mother. "We better go check in. See you soon."

She led a reluctant Jason over to her mother and father, who stood talking to several of her aunts and uncles. As she walked towards them, her mother separated herself from the group and hurried to her.

"Hi, sweetheart," she said, kissing her on the cheek. "And you must be Jason. It's nice to meet you."

"Thank you, it's nice to meet you, too," he said, his voice less than excited.

Well, he wasn't exactly wowing them. In fact, he didn't even seem to be trying to impress her mother. Her father would be the most critical one, her mother more laid-back. But so far, Jason was just being there, and that was a huge disappointment.

"Amanda tells us you work at Ramson and Company," her mother said.

"Yes," he answered.

Her mother stared at him. "What do you do there?"

"I'm a technical engineer."

Just then her father strolled over, and Amanda watched him size up Jason. Her mother introduced the two of them, and her father shook Jason's hand.

"Dear, Jason is a technical engineer for Ramson and Company."

"What kind of business do they do?" her father asked.

"Oil and gas equipment."

"That's a great business here in Texas," her father responded, making polite conversation.

Obviously, he didn't appear impressed with Jason either. She was just reading their body language, but so far her parents seemed to be less than thrilled with her date.

"Yes, it is. We stay busy."

Her father waved at someone. "Excuse me."

Amanda stood there with her mother. "Where is Aunt Rose?"

"They're not coming till later," her mother said, taking her by the arm and walking across the lawn.

"How long does this last?" Jason asked, looking bored as he followed alongside them.

"Usually until midnight," her mother said.

He turned and gazed at Amanda. "Babe, I've got to be home by five."

"Oh, I know I told you it would last all evening. After dark, we bring out the guitars, and everyone sings and dances."

"I don't sing, and I definitely don't dance," he said, raising his brows.

Amanda frowned, and her mother stepped away from the two of them to speak to another family member. Frustration seized her insides and wrung them out, while she kept a carefully controlled smile on her face. It wouldn't be good to have her first fight with Jason in front of the family.

"You can take me home and then come back," he said, looking into her eyes. "I've got things to do."

"This is our date day. What is going on after five?"

"I've got to work," he said.

She wasn't born yesterday, and he hadn't mentioned anything about working this weekend. Lying to get out of spending time with her family irritated her, but what could she do? "Okay, well, let me at least introduce you to the rest of the family."

She dragged him around the yard, introducing him to her aunts, uncles, and cousins, who politely spoke to him.

Afterwards, they sat with family members until her cousin Mary came up to her. "Hey, girl, come with me. You're needed in the kitchen." She glanced over at Jason. "I'll bring her right back."

Thirty minutes later, Amanda walked outdoors, hoping to find Jason with a coke in hand, standing around talking to her uncles or at least her father.

Instead, she found him sitting close to the pool, his phone out, playing a game. How could you bring someone around to show them off, when they didn't even try to blend in with your family? Was this how being married to him would be like when they visited her family?

"What are you doing?"

"Oh, there you are. I got bored, so I dug out my phone. I'm playing Bejeweled."

"I thought maybe you would get to know some of my family. I hoped you'd be talking to them," Amanda said, her insides tightening with frustration.

He looked around and shrugged. "Maybe later. Do they serve alcohol at these functions?"

"No, my uncle Jim is a pastor. Not going to happen at the family picnic at his house."

Jason snickered. "I guess not." He glanced at his watch. "When's lunch ready? I really need to get home by five."

Again, his insistence that he be home by five. Did he have another date tonight? Or was this just his excuse to get out of the family gathering?

Her uncle Jim came to the door. "Let's all gather around in a circle for prayer before we eat."

Amanda walked over to join in the prayer circle. When she glanced around, Jason sat in the same chair by the pool, his phone in his hand, still playing games.

"Jason, come on," she said, trying to keep the frustration out of her voice. She took her father's hand.

Her father looked down at her and smiled. "Coming around the family is always a good test."

She nodded, her stomach clenching, her insides seething. "Yes, it is, Daddy. Yes, it is."

Jason put his phone away, ran over and grabbed her left hand. "Okay, I'm ready."

Amanda glanced over at him and smiled, but somehow the smile didn't reach her heart.

~

Lacey sat in her office and glanced at her watch to see the time was after seven. Her last client had just left, and exhaustion oozed from her every pore. After her roller coaster weekend of highs and lows, Monday had drained her batteries of all reserves.

Now, she wanted to go home, heat up her TV dinner, and veg in front of mindless television. Something boring and dreadful where she could stare at the pictures and let her mind go numb.

She took out her keys, grabbed her purse and laptop, and walked to the door of her office. Opening it, she ran smack into Reed.

"Oh," she said startled. "Do you know how to knock?"

"Well, I would have if you hadn't opened the door," he said, his gaze giving her the once over in a way that left her warm and tingling.

Her breath caught in her throat, and her pulse started doing the mambo. What this man could do to her body had her yearning for his touch.

"I was just leaving," she said, all business, ignoring the signals from her body.

"I see that. How about I walk you to your car?" he asked, as he held open the door.

"Okay," she responded, not knowing how to react to him. She resisted the urge to wrap her arms around him and snuggle into his hard chest, as scenes from the other night flooded her memory, her body warming.

"I've tried to catch you all day."

She'd avoided him, not ready to have this discussion. "Monday is one of my busiest days." The office was quiet as they walked down the hall to the door that led to the corridor. "You didn't do any shooting today?"

"No, I worked on editing the film we took this last weekend. It turned out really good."

Relief washed over her, leaving her breathing deep and shallow. No more filming her seminars. They were almost done. "Good. I can't wait to see the finished product."

He held the door open while Lacey walked through and then shut it behind him. She turned and locked the door.

"Are you busy tonight? I thought we could go have dinner," he invited, his warm breath tickling the back of her neck as he leaned close to her.

She shook her head. "I can't." She turned and walked quickly toward the elevator.

He put his hand around her wrist, halting her in the hall. "Can't or won't?"

His touch sent her pulse racing, like the start of a gun or a race car engine. She gazed into his green eyes. The man wasn't stupid. He had to feel her standoff vibes. God, she wanted to go with him, but then her mind replayed Amanda's voice warning her about being involved with Reed.

She stepped away from him, needing to put distance between the two of them. "You know my belief on one-night stands. You know I don't sleep with someone without fully getting to know him and figuring out if we're compatible."

"Yeah, yeah, I know all about the twelve steps dating program," he said, clearly not willing to give up.

"No, it's a way to keep from getting hurt. I broke all the rules the other night," she said, remembering the feel of his naked body sliding down hers, skin against skin. Her heart rate skyrocketed like she was running a marathon. She pushed the thought away. She had to remain focused.

"And had a great time. Maybe your twelve step program needs a tune-up."

She stared at him as anger simmered through her on a low burn. Whirling around, she started walking toward the elevator. "My program doesn't need a tune-up. It works fine. I broke the rules of the program, that's all."

He kept up with her determined strides. When they entered the elevator, she punched the parking garage button.

He took a deep breath. "What now?"

"You do your documentary, and I continue to see clients and teach them how sleeping with someone without knowing them is not in their best interest," she said, not looking at him. Knowing if she stared into his emerald gaze, she'd be tempted to throw her program to the wind and fall into his embrace.

"Even when you enjoyed the other night?"

She turned to face him. "Don't do this. Don't lessen what happened the other night between us."

"I'm not. In fact, I want to do it again. I want to take you to dinner and then back to my place and experience the passion you can't deny exists between us once again," he said, reaching out to brush a piece of hair away from her face.

His touch made her catch her breath, the feel of his fingers on her face shaking her resolve.

"I can't."

"Why not?"

"Because I don't do sex purely for pleasure. I want a committed relationship between me and the person I'm sleeping with. And you have made it abundantly clear you do not want a committed relationship. It's better if I end this now, before I get hurt," she said, trying to remain focused on reaching the parking garage, ignoring the signals from her traitorous body.

He stared at her for a moment. "Yeah, we do want different things in life, but why can't we just have some fun together? We can't undo what's happened already, and I know you enjoyed it. Why can't you just live for the moment?"

Almost there, she kept telling herself, afraid to breathe in the small space, knowing the air was permeated with the scent of Reed. "Yes, I did enjoy having sex with you. But I'm the kind of woman who becomes emotionally involved, and you're the type of guy who just wants a fuck buddy."

The elevator bounced as it came to a stop, and the door opened.

"I'm very particular about who I sleep with. I expect more from him than just a rumble between the sheets." She turned and stared at him, his green eyes warming her insides, turning her legs into jelly. God, she wanted him so bad, but it was wrong.

"Do you want a relationship with me? Do you want to

settle down someday? Get married? Have children? Buy a house on the beach?" she asked, watching his facial expression to see his response to her demands.

His forehead scrunched up in a frown, and he didn't say anything.

"That's what I thought." She got off the elevator and turned to him. "It was fun, Reed, but it should never have happened. Let's forget it, so that one night doesn't ruin our working relationship."

"I don't want to forget the night we spent together. It was fantastic, and it could be again."

Her heart plummeted to her feet, and she knew she had to end this now. "I can't have sex with you again without a relationship."

He clenched his fists and said with deadly calm. "Then get prepared. There are all kinds of relationships that don't involve marriage. You want a relationship, then that's what you'll get."

He turned and walked away, leaving her standing in the parking garage, shocked at his outburst. Shocked at his declaration. What did he mean?

~

Reed stormed away from Lacey, needing time to think. He wasn't surprised at her reaction, but she'd sneaked into his thoughts all day at the oddest moments. He'd been unable to keep away from her and wanted to pick up where they'd left off the other night. The rational part of his brain expected her reaction today, but he'd held out hope she'd welcome him with open arms this evening.

And now he'd vowed they were going to have a relationship. What the hell was the matter with him? He didn't do relationships. Not since college when he'd thought it was forever, only to find out all it took was the promise of a sports car to tempt her away.

In his past, the objective had been to get the girl in bed and keep her there as long as possible. The objective here would not be any different. The high and mighty relationship coach would be enticed with the possibility of the two of them in a relationship, except the goal was to get her back in his bed.

And he'd do whatever it took to get her there.

His cell phone rang, and he glanced down at the number surprised. He picked it up. "Hello."

For a moment, he listened. "Where are you?" He responded to the answer with, "I'm on my way."

Tonight, maybe things had happened for the best, maybe it was good the lovely Lacey had denied him the pleasure of her company. But now, he had to come up with a plan to have a relationship with her and get Lacey back in his bed, before the documentary was complete.

There was no denying the attraction he felt for her was stronger than anything he'd ever experienced, but could it be because she was forbidden fruit?

~

Reed pulled up in front of the kid's house. Jose sat outside on the porch, his chin in his hands, his eyes swollen and bruised from the beating. Reed got out of his car and walked up the sidewalk to him.

"I'm sorry, Mr. Hunter," he said, glancing up at him.

The kid was tall and lanky, not muscular, more boy in a man's body. A boy who lived in a shithole of a neighborhood, where violence happened every day. Reed saw something in the way the camera and boy lived and breathed together. With training, the kid could find a new way of life without drugs and violence.

Reed eased down to the concrete porch beside Jose. "Looks like you took a pretty good beating. Are you okay?"

"Yeah, nothing that hasn't happened before," he said quietly.

"You want to tell me what happened?"

The kid sighed. "When the hall monitor wasn't around, the group of kids that Big Bob hangs with surrounded me after class. They grabbed my camera and started filming. When I tried to take it back, his homies took hold of me, and that's when the fighting started."

"Did you tell the principal?" Reed asked, knowing that regardless of what happened, this couldn't be good.

"It was my word against theirs. We all got ISS."

"What's that?"

"In school suspension."

"Yeah, that's not good." Reed sighed and patted the kid on the back.

"Even worse, they broke my camera. It won't turn on."

"Where's the camera?"

"In the house."

"How much of your film project is on there," Reed asked, angry that this kid couldn't seem to get a break from life. Yet, the boy was still trying to get the scholarship.

"All of it. I was almost done."

"Go get it."

The kid jumped up and went into the frame house. In less than a minute, he returned and handed Reed the camera. "They broke the lens."

Reed turned the camera over in his hands as he examined the case that held the disk. "But the disk is still inside, and it's not damaged. I'll do my best to get what you've shot out for you. In the meantime, I have an old camera in the car you can use."

The kid's expression lit up; the hang dog look gone. "You'd do that for me?"

"Here's the deal," Reed said, as he gazed at Jose trying to appear serious. "You've got natural talent. But unless you learn how to use that ability, then you're just a kid with a camera. I've been helping you because you're gifted and could learn an occupation that could take you away from all this. But you've got to help yourself and the way you do that is by staying out of trouble. Avoid fights. One more session with ISS or any other blemish of any kind on your record and the board at the Los Angeles Film School will not even consider you. Are we clear?"

"Yes, sir. I would have avoided trouble this time, but they took my camera, and my project is on there."

"I understand," Reed said, knowing a young man his age had testosterone overflowing. Fighting was survivor mode in this neighborhood.

"I'll see if I can salvage what you've filmed. In the meantime, you use the camera I'm going to give you. And stay out of trouble," Reed said, wondering if that was possible. Even good kids were dragged into situations that got them suspended.

"Yes, sir. Thanks, Mr. Hunter. I appreciate your help."

"Just win the scholarship, Jose."

"Mr. Hunter, I want that scholarship. I want to learn how to operate a camera and make films. I want to get out of here."

Reed saw the hunger on the teen's face. If ever a young man were trying, it was Jose.

"Then follow your dream. Stay out of trouble. Make sure your grades are good. I can help you, but I can't do the work for you. You have to want to succeed."

"Yes, sir."

Chapter Fourteen

Relaxing in her kitchen, Lacey took her TV dinner out of the microwave, just as the doorbell rang. She put the dinner on the counter and hurried to the door. If that were Dean, he would witness how a relationship coach expressed her anger.

She yanked open the door and jerked back in surprise. "Mom, I didn't expect you."

Her mother held up bags of Chinese food. "I estimated when I thought you'd be home and hoped you hadn't eaten yet."

"I was about to sit down and eat a Lean Cuisine."

"This is much better than a frozen dinner," she said, pushing past Lacey and entering the apartment.

Lacey shut the door behind her and led her into the kitchen, where she proceeded to empty the bags onto the dining room table.

"Do you have any plates?"

"Of course," Lacey said, willing her body to move and recover from the shock of seeing her mother in her kitchen. She'd been to Lacey's apartment once in the two years Lacey had lived here.

Pulling plates out of the cabinet, she handed them to her mother and then set out silverware. "What would you like to drink?"

Her mother dished Kung Pao chicken, fried rice, and egg rolls onto plates. "A glass of wine would be nice."

Lacey opened a bottle of wine and poured her a glass. Then they sat down to eat. "This smells wonderful and looks good."

"Hmm…it tastes good, too," her mother said, using the chopsticks that had come with the takeout.

The image of her mother sitting there in her loose blouse that came right out of the sixties, her long hair,

     Sylvia McDaniel

eating with chopsticks, made Lacey smile. How many women had a mother who did Yoga, meditated, burned incense, used chopsticks, and appeared young enough her looks said forties rather than fifties?

"You didn't say much about your break-up with Dean," her mother said between bites.

"No, Saturday was Kerri's day, and I wanted to concentrate on her."

"That was sweet."

"Is that why you're here?" Lacey couldn't help but ask. Did her mother expect to find her broken down in a puddle of tears?

Her mother paused, her gaze seeming to search Lacey's soul. "I'm here because you're my daughter, and I'm concerned about you. I know you find it hard to believe, but I love you. I don't like to see you hurt."

"I'm okay."

Her mother's brows rose in that questioning way Lacey hated. The one that doubted her response. The one she'd seen since childhood.

"Really, I'm okay, Mom."

"I see that," her mother said, frowning. "I thought you'd be heartbroken."

Lacey shook her head, wondering how much to tell her mother. "I broke it off. Dean is self-centered and way too concerned about prestige. I ended it."

Sharon held her chopsticks in her hand, her blue eyes focusing on Lacey. "Did my lecture on living together persuade you to break up with him?"

"No, I'm sorry to tell you that your motherly advice did not end this relationship. It was me," Lacey said, still sure she'd been right to break up with Dean.

Her mother sighed, picking at the chicken and rice. "I'm glad. Not because I didn't think Dean was a nice guy, but he wasn't right for you. You were more like brother and sister than a man and woman attracted to each other."

Her mother had voiced this concern more than once, and Lacey considered the validity of her comment. Nothing like Saturday night's sexual explosion between her and Reed had ever happened with her and Dean. While she usually wasn't one to compare one man to another regarding the art of lovemaking, the difference between Dean and Reed was astonishing. One gave her the sensations of riding a roller coaster and the other was more like being on a carousel.

Maybe her mother's comments held some merits.

Lacey wanted to learn more about this passion her mother spoke of and if the wild ride she'd experienced with Reed was this emotion. Not that she intended to tell her mother about Reed. Lacey wasn't ready for everyone to start speculating about the two of them.

"Mom, you said you always experienced passion. How did you know it was passion or lust when you met your husbands?"

A smile crossed her mother's face, and she stopped eating. Lacey could see her gathering her thoughts. "I've experienced lust. I've experienced passion. Lust is when I want to experience the physical, sexual side of a man."

She took a sip of her wine. "But when I experienced passion, there's an instant attraction that when they touch me, even casually, an electrical charge zips through my body, heightening all my senses. Even when we're just talking, there's something about that man that makes me want to spend all my time with him, only him. I'm starved for his company. And then when I'd get to the bedroom…*ay, caramba!*"

"Okay, Mom, thanks. I think you've answered my questions," Lacey said, not wanting to hear her mother's sexual exploitations. She was her mother, after all!

Still, her mom's description was exactly how she felt

around Reed. And then like a train wreck, it hit her.

Lacey was more like her mother than she'd thought.

In spite of her training, all she wanted to do was nail Reed. Not good for a relationship coach. Way too risky.

Stunned, she sat there her chopsticks in mid-air. The realization that possibly everything she believed about relationships was false, froze her. *No way! Couldn't be.*

Choosing a life-time partner could not be based on wild, reckless sex and fleeting emotional passion.

"Lacey, I know your business is to match couples up and help people find the right relationship. Knowing you, I'm certain you do a great job. But I want you to find the right person, and I hope enough passion exists between the two of you that the sparks are visible to everyone. I want you to be happy. I want you to marry and spend a lifetime with one man."

For the first time in Lacey's life, she was acting like her mother. She was crazy, passionate about Reed. And that scared the hell out of her. For just like her step-fathers, he wasn't a forever kind of man. And yet, she couldn't deny how much she wanted to see him again.

Lacey swallowed, tears clogging her throat. "I know you do, Mom. The funny thing is I think I may have experienced what you're talking about. It's scary. So very, very scary."

Her mother smiled. "I know, honey. I know. But it's wonderful too."

~

Lacey arrived at work the next day and didn't see Reed. She sighed. He wasn't there every day, but she couldn't help but look for him, just the same.

"Good morning," she called to her secretary.

"Good morning," she responded a quizzical expression on her face.

Lacey opened her office door, and the scent of roses smacked her in the face. She stared in shock at the four bouquets of roses gracing her desk. Setting her briefcase and purse down, she dug through each vase of flowers, searching for a card and found none.

She stepped back out into the hall and asked her secretary, "Did you see who brought the flowers?"

Her secretary grinned at her. "They were delivered this morning by Sunshine Flowers. No card. I looked."

"Call the flower shop and see if they'll tell you who sent them to me," she said and walked back into her office.

Dean had sent her flowers once, but she thought he was smart enough to know flowers wouldn't heal their relationship. And though they might have come from a client, she really didn't think so. Instinct told her Reed had sent her these roses.

He was throwing down a challenge and letting her know, *game on*. Like a cat chasing a mouse, he was pursuing her. She took a deep breath and let her lungs fill with the smell of the roses. Something about being pursued by a man made a woman feel good, especially when the man was smart and handsome man like Reed.

A smile spread across her face, and warmth like the caress of a ray of sunshine filled her. Memories of them wrapped together, skin on skin, moving, thrusting, and grinding as one orgasm after another swept over her. How could sex be so good with a man who didn't fit her criteria?

Lacey sat down at her computer and opened up her emails. The first one was from Reed.

Dear Lacey, You are cordially invited to dinner at my place tonight to dine on steaks prepared on the grill. After dinner, I'll give you a private showing of the clips I've edited so far. Dinner's at seven. Please let me know if you'll attend. Reed.

Her heart rate soared, while her brain screamed

warning. Going to his house was like giving a child matches. The chances of getting burned were almost one hundred percent. Yet, curiosity won out. She hit the reply button and responded.

Dear Reed, I'll be there. Thanks for the flowers. Lacey.

He'd known she couldn't resist the chance to see what he'd filmed so far. He'd known she'd have turned him down at the offer of dinner. But a chance to see some of the film was a guarantee she'd be on his doorstep at six fifty-nine.

Yet, sex was out of the question.

A complete no-brainer that she would not jump into bed with him, again. No matter how good the sex had been, her mind refused to go there. Now all she had to do was convince her traitorous body, especially when her mind kept replaying that night over and over looking for the answer to *why Reed?*

Later that evening, she stood nervously before his front door, a bottle of wine in hand, wearing a short, sundress and strappy high heels. She'd taken extra time with her appearance tonight, but wasn't willing to admit why she'd wanted to look special.

She took a deep breath and rang the doorbell. Reed answered, and she quit breathing at the sight of him. It wasn't fair a man could look this hot in nothing but shorts and a polo shirt.

"Hi," he said. "I'm glad you came."

"Hi," she responded. "You knew I would with the offer to see some of the film you've edited."

He grinned. "Nothing with you is a given."

She smiled into laughing green eyes, and a hum of sexual awareness vibrated through her. "Good response. But I bet you were pretty sure I'd come."

"Why don't you come in and we can continue this debate inside where it's cool," he said, opening the door wide.

"Great idea."

Walking into his home, she stared around in surprise at the decorations, the homey feel to the older home in a trendy, hip neighborhood close to White Rock Lake. The man had a good decorating sense with warm colors and tastefully arranged furniture. And no ugly blue recliner anywhere in sight.

"The home is a rental, but I hope to buy something when I move out to LA."

"You're moving to LA?"

"I'm considering it. I shoot all over the world, but that way I would be in the center of the entertainment industry."

She handed him the bottle of wine. "For dinner."

"Thanks," he said. "Come in the kitchen."

Putting her purse down, she strolled into the kitchen where he put the wine in the refrigerator and pulled out the steaks.

"I thought you only do documentaries," she said.

"I do, but right now documentaries are hot." He walked to the sliding glass door that led to a covered patio. "Let's sit outside in the shade, while the steaks cook."

Thank goodness. From the time she'd walked into the house, she'd worried where the bedroom was. How she had to avoid that room at all costs.

She followed him out the door. He carried the steaks on a platter outside. While she watched, he put them on the heated grill.

She sat down in a swing under the patio awning.

"Okay, in about fifteen minutes, we'll be ready to eat." He sat down across from her. "So, dear, how was your day?"

The way he said the words caused a smile to spread across her face. Like they were just an ordinary couple sitting down to catch up after a long day. But they weren't a couple.

"It started off, oddly enough, with four dozen roses from an anonymous sender," she said, staring at him, hoping he would confess he'd sent the flowers.

"Who is he? I'll kill him."

"You know who sent them to me."

He shrugged. "Bet they made you smile?"

"Oh yeah, they did," she replied with a laugh. Everyone who came in wanted to know who'd sent the flowers. Everyone thought they were from Dean, but she knew Reed had sent them.

"Then, I'm sure whoever sent them accomplished their goal," he said, not confirming or denying he'd been the sender.

But she was certain and knew they were part of the plan to seduce her again. Part of her welcomed the challenge and part of her wondered why in the hell she was sitting here with a man who did not share her goals and dreams. "What are you doing, Reed?"

"I'm cooking dinner."

"No, I mean between the two of us. Why are you pursuing me?"

"Don't you like it?"

"I asked you a question. You can't ask me one until you've answered my question."

"I'm pursuing you because it feels good. Because I want to and because I had a fabulous time with you the other night," he responded. "Now answer my question. Don't you like me pursuing you?"

She hesitated, wondering how she could get out of this one without telling the truth, but she knew her lagging response time spoke volumes. Finally, she answered truthfully, even though it revealed too much. "Yes, I'm enjoying your pursuit. But we both know it can't go anywhere because we want different kinds of a life."

"But you're enjoying it?"

"I said yes."

He leaned over and kissed her on the mouth, his lips covering hers. That electric charge her mother had spoken of zipped through her, causing her pulse to race and her breath to rasp in her ears. He tasted of sin and sweet barbeque, and she couldn't remember kissing a man with such abandon.

The grill made a sizzling pop, and he broke the kiss. "Oops, the steaks need turning."

Reed jumped up and opened the grill. After flipping them, he came back and sat down beside her in the swing. "Shouldn't be long now. Where were we?"

"Why are you doing this when you know we want different things in life? There's no future for us."

He turned and gazed at her, brushing a strand of her hair off her face, his gaze serious, his touch gentle. "You need to know where the path of your life is going to take you, that your future is all mapped out, and the right man handpicked, like you've gone to the grocery store with your shopping list. I, however, like to live on the edge. I want to explore this attraction between us. If it lasts one day, fine. If it lasts three days, even better. As for a lifetime, I don't make my plans that far in advance. No woman has ever kept my interest for that long."

She frowned, uncertain as to her response, knowing a lot of what he said was true. "But I don't want to get hurt. I know what a woman like me expects from a relationship. Your idea of living in the moment only means heartache for me."

He sighed. "Okay, let's make a commitment to continue seeing each other, until you feel your emotions are becoming entangled. You can end this at any time. You tell me we're done, and I'll stop pursuing you."

"What if my emotions are involved right now?"

He scrunched up his face and shook his head. "No way. I don't believe the relationship coach has let her guard down and is living for the moment. I think we had one night of rebound sex. You enjoyed the physical side of things."

Lacey did a quick check. No, her emotions weren't engaged yet, but she feared falling in love with Reed when he was up-front he only wanted sex, no relationship.

"Come on, coach. Live on the edge for once. Forget the twelve step program. Live in the moment. Let yourself go."

She'd never done this before. She'd never let a man take charge, knowing there was no future for them. With Reed, she was experiencing passion for probably the first time in her life, and she wanted to explore this emotion further. Just a little longer then she'd end this dangerous liaison that threatened her heart.

Lacey stared into his emerald green eyes and called herself ten kinds of a fool. "All right, but we move at my pace, not yours."

"God, I'll have gray nose hair and need a hearing aid before you're ready."

"Take it or leave it. Those are my conditions."

He leaned over in the swing and kissed her, his mouth sending her pulse skyrocketing. Never before had she been kissed so thoroughly that she wanted to forget the food and let him devour her. She wanted to be on the menu tonight.

When their lips separated, she felt woozy and knew she was in perilous territory. No matches were needed as the spark between them created enough heat to melt her clothes away.

She sat there, trying to compose herself and bring her breathing back under control.

"We'll start out with your plan, but I may try to escalate the pace," he said, his mouth close to her ear.

"I just bet you will," she said, wondering if she could

resist the temptation he presented.

~

Ty set up the lighting in the office next to Lacey's, where they had been filming some of her clients. He tested it against Reed's face.

"What's this girl's name?" Reed asked.

"Martha Jones," Ty said. "She used to be a client of Lacey's, but quit after her dates weren't getting results."

"And she's willing to talk about it on camera," Reed asked.

"That's what Ms. Jones said on the phone," Ty responded, adjusting the lights, checking his meter. "I'll be right back." He rushed out of the room, leaving Reed alone.

"Great." A twinge of guilt skittered down his spine. After having dinner with Lacey the night before, he felt like he was cheating. But this was business. And nothing, not even women got in the way of business.

His attraction to the relationship coach was intense. Seldom did women resist him, and her resistance made him want her more. He couldn't wait to get her back in his bed again. Last night he'd walked her to the door, kissed her soundly, and sent her on her way, surprising her that he'd not attempted to entice her back into his bed. But that was all part of the plan. Lure her in slowly and gently.

Reed enjoyed the chase as much as the next guy, and Lacey was the type of woman who would give him the run of his life. And when it ended, they would go their separate ways, both sexually satisfied.

A knock on the door interrupted his thoughts. "Come in."

The door swung open, and a young, fiery, red-haired woman dressed in an elegant pantsuit stood at the door. "Hi, I'm Martha Jones."

Reed stood and gripped her hand. "Nice to meet you,

Martha. Did Ty go over everything with you on the phone?"

"Yes, and he had me sign a release before I came in."

"Great, then let me explain to you how this works." Reed motioned for her to sit in the chair. "Have a seat here in this chair. I'm going to sit across from you, and while Ty films us, I'll ask you a series of questions. You answer them however you want. We want this to be like two friends chatting with the camera turned on."

"Will Lacey be here during the interview?"

This interview was supposed to show how the twelve steps didn't work for everyone. This was the first of the two bad interviewers he'd managed to find.

"No, it's going to be the three of us."

"Oh, I was hoping to see her."

Reed jerked and gazed at the woman, surprised she'd want to see Lacey. The twelve step program had not worked for this woman, so why would she want to visit Lacey? Especially if she was going to speak out against Lacey's system.

"Maybe afterwards, if she's available, you can visit her," he said, thinking he would be in the same room, just in case Lacey needed him. And then he realized he was being overprotective of the woman he would soon expose.

Ty chose that moment to step into the office. "Everything's all set. Are we ready to begin?"

"Let's get started." Reed sat in the chair across from Morgan.

Ty flipped on the camera, checked the lighting one more time, and then called, "Rolling."

"Please state your name for the camera and tell me how you met Ms. Morgan, the relationship coach."

The woman flipped back a lock of her red hair and shifted in the chair. "I'm Martha Jones, and I met Lacey through one of her dating seminars. I'd recently divorced and dated several men, but they all seemed like losers. Someone told me about Lacey's seminar, and I went," she said, not looking at the camera, but directly at Reed.

"Did you like the program?"

With a tilt of her head, she thought for a moment. "I learned what I wanted and needed as an individual. It made me rethink my life and how I searched for a mate."

Reed was surprised she seemed to like Lacey's program. What had gone wrong? "After the seminar, did your dates improve?"

"Yes and no. I began to meet nice men, but I couldn't find anyone I wanted to spend the rest of my life with."

Reed smiled. Now they were getting somewhere. "Did you think this was because of the system of dating Lacey promotes?"

"Oh no, she is right on about how you have to know yourself before you can find the right person to spend your life with. I mean, how can you expect to get what you want in life if you don't know yourself?"

For a moment, Reed felt a little stunned. For someone who didn't believe in Lacey's dating program, this interview seemed like a testimonial for the twelve steps. "What did you do once you realized your dates were still not what you wanted?"

"I did one-on-one coaching with Lacey," she responded candidly.

"And how did that work out?"

Martha smiled and twisted her hands in her lap. "Well, at the time, I didn't understand. I mean, I did everything she encouraged me to do. Every week we met and went over what I was going to do to find the love of my life. But nothing was happening."

"What did the coach advise you to do?" Reed asked, certain they were finally getting to the problem.

Martha shook her head, and then gazed at Reed

directly. "One day, Lacey asked me if I enjoyed being with my girlfriends. I went on and on talking about my girlfriends and how we had so much fun together. They understand me. They get me." Martha laughed. "She asked me if I ever felt that way about men?"

She paused, her eyes drawing together in a frown "At first I was stunned. I mean I've never really connected with men, and I've always enjoyed being with women. I've never had a physical reaction or even a connection to a man. I mean, it was so obvious, and I'd just ignored it my whole life."

"What?" Reed asked intrigued. How could a woman never have a physical reaction to men? He didn't understand.

She smiled at Reed. "Lacey asked me if I had ever considered that I might be gay."

Reed kept his face expressionless, working at not appearing shocked. "What was your reaction?"

"I got mad and walked out of her office."

Reed's insides tightened like they always did when he was about to get the scoop. Now they were getting somewhere. "Do you think the coach's question was out of line?"

"Oh, no. Later, when I'd calmed down, I started thinking about it. I let go of my preformed ideas of what being gay meant and analyzed myself. My likes and dislikes."

"But I thought you'd already done that in her seminar."

Martha leaned forward, like she wanted to make sure he heard her. "Yes, I had, but at that time, I thought I wanted a man. You see, Lacey is the first person to realize I'm gay. I couldn't find a man because I wasn't interested in men. I like women."

Reed sat there stunned. This was so not how he'd envisioned this interview. He'd wanted someone for whom the coach's dating methods had not worked for them personally.

"Martha, are you in a committed relationship now?"

"You know, I still did the twelve-step program like the Coach suggests, but I used it to find a woman and it worked." Her mouth morphed into a huge smile. "I've been in a committed relationship with Sarah for six months, and we're very happy."

Reed forced a smile onto his lips. This interview had not worked out the way he'd planned. Actually, it went against his assumptions and confirmed Lacey's program. "Thanks for speaking with us, Martha."

Ty cut the camera off, and they gave each other a glance. You never knew what would come out when you interviewed someone. He couldn't remember ever feeling quite so speechless.

No matter how he tried, revealing the relationship coach as shyster was not as simple as he'd hoped.

Chapter Fifteen

Lacey glanced over her list of bridesmaid duties. In the last week, she'd checked off every single item, except for the bachelorette party. That one still hung over her head.

She dialed her sister's phone number and heard her voice. "Hello."

"Hi, I'm calling to tell you I've now completed all my bridesmaid duties, except for the bachelorette party."

"Thank you. That's a relief to know. I'm beginning to understand the Bridezilla routine. Every day, more and more things need to be done, until you think your head will explode from the pressure," she said, her voice strained.

"Are you okay?" Lacey asked, concerned for her sister.

"Yeah, just bridal nerves. I'm sorry, I'm rambling on about me again. You were so sweet the other day and wouldn't discuss your break up with Dean, and here I am babbling about the beginning of our life together." She paused. "Are you all right?"

"Actually, I'm excellent. It's a huge relief we're no longer together," Lacey said.

"What? You're kidding me," Kerri said, shock resonating over the phone. "You thought Dean was the one."

"Yeah, I was wrong. I ended it."

"What happened?" she asked.

"He showed me how selfish he was. I didn't want to pay for him to live with me, while he made Mercedes payments."

"What?"

Lacey gave her sister the low-down on what went on between her and Dean.

"Oh, my God, I'm so glad you found out now he wasn't right for you."

"Yeah, me too. Mom came over the other night and

brought Chinese food. She was worried about me," Lacey said, clutching the phone. Still surprised at her mother's impromptu dinner. Even though they fought and disagreed, her mother always came through for her when she needed her.

"Wow. Did you guys work things out?"

"We did. On your wedding day, the two of us will be getting along fine."

Kerri released a heavy sigh. "Thank God. Now, I won't worry our wedding pictures will show the two of you having a screaming match."

"Oooh, that would make for interesting family chatter," Lacey said, laughing. "And think of the stories you could tell your children."

"Please. As the bride, I have enough to worry about. This is one less thing that will keep me awake at night."

Lacey paused, and the memory of Reed kissing her over dinner the other night sent a little tingle of awareness through her. "Kerri, I'm not asking for intimate details of your sex life with Matt, but you know how Mom goes on and on about passion. Are you passionate about him?"

Silence filled the phone line. "Why do you ask?"

"I'm confused. I've met someone who I'm so attracted to I can't stop thinking about him. When he touches me, I feel so alive, so turned on, I just want to rip my clothes off and jump into bed with him."

Her sister started laughing.

"It's not funny. It's damn confusing."

She continued to laugh. "Oh, my God, who are you and what have you done with my sister? I think you've found the right one."

"No, he can't be the one. He can't," Lacey insisted.

"Why, Lacey?"

"Because he doesn't believe in marriage. He doesn't believe in relationships, and he only wants to have sex.

He's not the man for me."

"That's a problem," Kerri admitted.

"I know," Lacey said, her mind telling her Reed would never work out, even though her heart and body were drawn to him. He was the most exciting man she'd ever met, and he was all wrong for her.

"That's the way I felt when I first met Matt. I didn't want to have a relationship. I didn't want to get married. I wanted to complete medical school, get my residency done, and become a doctor. Yet, being with him has changed my life. I still want to finish medical school and become a doctor, but I can't live without him. And I know you disapprove, but he's my soul mate, my best friend, and the man I want to spend forever with," Kerri said, a quiet determination in her voice. "I need him, Lacey."

Lacey sat stunned for a moment at the self-confidence she heard in her sister's voice. She'd never heard such steely resolve from Kerri.

"Wow, Kerri, maybe you should put that in your vows," Lacey said. "Even after witnessing what Mom went through, you want to take a chance with Matt?"

"Yes. And if your guy is even half as good as Matt and you're attracted to him, give it some time. He could change his mind."

Lacey couldn't imagine Reed changing. Nothing about this "thing" they were engaged in could be considered permanent. Yet, whatever this "thing" was, she couldn't deny the passion it evoked.

"I'm sorry I wasn't as supportive in the beginning as I should have been. I wanted to protect you," Lacey admitted.

"I know. And I love you for it. But I'm doing the right thing by marrying Matt. Give your guy some time, and if this budding situation is meant to be, things will work out."

"When did you become so wise?" Lacey asked,

surprised at how her baby sister seemed to have it together.

"I learned it from my big sister."

"Love you, Kerri."

"You too, Lacey. Now I gotta run, unless you want to help me pack boxes."

"Hell, no. I'll talk to you later."

~

The next day Lacey sat in her office, making notes on client's files, taking care of paperwork, and glancing at her watch. Her client meetings began at two. She hadn't had time for lunch. Booked until eight tonight, she would then crawl home exhausted and fall into bed.

She loved her job, but sometimes the amount of work was overwhelming. With her busy schedule of seminars and personal meetings with clients, she could fill up every hour of the day. Lately, she'd given herself one weekend a month free. No taking work home, no seminars, no answering client's desperate calls.

A knock on the door made her glance up. "Come in?"

Reed stood there with a basket of food in his hand. "Your secretary said you were skipping lunch today, so I brought lunch to you."

She smiled, her heart filling with an emotion she didn't want to recognize. No man had ever just dropped by with food to make her day easier. "Thanks. I'm starving."

He sat the basket down on her desk. "I didn't know what you like, so I bought ham and cheese or chicken salad."

"I love chicken salad."

He grinned at her and started for the door.

A part of her knew she should encourage him to leave, but she didn't want him to go. She wanted to spend time with him. Just the two of them.

"Is there enough for two?"

Reed turned around, and his eager smile sent warm vibrations dancing through her body. For heaven's sake, it was just a smile. But it packed a punch.

"I hoped you'd ask me to stay."

"It has to be quick. I need to finish these reports before my first session this afternoon," she said, unable to keep the smile off her face.

Reed began to pull everything out of the basket. "Ham and cheese for me." He reached in and grabbed the other sandwich. "Chicken salad for you. Some cups of fruit. Napkins and iced tea."

"You thought of everything," she said and reached for her sandwich. The man could give lessons to other men on how to make a woman feel special.

He sat across from her on the desk, unwrapped his sandwich and took a bite. After he'd finished chewing, he asked, "What did you think of the clips I showed you the other night?"

"They were good. It was a little embarrassing to see me in so much film, but overall you did a great job" she said. And she wasn't lying. The clips he'd shown her were excellent. She hoped the rest of the film would be just as good. But she felt uneasy talking about the film. Her career was riding on this project and the television show she so desperately wanted, which he knew nothing about. Eventually, she would tell him, but not until it was for certain.

"Thanks."

"What's next?" Lacey asked, taking a bite of her sandwich.

"We have a couple more individual sessions to film, and then we go off to the studio and start working on putting it all together."

"What sessions are you filming?"

"That couple…the one where he didn't want to marry

the girl, and she was pressuring him."

Lacey didn't have a good feeling about that couple. She feared they were not going to make it.

"Oh dear, I see them later this week. We could witness a break-up scene with them."

"I don't understand why she can't let things keep going the way they are currently," he admitted.

Lacey paused for a moment, thinking of how she could explain to him how a woman still needed to know she was the only person in a man's life. How a woman wanted to love one person for a lifetime, who gave her children and grew old with her. How could she explain this to Reed, so he understood from a woman's perspective?

"Reed, you've told me your parents have been married for many years. Have you ever asked your mother about their marriage? Have there been times they almost split up? Have you ever asked her about living with your dad? Would she have moved in with him?"

"Oh God, no. My mom is pretty opened minded, but she's said more than once, she would never have moved in with my dad because she'd still be waiting for that ring."

Lacey couldn't help but wonder if some of Reed's resistance to marriage he'd learned from his father.

"Hmm…I wonder why that is. My dad didn't want to get married, either. The story my mother tells is that she gave him an ultimatum. Marry me or get on down the road. He decided to marry her," Lacey said, taking a sip of iced tea, curious about Reed's family. "Does your father have any regrets?"

"Only when the Visa bill comes in."

Lacey laughed. "Your dad didn't want to get married?"

"That's what he said. When I was young, he told me I'd be crazy to marry anyone before I reached thirty," Reed said, before taking a bite of his sandwich.

"Why would he say such a thing?" Lacey asked. "Was

he thirty when he married your mother?"

"No. Dad kept telling me to sample as many women as I could before I stuck with one. And I've done my best," Reed admitted.

"Men think women are like flowers-pollinate as many as you can," she said., wondering about Reed's father. Sounds like he'd resisted marriage as much as his son.

"And women think men are like ATM machines. *Cha-ching.*"

"What do pollination and money have in common?" she asked.

He started to laugh, not answering her question.

"Did your dad tell you women think men are like ATM machines? After your comment about your mother and the Visa bill, I wondered. Some women make more than their husbands. When my sister becomes a doctor, she'll make more than her fiancé."

"True, but if women aren't dependent on a man for money, then why do they need us?"

To her, this was so easy she smiled. "Because we are created to procreate, and our bodies send secret signals to our brains, telling us to find a man and get pollinated. We are the gatherers, the people who keep the clan together, and help keep the testosterone at a level, so all hell doesn't break loose in society. We're the peacemakers, the keepers of the next generation. Without us, the tribe doesn't continue."

He nodded. "And there are always a few hunters in the clan who don't want to go with the normal rituals. They want to strike out on their own."

They had the most interesting conversations, and she was starting to learn more about Reed Hunter's background. It sounded so close to the type of family she'd dreamed of growing up in, but then he would reveal secrets about his father and mother, and she'd realize they were just like everyone else.

"True. They were either the bravest of the warriors, or they were killed and eaten by the animals." She gazed at him. "Which are you, Reed? A brave warrior or a schmuck who will be lunch for some animal in the jungle?"

He started packing up the basket and throwing away their dirty utensils. "Only time will tell, but regardless, I will go out in a blaze of glory."

She smiled at him. "Thanks for lunch. I appreciate it. I would have gone hungry, until I got home tonight."

"Any time." Reed leaned over the desk and kissed her, his lips brushing against hers in a way that left her hungry for more. Abruptly, he broke off and smiled at her, knowing he'd teased her, left her wanting. "See you in the jungle."

And then he was gone. Leaving her office lonely, silent, and her sexually aroused. Reed baited her, stirring her desires and making her want him. And damn it, his tactics were working.

She couldn't help but smile. He'd brought her lunch and made sure she ate on one of her busiest days. The man knew how to seduce a woman. He knew how to worm his way into her heart and her pants and then leave her wanting more.

~

Amanda followed Jason into the bar where his coworkers were gathered for a company hour she'd committed to weeks ago, before the doubts had begun to pervade her.

Tonight, he'd kissed her hard on the lips when he'd picked her up and told her, 'I'm going to have the best looking girl at the party and be the envy of every man there."

Sweet words, but were they enough to quell the doubts

assailing her?

Jason took her by the arm, and they stepped into the bar. For a moment, the darkness made it impossible to see, after coming in from the blinding sun. Finally, her eyes adjusted to the dimly lit sports bar.

"Hey, buddy, glad you could make it," an older guy came up and shook Jason's hand. "And you must be Amanda."

"Hi, nice to meet you."

He took Jason by the arm. "We've got a table here in the back. You guys get something from the bar. A group of us are playing pool."

In her three-inch heels, Amanda hurried to keep up with them. She followed Jason to the back, the two men talking the entire way, completely forgetting her as she trailed behind them.

They sat down at the table with a group of people. Introductions were made, and Jason got up and went to the bar. Amanda sat there making small talk, feeling completely out of her element.

When Jason brought back their drinks, he said, "Honey, I'm going to go play pool. I'll be back in a few."

Amanda frowned at him. "Sure, but don't be gone too long."

She chit-chatted with some of the women at the table, but their main topic was work, so she didn't have much to contribute. After an hour, she walked across the bar to the pool table.

"Jason, how much longer are you going to play?" she asked, working hard to keep the irritation from her voice.

"We're almost done. At the end of this game, I'll come back."

Amanda went to the bar and ordered herself another drink. She glanced around at the men who sat drinking beer and watching the televised baseball game. Strolling around, she checked out the different games they offered. At every table, people crowded around, playing their game of choice.

Finally, assuming he'd be done playing pool, she wandered back over to the table. No Jason. She sat back down, sipped the wine, and glanced at her watch.

Thirty minutes later, she walked back over to the pool table, where Jason now played a different guy. She waited until he'd finished the shot.

She stared her displeasure at him, turned around, and walked toward the door. At first, she didn't know where she was going. Her feet seemed to lead her in the direction her mind refused to acknowledge.

When she stepped outside, the sun had disappeared over the horizon. A valet stand with two guys parking cars sat on the sidewalk. Her feet carried her to the stand.

"Hail me a cab," she said.

As soon as the words were out of her mouth, her brain seemed to reengage. In less than a minute, a yellow cab pulled up to the stand. She entered the car, gave him her address, and sat back against the cushions.

After pulling out her phone, she typed a text. "It's over. Goodbye."

Hitting the send button, she leaned back against the cushion of the cab and released a deep sigh of relief. Damn, that felt good. Sometimes the mind was slower to accept what the subconscious knew. And her subconscious had been telling her for weeks this relationship was at the end.

Finally, her brain had caught on, and with relief, she let Jason go.

~

Lacey waited in the receptionist area of Chimney Rock Productions. This morning, Stan had called and asked her to come in; he had news for her.

Unlike before, she barely noticed all the pictures on the wall of the television shows he'd helped create and produce. This morning's call had her emotions springing from hope to despair. One moment, giddiness overwhelmed her and then the next despair, as she feared he'd tell her they were done. What if he'd called her to tell her they were no longer interested? What if he was dropping her and no longer pursuing a television show? What if he called her to tell her he'd found a network interested in her show?

"Ms. Morgan, Mr. Whittaker is ready for you," his secretary said.

Lacey stood, her knees quaking, as she followed his secretary into his office.

Stan rose from behind the desk and greeted her with a hug. "How are you?"

"I'm great," she lied, her stomach doing flip flops like it jumped on a trampoline.

He sat behind his desk, as she sank into the leather chair across from him.

"I hope it wasn't too much of an inconvenience for you to come down here this morning, but I wanted to talk to you in person about what's going on."

"No problem," she said, wondering about the urgency.

"Good." He took a deep breath, his gaze serious. "There's been a development I think you need to know about. One of the producers I've been talking to happen to be in Corpus Christi the same time you were doing a seminar there. She managed to get a ticket."

Lacey's hands begin to sweat. Corpus Christi's audience had been excellent and was one of their best seminars.

"What did she think of the Twelve Steps of Dating?" she asked, her stomach tensing, her heart racing with anticipation.

He smiled. "She called me that afternoon and said she thinks we're onto something. She asked for copies of your proposal. I over-nighted them to her, along with some of the tapes you'd produced."

"Oh, God! Has she looked at them yet?" Lacey said, still not certain this was good news he was about to give her.

Stan leaned back in his chair and smiled. "She likes your idea. She wants to see the documentary as soon as it's finished," he said, pausing. "And if the documentary has a good showing, she'll want you to come to Los Angeles and do a pilot."

Lacey couldn't restrain the thrill that filled her, letting it spill from her lips. "Oh, my God! Oh, my God!"

Excitement overwhelmed her, and she tried to subdue her enthusiasm. Her own television show! Everything she'd dreamed of and worked so hard to obtain could soon be within her grasp.

Stan smiled at her. "There are still a lot of things that could go wrong, but I'm getting positive feedback from her. I think once she sees the documentary, we'll be filming a pilot."

"That's fantastic. Thank you, thank you so much."

"Don't thank me yet. Let's wait until after this documentary comes out. That's still the key to everything. A good documentary means we're one step closer to getting you that television talk show."

Lacey took a deep breath and released it, trying to calm herself and think rationally. "Okay, I'm trying not to get too excited, but this is great news."

"Now the hard part," he said quietly. "She wants us to keep this under wraps for as long as possible. Which means, you can't tell anyone."

"Ohhhhh! The most exciting news of my career and you want me to keep it secret?"

"At least for now. That's why I called you in."

She wanted to tell Reed; she wanted to shout out the news to everyone she knew. Lacey sighed and shook her head. "Why?"

"Because we don't want the other networks to create a show similar to yours. If one relationship coach program is already on television, why would they need another one?"

"Okay, I understand. I'll keep my mouth shut. But you let me know the minute I can start talking about this."

He laughed. "I will."

But she had to tell Amanda. That woman could keep a secret better than any spy being tortured. She'd keep the news their secret.

Chapter Sixteen

Lacey stepped out of her office on her way to the interview room for her last session of the day, David and Jennifer, the couple dealing with commitment issues. This was also the last session Reed would film with Lacey. The documentary was almost done.

No longer would he be trailing her like a shadow everywhere she went. No longer would he pass her in the hallway of Mate Inc. The idea of not seeing Reed caused heartache so profound, she refused to think of the implications that pain meant.

She'd grown to like having him around.

She enjoyed his quick wit, his intelligence and his objective way of observing situations. He was spontaneous, fun, and damn good looking. Working beside him every day had slowly awakened every nerve ending in her body and wrung her emotions inside out.

If she were to evaluate how she felt about Reed, she feared her heart would soon be involved. The end of the filming would be a good time to stop her involvement with him. All she had to do was tell him, and he'd promised her he'd stop pursuing her. Her mind acknowledged the danger of their involvement, but her body longed to join with his again.

She halted outside the door, needing a moment to push aside her thoughts of Reed and focus on her clients. She loved her job, and this couple needed her help in facing their dilemma.

Opening the door, Lacey walked into the interview room, where Reed and Ty were busy setting up.

"Are we ready?"

"Just need to do a couple of lighting checks, and we're all set." They held the lights up to her face, and Ty read some kind of meter. Reed positioned the lights further away from her and turned them to make the lighting softer. Again, they checked the meter.

"All set," Ty said.

A knock on the door announced the arrival of her clients.

"Come in," Lacey called.

David and Jennifer walked in together and took a seat across from Lacey.

Lacey glanced at Reed, and a melancholy sadness rattled her. Their last interview together. She took a deep breath and pushed the thought out of her mind. "Are we ready?"

"Filming," Ty called.

"How are you guys?" she asked.

Jennifer shrugged, and David spoke up, "Okay."

Lacey leaned toward David, sensing a change in the couple. "You both look a little down today. What's going on?"

Jennifer sniffled. "He didn't do his homework."

Lacey glanced at her notes and turned to David. "I remember giving you three assignments. A list of how different your life will be without Jennifer, a list of what you like about your life with Jennifer, and a list of reasons why you can't marry." If he hadn't done his homework, then she doubted they would be together much longer.

"I tried, I really did, but I don't know why I don't want to get married. As for the other two lists, I don't want her to leave," David said, glancing at Jennifer.

"And your homework, Jennifer, was to write out a contract giving David a date as to when you're moving out if he doesn't agree to get married."

"I have it right here," she said, digging into her purse. "I gave him a week."

"A week," Lacey said, stunned by how quickly she was moving. Yet, that was her decision to make, and it looked like she'd already made up her mind.

"This has been a battle between us for six months. You are our last hope. I've already found an apartment. They're waiting for my deposit."

"Does that seem reasonable to you, David?"

He ignored Lacey and turned to Jennifer. "I've told you over and over I don't want you to leave. I love you."

"Just not enough to make it legal." She held a Kleenex to her eyes.

"David, what is holding you back from marrying Jennifer?" Lacey asked again, trying to find out this man's resistance. If she knew his reasons why, then they could work to overcome them.

"Marriage scares the hell out of me."

"Knowing you'll lose Jennifer, your fear of commitment is more important?" Lacey asked.

He stared at Jennifer and tried to take her hand. She pulled away. "I love you, but I don't want to get married. I want things to stay the same."

"But if Jennifer moves out, life won't be the same."

"I know that," David said, his eyes flashing anger.

Lacey observed the couple, wondering what she could do help them. She tapped the end of her pencil on her notebook. "What if Jennifer became seriously ill and couldn't work any longer. David, what would you do?"

He shrugged. "If it were for a short time, I'd probably take care of her."

"What if Jennifer became paralyzed?"

He shook his head. "I couldn't handle that. She'd have to go back to her parents. They have resources I don't."

Lacey nodded, setting the trap. "Fair enough."

"What if Jennifer got pregnant? What would you do then?" Lacey asked and then whirled on Jennifer. "Not that I'm advocating that at all. I'm not."

"I don't want kids," David said quickly.

He wouldn't care for Jennifer if she was paralyzed, and he didn't want children with her. For a moment, Lacey sat there and let his words resonate in the room, hoping Jennifer would come to the conclusion on her own.

In horror, Jennifer recoiled, physically moving away from David, her eyes widening. "You know I want children, a family. I've said that since the first day I met you."

David squirmed. "Yeah. I was hoping you'd change your mind."

Her eyes were wide with indignation. "Change my mind!" Realization echoed in her voice. "You don't love me. I'm convenient. I'm someone who cleans the apartment, cooks, and gives you sex. It's all about you."

"Oh, Jenny. How many times do I have to repeat it? I love you."

She shook her head. "No! Both of your answers clearly show you don't realize that when you love someone, you put her needs first. I'm just someone you come home to."

"Well, you're not putting my needs first by demanding we get married." David raised his voice in anger and looked at Lacey for confirmation.

Jennifer all but exploded. "I've put your needs first for the last two years. Now it's time for me to think about how much longer I should wait on you."

David didn't know how to respond. He sat there unable to say anything, but Jennifer was just getting started. "I have your dinner cooked when you come home. I do your laundry. I clean the apartment. I pay the bills. All I asked of you is to love me and consider my dreams."

Lacey watched as David struggled for words. He sat there, his eyes downturned, his lips pursed. Silence stretched into minutes.

Jennifer picked up her purse and stood. "I'm done. He's not going to change, and I'm tired of trying. I'm leaving here to go put down a deposit on the apartment. The movers will get my stuff next weekend."

David glanced at her. "I'm sorry. I do love you."

"I'm sure in your own way you do, but it's not enough for me." She glanced at Lacey and let out a deep sigh. "Thanks, you've helped me make a decision."

Lacey rose from her chair. "You're welcome." She walked Jennifer to the door and then halted. "Are you all right?"

"I'll be okay."

"Good. Give me a call, if I can help you in any way."

"Thanks." Jennifer went out the door.

Lacey knew that was the end of Jennifer's relationship with David. A sense of failure filled Lacey, leaving her sad. She hated to see her clients not make it together.

David continued to sit in the chair and stare into space.

"Are you all right?" Lacey asked, sitting back down across from him.

"I wish I could have married her, but I couldn't."

Lacey nodded. "Is there anything else you want to talk about?"

"No, but I don't want to go home. I know I'll be alone. She won't come back."

"No, I think it's over," Lacey confirmed.

"What do I do now?" He looked confused almost lost.

"You take some time to evaluate why you didn't want to marry Jennifer, before you get involved with anyone else. Many women want the safety and security of marriage. You may never want to marry, but you need to let the woman know that right up front, before you ever get involved again. And you need to tell them you don't want children."

"I *did* love her."

"I'm sure, in your own way, you did." Lacey wanted to show him she wasn't taking sides, but it was hard. She wanted to yell at him that he was a dumb schmuck for not seeing what a beautiful wife and mother Jennifer would have been. His loss.

"But I didn't want to marry her."

"I understand."

With that, he rose and started for the door..

"Good luck, David," Lacey called.

"Thanks. Goodbye Lacey," he said and walked out the door.

Lacey closed her file, leaned her face into her hands, and sighed. She hated it when she was unable to resolve the issues of one of her clients. She hated it when she watched a break-up, and she hated it when two people could not work out their issues.

David was afraid of commitment, and Jennifer had reached a time in her life when she needed something more. At an impasse, neither one could win.

And neither one would be happy for quite some time.

Reed stepped in front of the camera. He touched her on the arm, and she jumped.

"Are you okay?" he asked.

Involved with helping this couple, she'd completely forgotten about the camera in the room. She gazed up at him. "I'm sorry. I hate it when I can't help a couple."

He sat down across from her and leaned toward her. "What went wrong with this couple?"

Lacey straightened and remembered the documentary. "Some issues can't be resolved. He didn't want to get married, and she was at a place in her life when she needed a commitment from him to continue in the relationship. He wasn't willing to give her what she needed."

"Why couldn't she wait?"

She frowned and wanted to ask him "Really?" but knew the cameras were rolling. "She'd given him two years. She could have given him twenty more, and it wouldn't have mattered. I think deep down she knew David would never marry her. I don't think he understands love. It's easy to say the words, but the truth lies in your actions. David enjoyed what Jennifer did for him, but if this had been real love, he would have done more to save the relationship."

Reed stared at her, his green eyes warming her insides making her feel, safe and secure. Once again, she felt at ease in front of the camera.

"Give me your definition of love," he asked.

There were as many definitions of love as there were kinds of love, but the emotion between a man and a woman was both simple and complex. She took a deep breath. "Love is putting the other person's needs before your own. When you're in love, you're not selfish, and your partner is your best friend and wants the very best for you. Being with him makes you a better person."

"But she was putting her needs before his."

"In a way, yes. But she had put his needs first for two years. It was her turn, and he was unwilling to satisfy her need for commitment before his fear of marriage. If he'd loved her, he would have put his fears into perspective and married her. Just completing the simple homework assignment I gave him would have shown her he was willing to work on their relationship. He chose to ignore her needs, and it cost him a relationship."

Lacey watched Reed struggle to understand, his forehead wrinkled, and his brows drew together. Could this be part of his problem with love?

"Love is putting your best friend's needs first," he said, quietly as he contemplated the thought for the first time.

"You want the best for your partner, and you want her to be happy. And sometimes that means doing things that are not in your comfort zone. Like marriage."

"Like bungee jumping?" he asked.

She laughed. "Yes, exactly. Or loving your partner enough to know that bungee jumping could send her over the edge, so you ask your buddy to go do it with you instead."

"Hey, I got you to smile," he said, his voice sincere.

She ducked her head before raising her gaze to stare into the depth of his soul, feeling scorched by the heat reflected in his eyes. She wanted to dive into that head and let it take her away. "Yes, you did."

Ty called out, "Cut! You two were getting sappy, and I thought we're done."

"Good call," Reed said. "I've got one more client who has agreed to talk to us, but not during a session. This is a wrap for you," he said, the mood shifting back into work.

She let out a sigh, as tension left her body. "That's a relief. Though, I will miss you guys hanging out here. Usually, there are only females in the office and having some testosterone around has been different."

Reed smiled. "The flower smell does seem to be a little less in here now."

"Oh, that will change once you're gone."

He gazed at her, unclipping the microphone from his shirt. "What are you doing later tonight?"

"Going home and resting."

With a tilt of his head, he said, "I hate to eat alone. Want to grab some dinner?"

She should say no, but she hated to eat alone as well, and after today, she wouldn't be seeing Reed. Why not one last celebration? "Okay, but I need to run home. Pick me up in an hour?"

"See you then."

~

Everyone had left for the day as Reed took the elevator down to the garage. One more interview before he moved to the studio to begin putting the film together, splicing and editing and trying to come up with a documentary that showed how relationship coaches were people without doctorates, who really didn't know how to guide lives.

However, he was having more difficulty remembering the reason for the documentary other than he'd enjoyed watching Lacey work with people. Observing her today, with the break-up of that couple on camera would be excellent viewing.

He stepped off the elevator, and Jose walked toward him.

"Hey, what are you doing here?" Reed asked, startled to see the kid.

A dejected air permeated the kid's expression. "I'm done."

Reed frowned. "You finished your assignment?"

"Yes. But I quit."

Reed stopped walking and stared at the kid. "What happened?"

Jose pulled an envelope out of his pocket and slammed it into Reed's hand. The return address was the Los Angeles Film School. Reed opened the envelope and read the letter that started with, "We regret to inform you…"

"Damn!" he said.

Anger vibrated off the young man, his eyes dark with disappointment, his body tense. "You said I had talent," he spouted, his tone cocky.

"You do."

"Then why did I get rejected?"

"Even people with talent get rejected. It's part of life."

"They don't want me because I'm Hispanic."

"You are talking about one of the most liberal arts schools in America. I doubt very seriously they have rejected you because you're Hispanic. I don't know why they declined you. I don't like it any more than you do,"

Reed said, running his hand through his hair as he stared at the letter. He turned it over in his palm, resisting the urge to crumple it and throw it as far as he could.

The kid groaned. "I'm going to have to work with my father. I don't want to mow lawns."

Reed hung his head, as guilt swept over him. He'd only wanted to help Jose, and now it seemed he'd broken the kid. "Give me some time. I can't make any promises. I need to think about where we go from here. You've got natural talent, Jose. Let me see what I can do."

The kid's eyes filled with tears. He shook his head, trying not to cry. "I believed in you. And it got me nowhere!"

The words ripped Reed apart. Maybe he wasn't meant to teach children. Maybe he should have never helped this kid.

Before he could respond, Jose turned and ran out the garage.

"Jose! Wait!"

But the kid ran on, leaving Reed standing in the garage, wanting to smash his fist against anything. The kid had talent, and now Reed feared he'd only given him false hope.

~

Lacey spent extra time refreshing her makeup and changing her clothes. Her time with Reed was coming to an end. She forced herself to say the words to herself in the mirror. Though the attraction between them was strong, he was not interested in a permanent relationship, and she couldn't continue to see him without her emotions becoming involved.

She would tell her clients to walk away, and so after tonight, that's what she would do. Tonight was her last special treat with Reed. Dinner and then at the end of the night, she would call it quits with him.

Her mind knew it was for the best. Her body thought she was crazy.

The doorbell rang, and she hurriedly put lipstick on, grabbed her purse, and ran for the door. She pulled it open, eager to spend the evening with Reed. He stood before her, hands in his pockets.

"Hi," she said.

"Hi." His voice was dull and flat. For the first time, she noticed he seemed to have a dejected air about him.

"Hey, you okay?" she asked, as she opened the door to let him inside.

He came into the apartment and sank down on her sofa. She set her purse down on the floor and then sat on the couch beside him. "What's wrong?"

He glanced at her. "I think I should go home. I'm not going to be good company tonight."

"Are you all right?"

Something was definitely wrong.

"I'm fine," he said, leaning his head back, looking up at the ceiling. "It's one of my students."

"What happened?"

"As I was leaving the office, Jose showed up."

"Jose?"

"Yeah, my best student. Remember the kid who filmed the old couple and the humping squirrels?"

"How could I forget?"

"I've been working with him to get him a scholarship with the Los Angeles Film School. The kid is good. He's a natural and this college rejected him. He's gotten into trouble a couple of times and his grades weren't the best, but the kid has such natural talent. I thought someday he'd be a great filmmaker. We even submitted a short film to the school."

Her heart overflowed with empathy for Reed and his

high school kids. He gave so much to them, and they in
return worshipped him. Now, one of them had suffered a
terrible setback, and he grieved for their loss.

"And you feel sad for him."

He looked at her. "Actually, I feel pissed. They don't
know what a great filmmaker they're turning down. I mean
the kid is poor as a dirt farmer. His father works for a
landscaping company. I wanted to help him get ahead in
life. To give his family a chance to get out of poverty."

"How is Jose taking the news?"

The kid must be devastated. He'd lost a chance to
escape the poverty he'd been born into.

"Not well. He's mad at me for getting his hopes up. He
ran away so I wouldn't see him cry."

"You did everything you could. You tried to make a
difference for this kid. You should be proud of the fact you
were helping him."

He clenched his fists and turned his gaze upon her.
"But I didn't help him. I only got his hopes up to have them
dashed. I'd be pissed, too."

She reached out and touched him on the arm, running
her fingers up and down his strong forearm. "Reed, you
gave him hope. You did more than any of his other teachers
did. You showed him a way to get out of his poverty."

"I wanted him to get the scholarship. I hate losing,
especially when I know I'm right."

"Then help him get into a community college. Maybe
he needs to prove to the administration that he's serious
about changing his life. Get him a school loan. Help him
with the tuition if you have to. See if the studio has a
scholarship."

He stared at her in shock. "You know, I'd forgotten all
about the studio. They may have a scholarship program.
They may even have an intern position where he could
work and go to school part-time."

"He could work for you part-time."

A smile flitted across his face, and his gaze spiraled warmth throughout her. He pulled her against his chest, and she wrapped her arms around him.

"He could," he said. He leaned toward her, and his mouth covered hers. She sank into his kiss as her heart rate accelerated.

No, no, no, she couldn't let herself go. She couldn't give into the sensations skyrocketing through her breasts down into her center. Her body remembered his touch, remembered the pleasure in his arms as she melted beneath his kiss.

Her brain rebelled. She shouldn't let this go beyond a kiss. She shouldn't let this go beyond a touch. She shouldn't let this go beyond…

His hand reached beneath her blouse, his fingers skimming across her bare skin. His lips continued their assault on her mouth, wringing a moan from her.

This had to stop now.

Lacey broke free. *Oh God, I need to clear my mind.* "I think we better go eat."

He leaned back against the couch, his breath ragged and uneven. "Let's go."

She stood, her legs shaky, her head still fuzzy. She needed to put some distance between them, or she'd be lost to his magical touch.

He stood beside her, and then he reached out and brushed a piece of hair from her face. "Thanks."

"For what?"

"For making me feel better about Jose."

They were almost to the front door. She looked at him, and he bent his head, kissing her softly on the lips. His words and his kiss sent her plummeting over the edge into a pool of heat.

She leaned into his kiss and grabbed the front of his

shirt. She needed him. She wanted him with a passion that could not be denied, to experience the pleasure of his body again. One more time and then it would be over, and she could go back to being the safe relationship coach, who didn't feel passion for any man.

Just once more she needed to experience his arms.

Her mouth came away from his. "I'm not hungry for food."

He sighed. "Thank God." He took her hand.

She looked at him. "I'm crazy for doing this."

"And I'm crazy with need for you."

~

Reed needed no urging to feel her arms around him again. The long day filled with drama and life-changing events had left him drained. He needed someone to remind him of the good things in life. He needed Lacey, and that thought rippled through him as he led her down the hall to her bedroom.

He had waited a long time for this moment, when Lacey acquiesced and gave herself to him again.

In her bedroom, he took notice of the bed centered in the room, but his focus remained on this woman in his arms. The need for her to touch him drove him, as he turned her to face him. Her lips begged him to kiss her, but instead, he focused on slowly unbuttoning her blouse and then sliding it down her arms, before he tossed it to a chair.

Her pebbled nipples beckoned him through her bra, and he closed his mouth over the silky lingerie, sucking her through the clothing, while his fingers pushed her breasts together.

She gasped and let her head fall back.

Releasing her breasts, he unbuttoned her pants, slid down the zipper, and let them drop. She stepped out of her shoes and pants, leaving them in a pool on the floor.

Lacey stared at him, a warm smoky depth to her gaze. She wanted him as much as he needed her, and that filled his chest with pride.

Reaching behind her, he unhooked her bra and slid the straps over her arms, letting her breasts fall free. God, she was beautiful, standing before him in nothing but her panties.

He kissed her, his mouth covering hers, his tongue teased her while his fingertips caressed her silky skin. Ginger and lilacs permeated the room with a spicy, sweet scent, that tantalized him.

She broke the kiss, her eyes glazed, her breathing harsh. Her fingers trembled as he watched her unbutton his shirt. He wanted to rush her, to push her hands aside and hurry the process, but knew half the fun was teasing one another, pushing each other to the limit, until they both were frenzied with need to climb that summit together.

Reaching inside his shirt, she ran her fingertips across his chest, his skin tingling wherever she touched. He closed his eyes and willed himself to stand there and let her slowly push his shirt down his arms until it fell to the floor.

She reached for his jeans and struggled with the button and then slide his zipper down over his hard erection. He stood, clenching his fists to control the desire to throw her onto the bed and get on with the seduction.

Her fingers reached inside his briefs as she slid his jeans and shorts down his legs. His erection sprang free, hard and heavy with need. He did math problems in his head to slow the release he felt rushing at him. Just a touch would send him over the edge.

Leaving his shoes with his pants, he stood naked before her. He reached over and slid her panties down, until she stood naked too.

For a moment, they stood there, staring at one another. Her long legs, her sweet, sweet breasts, her rosy areolas, puckered and waiting for his kiss. And then he couldn't stand it any longer, he had to have her.

He picked her up. As she wrapped her long legs around his waist, he carried her swiftly to the bed. There he laid her down gently. His mouth covered hers in a kiss that should have set the coverlet on fire.

She tasted of sweetness, her perfume wrapping them in a sensual cocoon of pleasure as his mouth plundered hers. Why with Lacey did lovemaking seem more intense, more satisfying? Why did he feel like he'd come home? Why did he feel like this was where he belonged?

He broke the kiss, his mouth trailing down her chest to her breasts. Taking her nipple in his mouth, he sucked the kernel, tasting her delicious flesh.

"God, I can't get enough of you," he whispered.

"Hmmm…" she moaned. Her hands clutched his hair, and she moved her body until his penis fit between her legs. Nothing would please him more than to shove himself deep inside her and be enveloped in her warmth, but not yet.

Reed wanted to hear her moan, he wanted to see her climax, and he wanted to be inside her. But more than anything, he needed to know her passion was as great as his. And he would do everything he could to make sure she lost complete control.

With gentle pressure, his fingers reached inside her center, and her hips rose with pleasure as she moaned. Like a gentle ride, he teased her, until she lifted his head from her breasts, her breathing ragged.

"Condoms are in the nightstand. Get one now," she commanded, her breathing frazzled and uneven.

He smiled and reached over, opened the drawer and pulled one out. Quickly, he tore open the foil packet and slid the latex over himself.

His mouth covered hers once more, and this time, he

slid his body over hers, touching skin to skin. He pushed himself inside her, and she welcomed him, wrapping her legs around his waist, giving him deeper access.

"Oh, yes," she said, whispering into his ear. "There."

Somehow, he held back as he met her rhythm. He wanted her to soar to the highest heights and be right there beside her, holding her, caressing her. All the while, he held a tight rein on his own release, waiting until he knew she was ready to fly.

In no time, he felt her clench around him, squeezing him as he knew she climaxed. Then he let himself take flight, joining her as they raced toward the moon, knowing he'd never experienced pleasure like this before. Knowing no other woman had reached inside and touched his heart and found it wanting. Only Lacey had the power to break down his barriers and make him feel needed.

Tightly, he held onto her as he shook from their lovemaking. Pushing himself even deeper into her.

When it was over, he rolled over onto his back and tried to catch his breath. His body shook as he glanced over at Lacey. She lay on her back, her breathing ragged, her eyes closed.

A rush of tenderness, swift and protective, swept over him, leaving him in shock. His chest tightened with the need to hold her close. Normally after sex, he didn't feel anything but tired. With Lacey, he wanted to pull her to him and hold her. He wanted to keep her close. He needed the touch of her skin against his own. He wanted her right where she was. Beside him.

Lacey Morgan was getting under his skin. She was breaking down his barriers. She made him feel emotions he'd never felt before and that frightened him to his very core.

Chapter Seventeen

Lacey awoke the next morning feeling glorious. That was the only way to describe how she felt after spending the night in Reed's arms.

After the first time they'd made love, they'd gotten up and raided her kitchen and made nachos with beans and guacamole. Then they'd gone back to bed, and he'd had her clutching the sheets and screaming his name.

Later, they'd filled up her bathtub and soaked until their skin was wrinkled like prunes. Then they'd fallen asleep in each other's arms.

This morning, he'd woken her early and said he had to go. He'd kissed her and told her not to think that they were done. But with the glorious feelings this morning, Lacey also realized she was falling for Reed-hook, line, and a broken heart in her future. She didn't do casual sex and limited her sexual partners to men she was in a serious relationship with. To her, sex was an emotional joining, and she couldn't just be someone's fuck buddy.

She sighed, got up and started getting ready to go to the office.

An hour later, she walked in as Amanda rounded the corner. Lacey handed her a cup of Starbucks.

"Vanilla Latte skinny, just the way you like it," Lacey said.

"What's up? That drink is code for we need to talk."

"You got it, sister."

Amanda laughed and followed her into the office. She took a seat across from Lacey's desk. "What's so urgent?"

"I'm worried about you," Lacey admitted. She'd known something was wrong with Amanda, but had not had the chance to talk to her. This morning, she was making time for her friend.

"Me?"

"Yeah, you've been quiet lately. What's going on?"

Amanda shook her head. "I think I'm going to become celibate," she said with a short laugh. "I broke up with Jason."

"Oh, I'm sorry. He seemed so perfect." Lacey sipped from her coffee. "But then, so did Dean."

"Yeah, seemed and is, are too different things. We were going nowhere. So I ended it."

"Are you okay?"

Amanda didn't look broken hearted, but Lacey had known something wasn't right. Now she understood.

"Actually, I'm fabulous. I'm certain I did the right thing. My next step is contemplating joining a nunnery. How do you think I'd look in a habit?"

"Drab."

"Finding a man who fits my needs, gets along with my family, and is a good guy doesn't seem to be happening. Maybe I should sign up for our matchmaking services."

"Amanda—"

"I know, I know,. I'll find someone when the time is right."

"You deserve someone who is good for you. Obviously, Jason wasn't. You have to kiss a lot of toads before you find your prince."

God, there were more toads than princes and even the princes had issues. Just like most women had problems they needed to deal with. Dating wasn't fun, exciting, but rather nerve wracking.

"The toads are going to have to do without me for a while."

Lacey laughed.

"You're in a chipper mood this morning."

"Yeah, I am, though my reasons for feeling so good could come back to bite me in the butt at any moment."

Amanda groaned. "Oh, no."

"Oh, yes. I slept with Reed again."

"Lacey!"

"Yes, I know. He's not interested in marriage. Or even a steady relationship for that matter. But when he touches me, my body turns to hot liquid, and I can't get my clothes off fast enough."

"Oh, if this gets out."

"I'm in so much trouble, Amanda. He makes me feel things I've never felt. He makes me scream with passion. I don't recall experiencing anything like this before."

Amanda frowned and stared at her like she had two heads with snakes crawling out of them. "You've never acted like this over a man before."

"Men don't usually affect me this way."

"Oh, no."

"Yes, I know." Lacey repeated, shaking her head, unable to believe she had left herself so vulnerable. "I'm a relationship coach, a counselor, who is not following my own advice. I'm falling in love with Reed Hunter, and he's going to break my heart."

~

Reed stared at Stephen Bridges, his last interview for the documentary. A man who had a negative experience with Mate Incorporated. He already didn't like the guy, and he'd only met him five minutes ago. He'd come in with an arrogant attitude, insisting they shine the camera on his right side as that was better than his left side.

Reed had Ty rearrange the room, so the lights were arranged to show off Mr. Bridges' right side, which was just as ugly as his left side.

Then he'd tried to have them sign a release saying he could not be sued.

"Sorry, Mr. Bridges. I don't sign releases without my attorney looking them over. Now we can either film your story today, or we can decide this was not in your best interest and go our separate ways."

The man frowned at Reed, his thinning short hair and hawkish eyes staring at him. "Sarah told me you'd be a fool to sign anything, but I wanted to try anyway."

"Sorry, I don't sign releases." Reed paused. "Who is Sarah?"

"Oh, she's a girl I met while doing the matchmaking service."

"You're still seeing someone you met while going through Ms. Morgan's service?"

"Oh yeah, Sarah's great. I didn't like the service, but since I'd paid for it, I felt I might as well use it."

Reed didn't say anything for a few moments, his gut twisting with guilt. The memory of Lacey curled in his arms came rushing at him like a missile, and he felt its explosion around him.

Reed focused on his job. His personal feelings had no place in the workplace when he was filming. Yet, what he was doing would harm Lacey, and he was struggling with that knowledge.

"Are we ready to begin?" he asked the gentleman.

"Sure."

Ty called, "Action."

"Today, I have Stephen Bridges, a client of Mate Inc. Tell me how you got involved with Mate Incorporated."

The man crossed his legs and cleared his throat. "After being in a serious relationship for over a year, we broke up, and I didn't know how to go about meeting other women. I signed up for the Twelve Steps of Dating Seminar."

"And did you learn anything about yourself at the seminar?"

"Oh yeah, Lacey spends a lot of time on making sure you know who you are and what kind of relationship you're looking for. I confirmed what I already knew about myself. The seminar was a waste of time for someone like me."

Reed tried to stay focused, but he wanted to wipe the smile off this arrogant, pompous fool. "What did you do after the seminar?"

"I signed up for the matchmaking session. I also started attending the Friday night get-togethers. Let me tell you, those Friday night parties are filled with women desperate to find a man. You can get plenty of action there, if you know what I mean." He raised his brows in a lecherous way that made Reed want to puke.

Reed ignored his comments. "What about the matchmaking service?"

"Totally bogus. They made me take a personality test and gave me four letters and said this type of woman would suit me best. Hell, I know the kind of woman I want. Blonde, big boobs, and has a job. That's all I need to know."

Reed wanted to turn the camera off at that moment, but decided to forge ahead, knowing very little of what this Neanderthal said would show up on the film.

Were all men this way about women? Had he treated women this way?

What the hell was wrong with him? He'd never questioned his actions before. Could Lacey's relationship advice have changed his subconscious?

"Did you get any dates from the service?"

"Oh, yeah. I went out with two of the homeliest women I've ever seen. If you want to meet some dogs, believe me, sign up with a dating service. I expected women as hot as Lacey."

Reed took a deep calming breath. If he didn't jump out of this chair before the end of the interview and throttle this man, it would be a miracle. And he would be doing women world-wide a favor.

"Okay, did you have any good dates from the service?"

"A couple, but one girl told me I was not her type, and the other one won't return my calls."

Smart woman. "How did you meet Sarah?"

"Oh, I met Sarah at the Friday night gathering. We stood around making fun of everyone in the room."

"That's nice." The sarcasm was lost on the man. "What exactly is your complaint against Lacey?"

"It's the way they do things. I didn't need to take a personality test. I didn't need to be psychologically evaluated to make sure I'm not a stalker. I paid them good money to get me dates and find someone compatible with me. Sarah is the only person I still have a connection with."

"Did you speak with Lacey about your dissatisfaction?" Reed knew she tried to make every client happy and would go out of her way to help satisfy someone if they didn't think they were getting their money's worth. Yet, here sat this ignorant soul.

"Yes, and she told me she would refund my money. She does that with clients after six months if she is unable to find them anyone to date."

"That seems more than fair. After all, you had two dates."

"But I expected ten or more."

"Maybe she didn't have anyone who fit your profile."

"Profile, personality test, whatever. I expected to date women. Lots of gorgeous women."

Reed had to wait a moment before he could respond without pounding the weasel. "Did you take the refund from Lacey?"

"Hell, no. Not at first. I told her I wanted dates."

"And how did she respond?"

"She told me she didn't have any clients who would fit my criteria. She sent me my money back!"

Reed had to bite his tongue to keep from laughing. He

could hear Lacey saying this to him in a professional voice, knowing he wouldn't get that she didn't have anyone who would want to date him. Or that she would inflict his personality on.

"How would you describe your experience with Mate Incorporated?"

"Totally frustrating. She needs to be shut down and put out of business."

"Even after she refunded your money?"

"She played with my emotions. I expected to meet a hottie." The man spat like a drama queen in men's clothing.

At the end of his patience, Reed wanted to walk him to the door and tell him to never come back.

He made the cut motion to Ty.

"Okay, thank you for coming in, Mr. Bridges."

Reed had to end this session or find himself in jail for trying to pound some bloody sense into this fool. How did Lacey put up with idiots like this?

"We're done? That's all? I was just getting started."

"We have everything we need."

The man stood and gathered his belongings. "I hope you run that bitch out of business."

Reed felt his fists clench at his sides. He took a deep breath to keep from slamming the man. The brothels he'd filmed in Russia hadn't left him feeling so slimy and dirty. "Goodbye, Mr. Bridges," he said and deliberately closed the door on him.

Stepping from behind the camera, Ty came out laughing. "That dude was a trip."

"I wanted to punch him."

Ty looked at him in a weird way. "I don't think he helped us show her in a bad way."

Reed had to resist from telling Ty to dump the film. He so wanted to tell him to destroy this interview, but he knew he couldn't. "Would you date a creep like that?"

"No, I don't date other men. I like women."

"I guess we saw what women have to deal with from our sex all the time."

Ty stared at him and shook his head. "You're going soft on me, buddy."

"What do you mean?" Reed asked, a strange ache gripping his stomach.

"Are you sleeping with Lacey?"

Reed frowned. What could he say? Ty sometimes acted ignorant, but he was as intelligent as they come. He would know the truth.

"Shit!" he said. "You're sleeping with her again. I knew I had a bad feeling about this film. This is going to turn out to be crap, isn't it?"

"I don't mix business and pleasure. Business is business, and pleasure is kept strictly separate," Reed said, straightening his shoulders and gazing into Ty's eyes.

"Yeah, and my grandmother smokes pot."

Reed smiled at him. "You never told me that before. That's a new revelation."

"You're lying to yourself and me. I can see it on your face. You're starting to care about this girl. You're falling for her."

Panic crept over Reed like ants on candy. She was just another woman he enjoyed sleeping with. Still, wow, he did enjoy being with her. "Hey, you're talking to a man who has not had a serious relationship in years."

"Sure." Ty looked away and begin to pack up the equipment. "If you don't get your act together, we're going to crash and burn."

"You say that about every film. This is going to be our best film yet."

"I sure hope so. I'm looking forward to that beach in Hawaii. I'm hoping Graham doesn't fire our asses."

~

Lacey had just turned out the light in her bedroom when the phone rang. She jumped on it, hoping it was Reed. She hadn't heard from him all day, and tonight, she'd been disappointed he hadn't called. But until this moment the phone had been silent.

"Hello," she said, her heart rate accelerating with hope.

"Hi," her sister said, her voice sounding odd.

"Hi," Lacey responded, sitting up in bed. "Is everything okay?"

The phone went silent.

"Are you all right?" she demanded.

"Yes."

"What's wrong? You never call me this late."

"Matt is out with his friends. They're doing his bachelor party tonight," Kerri said, her voice tired and strained. "The wedding is two weeks away."

Lacey didn't say anything and just let Kerri talk. As she listened, she felt torn. She had come to accept this wedding, and now, what if Kerri decided to back out?

"I spent tonight packing, trying to get ready to move. Usually he's here with me."

"You spent the evening alone?"

"Yes."

"You must have enjoyed some time to yourself."

"No, I didn't."

"Kerri, what's going on?" Lacey asked.

"I don't know. I sat here all night wondering if I was doing the right thing. I mean you're right. We grew up with so many step-dads and step-families. I don't want that for my children. I started having doubts."

"Do you love Matt?"

"Yes, with all my heart."

Lacey smiled. Her sister had a case of pre-wedding

jitters. She could try to talk her out of the wedding, but Kerri wanted to get married. Lacey just needed to be there for her sister.

"I think it's normal for you to get scared before the wedding. This is one of the biggest decisions of your life. And we're all human and prone to errors," Lacey said, determined to support her sister during this moment of doubt.

"But you and I made a promise we wouldn't do this to our children."

"We were kids when we made that promise. We had no idea how tough relationships could be, how hard it is to find the right person, how many people could possibly look like the right one, only to be an imposter."

"What if Matt is an imposter?"

"Do you think he's a phony?"

"No, I can't imagine my life without him."

"Do you feel passionate about him?'

"When he walks into the room and I see him, I get goose bumps," she admitted.

"I think you're afraid. Until tonight, you were defending your decision to marry."

"I don't want to make a mistake."

"None of us do. But we make the best decision we can at the time with the knowledge that we have. It's all we can do."

Isn't that what Lacey was doing with Reed? She knew he didn't believe in forever after. She knew he didn't want to get married. Yet, the two of them had spent two glorious nights together, enjoying each other. What the hell was she doing? For once in her life, she was experiencing passion.

There was a moment of silence on the phone.

"Do you think I should marry him?"

"If you love him, you're passionate about him, can't live without him, then marry him."

Her sister sighed on the other end of the phone. "I knew that in my heart, but my mind questioned everything. I knew you would help me," her sister said, sounding relieved.

"I want you to have a great life with Matt. I want you to become a doctor, but more than anything, I want you to be happy. If you love him as much as you say you do, marry him."

"Oh, Lacey, thank you. I needed to hear that. Someday I hope you find someone who will make you as happy as Matt makes me."

"Me too," Lacey said. "Tell me about the wedding?"

"Everything is ready. All we lack is the bachelorette party, and you're in charge of that."

"Do you have any requests?"

"Yes. No strippers. No comedy clubs and no sex toys." She laughed. "I know it sounds boring, but isn't that what everyone does and I don't want the usual. I want a day at a spa with my girlfriends and then a nice dinner with a lot of good wine."

"Sounds great and perfectly boring. Something I can handle."

"But that's what I want."

"Then that's what we'll do. Give me a list of friends to invite, and I'll take care of the rest."

"Oh, and one more thing."

"Yes?"

"You'll have to invite Mom, or she'll get her feelings hurt," Kerri said.

"Are you okay with that?"

"It doesn't bother me."

"I'm okay with it. Just be prepared for her to say you need a stripper."

"No strippers."

Lacey laughed at her sister. "You know, in some ways

we're very lucky. We have a mother who knows how difficult it is to find the right man."

"Yes, and we've seen real life lessons on why it's important to find a man who fits in with your family and your life."

Lacey yawned. "Yes we have. Are you going to be okay now?"

"Yes, I know I'm making the right decision," Kerri said, her voice once again sure and determined.

"I'm going to miss you when you move to Tennessee."

"I know. You'll have to come visit me."

"When you have time off," Lacey said.

"Yes, life will be crazy for a while."

"Dr. Kerri Stevens."

"Has a nice sound to it, doesn't it?"

"Yes."

There was a pause. "So, how is Reed Hunter?"

Lacey didn't say anything for a moment. She took a deep breath, not wanting to reveal how confused she felt about him. "Too good. I think I'm falling in love with him."

"Oh, Lacey, that's wonderful."

"I hope so, Jennifer. I truly do. I've never felt so drawn to a man, yet so fearful. He doesn't want a relationship, and I feel the need to be with him. I'm in way too deep, and I'm scared."

Chapter Eighteen

Lacey gazed around the Gridiron bar, waiting for Reed. He'd called this afternoon and said he had news about the documentary and couldn't wait to see her. They'd agreed to meet here and then go to dinner.

Men sat in groups, watching the big screen television, playing pool or air hockey, drinking a beer and socializing. Few women graced the bar, and most of them were young, single, and on the hunt.

Testosterone seemed to hang in the air, like an invisible smoke screen. This was not the kind of place she liked to hang out at, but she sat, waiting for Reed and studying the male species.

A tall blonde walked up to her table. "Aren't you, Lacey Morgan, the relationship coach?" she asked.

"Yes, I am."

"Hey, I'm Blair Roberts. I took your seminar. It changed my life," she said. The woman didn't look like the type to have any trouble getting dates. But everyone had trouble with relationships at some time in their life.

"For the better?" Lacey asked, always curious how she affected someone's life.

"Yes. I ended a dead end relationship," she said with a shrug. "It was for the best."

Lacey studied the beautiful woman, wondering at the man who'd let her get away. "Are you doing okay?"

"Yes, I am. Tell me what's new with Mate Incorporated. Are you doing more seminars?"

Lacey smiled, pleased that people wanted more information about her business. "Thanks for asking. We've been working with a filmmaker doing a documentary on our company. In fact, I'm meeting him here now."

"Oh, really. A documentary. The man I used to date was a documentary filmmaker."

A warning tingle zipped down Lacey's spine from her head to toes. How many filmmakers lived in this area? "That's interesting. Reed Hunter is who I'm working with."

The girl's face went white, and she sank down onto a chair across from Lacey. "Reed is the man I broke up with." Blair frowned and shook her head, her brows raised in horror. "Oh, my God. He doesn't believe in relationship coaches or even permanent relationships. Are you sure Reed is filming your documentary?"

"Yes," Lacey said, feeling the floor tilt like a ride at the fair, sending her stomach dropping to her feet, her equilibrium so off balance, nausea gripped her. "It's true he didn't believe in relationship coaches when he started filming, but I'm certain after everything, he believes in them now."

When had he told her he believed in what she was doing? Had he ever said anything about what she did that conveyed his belief? No.

Blair shook her head. "Not the Reed Hunter I know. Juliet and I attended your seminar together, and she left her boyfriend, as well. In fact, Reed works for Juliet's boyfriend."

"Graham Productions?"

"Yes. When I came home from your seminar and started working the step program, he freaked. He told me I was listening to a woman who wasn't a therapist. After your program, I realized he liked having sex with me, but there would never be a future for us. Reed is a serial dater who expects fringe benefits. He doesn't believe in marriage."

Lacey took a sip of her iced tea and tried to calm her nerves. It was true. She'd forced the fact that Reed didn't believe in marriage from her mind. Hoping like a naïve schoolgirl, she could change him. The exact thing she warned her clients against. "He told you he didn't believe in relationship coaches."

Blair's eyes widened, and she nodded. "Oh, yes. But I never thought he'd do a documentary on you. Juliet told me Graham promised her he'd get even, and I think this is how they're doing it. They're filming a documentary to prove us wrong. To show you as a fake."

Did she believe this woman or was this some awful prank she was playing on her ex? After all, she claimed to have a past with Reed. What did Lacey do now? Her television show depended on the documentary Reed was producing, and yet now, she was uncertain he'd ever meant this documentary to be about the people she helped, but rather an attempt to do an exposé.

And worst of all, she was falling in love with him. Now, he would strip away her dreams, leave her heart damaged possibly beyond repair, and she had no one to blame but herself.

"He's meeting me here." Lacey glanced at her watch. "Any moment now." She should never have abandoned her own advice.

Blair sat across from her, staring at her in shock. "Oh dear, this could be a cozy reunion." She gazed at Lacey and then reached out and touched her on the arm. "Watch out for Reed Hunter. He's a smooth talking devil who will string you along while sucking the life right out of you."

Lacey couldn't say anything. She knew suddenly the woman was right. With Reed, she'd experienced passion for the first time.

"He's got a good heart, beautiful smile, and he's a very talented filmmaker," Blair added. "But if anyone can make your business look bad, it would be Reed. And if you let him, he will break your heart. I know. I've been there." She slid off the chair and stood.

Lacey tried to remain detached and think logically, but her mind was whirling faster than film in a camera recording every nuance of what this woman told her. "Thanks for telling me, Blair. I appreciate your honesty."

Was this just a bitter old girlfriend or could everything she'd just said be true?

"I better go before he shows up." Blair scribbled on a napkin and handed it to Lacey. "Here's my phone number. If I can help you with anything, you call me."

Lacey nodded. "Thanks."

Blair glanced around the bar. "Oh crap, he just walked in."

Lacey watched Reed walk between the tables. His gaze met hers and the smile that had been on his face as he searched for her was suddenly replaced with his eyes drawing together in a frown that went from his mouth to his forehead.

Just that change of expression was enough to confirm her suspicions.

Her stomach clenched; her blood seemed to freeze in her veins. Suddenly, she feared Reed Hunter had intended to make her business look bad all along. Everything she'd worked so hard for hung in the balance.

He reached the table. "Hi, Blair. Lacey."

"Hi, Reed," Blair said.

Lacey didn't say a word; her mouth felt frozen.

"She knows everything, Reed."

"What did you tell her, Blair? Your side? Or mine?" he asked, his eyes darkened into a burning emerald.

"She knows you're making this documentary to show how relationship coaches are frauds."

"Who said I was going to make Lacey look bad? Documentaries show the public what is going on and let them make the decision as to whether or not this subject is harmful or helpful," he said, his voice low and controlled.

"Drop the bullshit," Blair told him. "You were mad when I left."

"Blair, it was over between us before you left."

"You didn't want me to leave, and you were mad I let someone convince me that you would never marry me. You were mad you lost. You were mad we weren't going to have sex any longer."

"You think a lot of yourself."

Lacey couldn't take it anymore. She didn't want to listen to the two of them argue over who was right or wrong. She didn't want to listen to how this beautiful blonde bimbo had crawled out of Reed's bed before he'd crawled into Lacey's. With a flash of Reed's beautiful smile, she'd forgotten all of her teachings and had sex with him. Now she was getting a lesson in heartache.

The reality was he'd deceived her, and she'd let him.

Sliding off the chair, she grabbed her purse. They both turned to look at her.

"Where are you going?" Reed asked.

"I'm out of here."

"Lacey! Wait!"

The distance from the table to the door seemed longer than a football field but was shorter than a first down. The sounds of the TV pounded inside her head, reminding her of all the reasons she didn't like sports bars.

Pushing open the front door, she walked out into the twilight and took a deep cleansing breath, hoping it would clear her mind. But instead, her chest tightened. It was over. He'd deceived her. He'd played her for a fool.

And she'd slept with him.

With her eyes focused forward, she all but ran to her car.

Suddenly, Reed grabbed her arm from behind. "Lacey, please stop. Let me explain."

She whirled around. He was alone. "Explain what?"

"Explain that it was over between me and Blair before I started filming the documentary."

"But isn't it true you decided to film my company because of your break-up with Blair? That my seminar helped her to decide not to wait for you any longer?"

He stood there biting his lip, shuffling nervously, not saying anything.

"Is it true that you don't believe in relationship coaches because I don't have a counseling degree? That we're just soothsayers spouting bullshit?"

Again he only stared at her. He opened his mouth to speak, and nothing came out.

"Is it true that after Blair attended my seminar, she realized you were not what she wanted in a relationship and decided to move on? You didn't want her to leave. You wanted her to stay and continue on as before, but she wanted more."

~

Reed felt his stomach clench as he stood there, unable to say anything because everything she'd just said was true. He didn't know how to respond to her without lying even more, so he just stared, watching the hurt blossom on her face and knowing he'd caused her pain.

He was a moron. A complete idiotic moron.

"You had no intention of showing the business I've created helping couples find the right love and make the best decisions. No, it's going to show I'm someone without a Ph.D., offering advice and leading them down a pathway littered with platitudes and misguided advice. Kind of like how you presented this project to me."

For the first time since he was a child, Reed felt shame for what he'd done. Her words made him sound evil and narrow-minded. He didn't like seeing Lacey almost hysterical, yet quietly getting her point across like the slide of a cold blade into his heart. He hated hurting her.

"Graham Productions hired me to film your company,

Lacey. I'm just showing your profession and letting the viewer see what you do," he said, knowing it was a lie.

A car pulled into the parking lot, its headlights flashing across his face.

"Do you believe in relationship coaches?"

He stared at her. What could he say? Whatever he said, Blair had obviously told her the truth. No, he had never believed in relationship coaches, but then he'd met Lacey, and she was different. "I believe in you."

"Bullshit!" she said, with such vehemence he took a step back. A lone tear made its way down her cheek. "I made such a mistake with you, and now, it's going to cost me everything. My business, my career, even my heart. Because you see, after the other night, I realized I was falling in love with you. You made me love you, damn it. Now, I don't know what to do."

Her words slammed him, leaving a giddy sickness. She loved him. She admitted to loving him, and with a sudden realization, he knew he didn't want to lose her.

Another tear trickled down her cheek. She yanked opened the door to her Prius and climbed in. "In case you haven't figured it out, we're done. I'm going to my attorney to see if there is any way I can stop this film. Get your cameras, your equipment out of my office by tomorrow, or so help me God, I will trash them."

"Lacey, don't go! Let's talk about this."

"There's nothing left to say. You lied to me. And I'm going to lose everything as a result of your deceit. Don't come near me again."

"Wait! We need to talk."

She started the car and put it in reverse. He jumped back, as she almost ran over his foot when he tried to stop her.

He wanted to smash something. This was not how it was supposed to end. This was not how they were supposed to spend the evening.

This was not what he wanted.

And yet, everything she'd said was true. She loved him. She'd given him her heart, and he'd treated it badly.

He felt like a creep for lying to her the way he had. Ty tried to warn him this was going to end badly, but he hadn't thought it would end this way. He hadn't thought it would end so soon.

He glanced at the bar and knew he couldn't go back in there and see Blair again. He hated that woman.

She'd managed to get her revenge. In a sudden flash, he knew she'd managed to ruin his life. She'd told Lacey the truth, and now she wanted nothing to do with him.

A cold loneliness washed over him as he watched Lacey's Prius drive into the distance. What did he do now?

~

Lacey drove straight to Amanda's house, needing her friend, needing her comfort. They had to somehow come up with a plan to save the business. But Amanda couldn't save Lacey from the heartache that threatened to overwhelm her.

In a mindless daze, she drove until she found herself sitting in front of Amanda's apartment, letting the tears she'd held at bay stream down her face.

She'd fallen in love with him. She'd ignored her own advice, skipped the steps, slept with him, and given him her heart, only to have him break the fragile organ.

Unable to move, she leaned her head on the steering wheel and let the tears spill down her cheeks, sobbing for the love she'd given to a man who wouldn't return the emotion. Knowing in the process, she'd endangered everything she loved in her life.

Passion was a reckless emotion that only wreaked havoc on you and did nothing to help in choosing an appropriate mate. Sure, her mother lived for passion, but not Lacey. Never again, would she let passion control her. Never again, would she choose a passionate relationship over the safe twelve step program she had created for her clients.

She knew better.

Now, she had to face Amanda and tell her the business was doomed. Somehow, they had to figure out a plan to save this business she loved. She had to figure out a way to stay sane the next few months, while her business was dissected on film and her reputation slaved in front of the masses.

Lacey wiped the tears from her cheeks and blew her nose. She needed to get away. She had not taken off anytime in the last three years of building this business, but now after her sister's wedding, she wanted to escape.

She needed a break, yet now more than ever, she had to enjoy each day because her business might not have a tomorrow.

Opening the car door, she stepped out and made her way up the steps to Amanda's apartment. What if her friend wasn't home? What if she'd gone somewhere? She needed Amanda.

Lacey rang the doorbell.

A few minutes later, the door opened, and Amanda stared at her, her eyes widening in horror. "What the hell is wrong?"

Tears clogged her throat. "I fell in love, and I've ruined everything."

~

The next morning, sitting in the office, rage consumed Amanda. She'd spent the better part of the night reassuring Lacey the business wasn't lost. Her reputation wasn't ruined, and she hadn't been crazy to let passion overrule her head and go with her heart.

Okay, so maybe that last one she'd had to really stretch for her friend, but she loved Lacey and would have done anything to help her. She'd never seen her so distraught.

Now, Amanda sat here at the office, waiting for Ty, who had called earlier and said he was on his way to pick up the cameras. She'd gone through their equipment looking for the film, but the cameras were empty.

If they had left the film in the cameras, she would have cut it to shreds.

Amanda wanted to rip Ty and Reed to tiny pieces, but that would make the news at seven, and she was already trying to find a way to finagle this publicity nightmare. So far, she hadn't come up with any ideas as to how to make this situation look good in the press. And the television show might as well be history because certainly no one would want to put them on television with the trashing they'd receive with this film.

"Ty's here," their secretary called out to her.

Amanda marched into the room where Ty was kneeling on the floor, packing everything up. "I need you to be honest with me."

Ty glanced up at her. "Hmmm, Reed warned me I could be walking into a war zone over here. Are you the first strike team?"

"Look, because of Reed, I spent the night consoling my friend over how we could save her business. So yeah, you could say I'm the first strike team, and you're about to be toast," she said, standing over him. She'd never wanted to drop kick someone before, but she felt that need now.

"I see all of my cameras are open."

"That's because I searched everywhere for the film."

"Any film we shot that day has to go into the film safe at night. It's not here," Ty informed her.

Amanda crossed her arms, still standing above Ty as he

locked everything into the cases he'd carried in. "Tell me the truth. How did Reed shoot this film? Does he make my friend's business look bad?"

"I'm not at liberty to talk about this with you or anyone else," Ty said, avoiding eye contact.

"I don't give a damn about your liberty. I need to know how to prepare my friend and her business. The place that I come to every day to work. I need to prepare her and the business to face the press. Did Reed set out to ruin Lacey?"

Ty stopped his packing and sighed. "This is what I was told to say. We film documentaries. We show the business and let the viewers decide whether or not this is a legitimate bus—"

"Legitimate?" Amanda said, almost shouting. "You know damn well we're legitimate. You know we care about our clients and do everything we can to make sure everyone has a good experience with our firm."

Amanda stood just inches from Ty, looking down at him, her voice almost screaming. She so wanted to rip every long burnet hair strand from his head. Lacey was hurting because of these two.

Ty shrugged, his packing increasing with speed. "I'm just the messenger. I told you I can't say anything."

"You could be honest with me and tell me the truth. You could give me some indication of how Reed has shown Lacey. Did he show her in a bad way?"
"Look, Amanda. I like you guys. This has been a fun place to come to every day, but I'm just the cameraman. I don't decide how the film is presented to the audience. All final editing is done by Reed. He's the editor; he's the moneymaker. I just shoot film."

Ty's position was a lot like Amanda's, and though she was still furious, what good would it do to remain mad at Ty?

"But you know the intention of this documentary. Did

he deliberately lie to Lacey?"

Ty put the last camera into its case and clicked it shut, locking the box. He gazed up at Amanda and sighed. "I will deny I ever told you this if anyone asks. Let's just say it doesn't look good. Graham Productions is in charge of the film."

Amanda wilted, all the anger draining her. "She's crushed. She loved him and now feels betrayed."

Ty stood and begin to pick up the cases by the handles. "Reed is not a man to fall in love with. He's a heartbreaker. I wouldn't let my sister or any woman I cared about near him."

"This is the first time she has ever let herself completely go without going through the twelve-step program, and now, all it's done is break her heart. And probably cost her, her business," Amanda said, clenching her fists her heart aching for Lacey. For herself and all the hard work they'd put into this business.

Ty shrugged. "I don't know what to tell you."

"You can go back and tell Reed Hunter I hope he rots in hell," Amanda said, as she walked out of the room.

Chapter Nineteen

A month passed, and Reed kept thinking any day now, things were going to get better. He kept thinking any morning he would wake up and be himself again, but each day only seemed to make him gloomier. And then he would go into the editing room and see Lacey's face on film, and a deep sadness would overwhelm him.

At first, he'd tried to contact her, but she wasn't taking his calls. According to her secretary, her response had been that he could go fuck himself.

Lacey's crew had circled around her like a protective shield. They weren't letting him near her. And he wanted her like his next breath. He had shown up at her office with flowers. Her secretary and Amanda had made it very clear he was no longer welcome. They had thrown his flowers in the trash, shown him the door, and told him they'd call the police if he returned.

For the first time since he'd graduated college, even sex didn't seem to hold the interest it once had. He felt lost and rambled around his house every day, trying to get interested in his life once again. Not once did he think of going out to chase women. It no longer held any appeal.

Never before had a woman disrupted his life in such a way. The break-up of his engagement had been a cake walk compared to the pain he'd experienced in the last month. He'd lost ten pounds, wasn't sleeping well, and had no clue what he would do when he finished this documentary. Always before he'd had two or three ideas ready to start on once he finished editing the current film.

This time, it seemed nothing inspired him. This time, he felt like a fish out of water, flopping on the bank of life, gasping for his last breath.

How could one woman cause so much pain? How could one woman disrupt his life so much? How could one woman make his heart ache with longing and regret?

But he missed Lacey with every breath he took. Ty had been right. This film hurt. Looking at Lacey day in and day out, trying to find the right angle on the story, hurt too much. He'd been unable to edit more than five minutes, before he walked out of the room and turned off the light.

He was a selfish bastard who used women for sex, until one woman had completely disrupted his life and made him realize his destructive ways. Even that last character he'd filmed had more integrity than what he'd done.

Lacey made him a better man. She made him think of things in a different light. She saw the good in him, even when he was at his most disastrous, attempting to tarnish her good name and reputation.

And God help him, he loved her. He'd sworn never to experience this weakness again. Yet he loved Lacey, pure and simple. And that was the reason he hurt so bad. Because like before, an overwhelming sense of sadness and loss filled him.

He'd screwed up royally and hurt the person he loved.

Settling down with just one woman had never been an option he'd considered since his broken engagement, but now, if that would bring Lacey back, he would gladly reconsider.

He was hurting, and he'd done nothing but bring this pain upon himself. Somehow he had to get over this crippling depression.

Flipping through the morning paper, trying to get the energy to go in and start editing the film, he came across an ad for one of Lacey's seminars. His stomach clenched at the cancelled stamp across the seminar, and a phone number telling people where to call to receive a refund.

Why would she cancel a seminar? Why would she give up on doing what she loved? Unless she was sick or injured. What if she'd come down with some catastrophic disease and was dying?

God, she had to be all right.

He yanked his cell phone out of his pocket and called the office. "Hello. Amanda, please?"

A few minutes later, he heard her voice. "This is Amanda."

"Is Lacey okay?" he asked.

Silence greeted him.

"I've got to know."

"No, dick wad, she's not okay. She's quitting the business. Are you satisfied?"

The news stunned him. He stared at the phone, not knowing what to say. An overwhelming sense of sadness overcame him. "Could we meet somewhere and talk?" he asked, desperate to hear in person why Lacey would give up the business she loved.

"Why would I do that? So you can get more ammunition for your film?"

Reed cringed inside, his chest aching, knowing he deserved her mistrust. "No, I'd like to talk."

Amanda paused, and he thought she was going to tell him no. A long minute stretched out to what seemed like forever.

"Meet me at the Starbucks on Main Street in half an hour."

"I'll be there."

The phone clicked, and the dial tone echoed in his ear. What would he say? He didn't know, but he had to find out why Lacey was quitting the business she loved. Grabbing his keys, he ran out the door.

He raced to the meeting with Amanda, speeding and even ran a red light, knowing he had to get there. He parked the car, walked into the coffee shop, and hurried over to Amanda, waiting in the corner.

"Hi," he said.

"Make this quick. I've got to get back."

"Why is Lacey cancelling her seminars and quitting the business?" he asked, slumping down into the chair across from her.

Amanda shook her head like she couldn't believe he would ask this question. "Lacey thinks if she's barely visible when your film comes out, then maybe she might survive. She's quitting for a while."

"Why wouldn't she do as much business as possible before the film comes out?"

"Because she's hurting. She's lost the desire to do what she loves. She is going to close the business. She's lost weight. She's accepted the loss of the television show."

Reed stared at Amanda. "What television show?"

"For months she's been meeting with a producer who was shopping the idea of a talk show. It was the reason she did the documentary. The studio was interested in doing a pilot program. They were waiting for the documentary to come out before they started filming."

"Lacey never mentioned a television show." How many of her dreams could he somehow have managed to squash?

"That's because they told her to keep it quiet."

"But, I would…"

"You would have done what? Filmed more clients who don't like Lacey? Done more shooting to show her at a disadvantage? What? How much uglier can you be?" Amanda asked, her face filled with anger. "You're going to destroy her because you got dumped and that tanked your ego."

Reed stared down at the coffee before him. She was about to get a television show, and now he was destroying her business and her dreams. He couldn't do this any longer. He didn't want to hurt her. "Okay, I admit it. I'm an ass. Call me names. Do whatever you think you have to. I wake up each morning, knowing something is missing from my life. I want to make this right. What can I do?"

Amanda sat back and stared at him like he had two heads. "Are you just saying this or do you really mean it?"

Reed didn't know how to convince Amanda. "I can't stop thinking about what she said to those clients of hers. How love is putting the other person's desires before your own. How loving the other person makes you a better person."

"Go on."

Reed suddenly knew what his subconscious had been trying to tell him for weeks. And he knew what he had to do. "Love is-I know what the hell I have to do."

Amanda shook her head. "You frighten me. I don't trust you."

"I don't deserve your trust. But I'm going to make this right." He stood. "I've got to go. I know what I have to do."

~

The phone rang, waking Reed up from a deep sleep. He glanced at the clock, it was after midnight. He picked it up.

"Hello," he said, his voice groggy with sleep.

"Is this the only way I can get you to answer my calls? Call you at midnight?"

Reed sat up in bed, dreading this phone call. "Sorry. I've been busy working on the film."

"You're almost done?"

"Yes, sir. It's in the final stages," and you will never be happy with what I've done, he thought. "I should be finished very soon."

"Great. I'm going forward with the plans then for the opening night showing. When can I see the film?"

Reed knew he was going to be fired. He'd never get to do the exposé he dreamed of doing, only because he would soon no longer have a job. "Give me a couple of weeks, and I'll give you a date for a private showing. Just you, Lacey, her staff, and a couple of other people."

"You're going to invite her to the private showing?" Graham asked.

"Why not? It will be good for her to know what she's going to be facing."

Graham chuckled. "I like the way you think. I'll be in Spain the next two weeks."

"Why don't we schedule the showing for after your return," Reed said.

"But that means I won't be able to see the film until the night of the private showing."

"Graham, you'll enjoy it that much more. You'll see how we got the bitch."

There was a moment of silence on the other end. Would he agree to wait and see it at the same time as everyone else?

"You know I wouldn't usually do this, but we were both burned by this woman. I trust you, Reed."

Reed smiled. Problem solved. He'd be fired, but still, there would be nothing Graham could do to stop the showing of the film Reed wanted to produce. "Graham, I have one more request. Would you donate ten percent of the proceeds from this film to a scholarship fund for young filmmakers?"

"What, are you crazy?"

"No, I want to help kids who need a way to get to college."

"And who's going to oversee this scholarship fund?"

"Well, that's why I thought we would name it the Juliet Fund, and maybe your old girlfriend, who was an accountant, would manage it for us."

Graham laughed. "You're a sly dog."

"No, I just thought that maybe after Juliet sees the film, she'd come back to you. You know when she sees how wrong she was about Lacey, and then you could get her to manage the scholarship fund."

There was a pause on the line.

"Unless you've moved on to someone else."

"No, I'd take Juliet back in a heartbeat."

"Well then, maybe this will bring her back into your life."

"Are you feeling okay?" Graham asked.

"Why?"

"I never thought I'd see the day you were trying to help bring a girl back into the relationship? Are you going to invite Blair?"

"Hell, no," Reed said. "My relationship with Blair never had a chance, even long before she ever took Lacey's seminar. I just wanted to see if maybe you and Juliet could get back together."

"Thanks, Reed. I'm surprised. But I like the idea and maybe she'll see reason."

"Let's hope so. We're all set for the private showing?"

"I can't wait," Graham said, laughing. "Watching Lacey Morgan go down is going to be quite enjoyable."

Reed sighed knowing that documentary would never be seen if he could help it. "Have a safe trip to Spain, and I'll see you at the private screening."

~

Two weeks after his meeting with Amanda, Reed stood in front of Jose's family's home, knocking on the door. He'd buried himself in his work, and now the film was in production and would soon release.

He only hoped he wasn't too late.

Jose opened the door and stared at him. "What do you want?"

"Can we please talk?" Reed said, knowing the kid was still angry he hadn't received the scholarship.

The boy walked out the door and closed it behind him. "Graduation was over weeks ago. What are you doing here?"

"I came to check on you. What are you doing this summer?" Reed sat down on the concrete steps, while Jose walked out in the yard, his hands in his pockets, his gaze down on the ground.

"I'm working with my Papa, doing yards."

"How do you like it?" Reed asked.

The kid raised his gaze to Reed, his brown eyes flashing with anger. "I hate it."

"Are you still filming?"

He shrugged. "When I get a chance."

Reed nodded. "Can't give it up, can you?"

Anyone who loved working in film had tried several times to give it up and had been unable. It almost felt like an addiction. It traveled with you everywhere.

"No, I've tried, but it makes me happy." Jose stared at him. "Why are you here?" he asked.

"A wise lady told me I should help you, and at the time, I didn't know how. I did some research and didn't really find what I wanted. And then yesterday, an idea came to me," he said, watching the boy stub his Nikes in the yard.

Jose glanced up at Reed, seeming curious.

"I have a film coming out in the next two weeks. A film about changing people's lives for the better. What better way to demonstrate my interest in helping people than to give a scholarship based on the ticket sales of the film?"

The kid's eyes widened, and he stared at Reed.

"Ten percent of the gross film sales will be put in a special fund that will go to a young man or woman studying filmmaking." Reed paused. "Do you know of anyone who is interested?"

A smile broke out on the kid's face, and he laughed. "That's a dumb question. I want that scholarship. I want that chance to go to filmmaking school." He jumped up in the air and yelled, shaking his fists, excitement gleaming from his face. Then he stopped and gazed at Reed. "You were thinking of me, weren't you?"

Reed stood and ruffled his hair with his hand, feeling certain Jose would take advantage of the program, and soon would be on his way to making films for a living. "Yeah, buddy. I was thinking of you. In three years of teaching, you're my best student. I think you have what it takes, and I want to help you. There will be some stipulations that your grades have to remain high, but other than that, you just go to school."

Jose clasped Reed's hand and then awkwardly pulled him to him and slapped him on the back. "Thanks, Mr. Hunter. Thanks for helping me. I can't ever repay you."

"Sure, you can. Graduate."

"Oh, yeah," he said, running up the stairs. "I've got to tell Mama and Papa."

Reed watched him rip open the door, screaming at the top of his lungs.

"Mama! Papa! I got a scholarship. I got a scholarship."

A warm sense of happiness came over Reed. Ten percent of the gross sales would more than put the kid through school, especially if this film took off like he thought it would.

He walked toward his car, lightness in his step. Listening to Lacey and taking action on her advice made him a better man. Now he had to get her back.

$\sim$

Lacey's office phone rang. She picked it up. "Lacey Morgan."

"Lacey, Stan Whittaker of Chimney Rock Productions."

Her heart skipped a beat and then raced to catch up.

The man who had talked her into doing the documentary. The man who had promised her a television show if the film did well. And now, here he was on the phone and what did she tell him?

"You didn't call me and tell me about the private screening. I just heard about it. I'm calling to see if you want me to pick you up in the company limo."

"Sorry, Stan. I just learned of the date myself. I've already got plans that night," she lied. Why should she attend her own public flogging? There was no need for her to see how Reed had slain everything she loved. Including their relationship.

There was a long moment of silence on the phone, and then he let out a sigh. "Lacey," he paused, "in order for me to sell this idea, I need you at that private screening, smiling and saying thank you. You're the star. You have to attend."

Lacey gritted her teeth. "What if the movie is horrible?"

"Then we still get the publicity of your first bad film," he said. "It's going to be fine. What time do you want the limo to pick you up?"

"Six-thirty."

"That doesn't give us much time to schmooze. How about six?"

"Whatever," she said, instantly regretting the word that sounded so indifferent. She felt anything but indifferent. "Arriving in a limo sounds grand."

Frankly, she didn't care how they got there, as she felt sure she'd be going home by taxi, once Stan saw the diabolical film.

"My wife and I will pick you and your manager up the night of the screening. We'll see what Reed Hunter has put together. If this film takes off like I'm hearing, you should have your own show very soon," he said, his voice excited.

But Lacey was unable to muster any enthusiasm. "Oh,

it's going to take off all right."

He laughed. "The buzz around town says it's his best film."

Lacey cringed. Was the film good because it showed her business with all its faults? "Buzz is good."

"Yes, it is."

"Great. See you then."

Lacey hung up the phone and moaned. How would she get through that night? How was she going to see Reed again without crying? What would she do if she lost everything?

~

That evening, Lacey knocked on her mother's door. Since her sister had married and moved away, Lacey tried to spend one night a week with her mother. Normally, they went to dinner, but tonight, she didn't have the energy to do much of anything.

Disaster loomed on the horizon, and like a bad movie, she could only stand there and let the tsunami overtake her.

Her mother opened the door and stared at her. "Hi, sweetheart."

"Hi, Mom."

"Come in, and I'll pour us each a glass of wine," she said, pulling Lacey in and closing the door.

"Bring the bottle," Lacey said, walking into the living area and slumping onto the couch.

A few minutes later, her mother sat the bottle down on the table. "You look tired."

"I'm exhausted."

"How long before you get over Reed Hunter?" her mother asked.

Tears pricked the back of her eyes. "You never beat around the bush, do you, Mom? You just come out and ask."

Her mother sank down across from her. "You're letting this man make you a wreck. I'm worried about you."

"There will be a private screening next week," Lacey blurted out.

"Oh," her mother said, that single word hanging in the air around them weighing a ton. "Are you going?"

Lacey hugged her arms around her middle. "I have to. Stan Whittaker, the producer interested in getting me my own television show, he wants us to go together. He's arranging for a limo to pick me and Amanda up. Do you want to go?"

"Yes," she said quickly. "I think you need all the support you can get. We'll show up in force and make Reed Hunter realize what he's missing out on."

Or make Reed Hunter see how he'd made her a wreck. She'd never suffered such a broken heart until Reed.

Her mother raised her chin, defiance sparkling in her gaze.

"Mom," Lacey said, fighting the tears that threatened to fall. "I just don't know if I can face him. I fell in love with him, and those feelings haven't gone away. Even after three months, the pain is just as sharp."

"Oh, sweetie," her mother said, coming to sit beside her and pull her into her arms.

Lacey let the tears flow, the open wound in her heart flowing unheeded. "You…you said that passion could cause pain, and now I know what you mean. This hurts so much."

"I know, baby. I know. But if you don't experience great passion, then you would never know what it's like to live with a great love."

"I don't think I want to experience either one ever again."

Her mother laughed. "I understand. I wish it would have worked out for you and Reed."

"Thanks, Mom. But how can I still love a man who wants to hurt me? Am I pathetic or what?"

"No, honey, you're human. You gave away your heart to a man who didn't know what he had. You're a wonderful woman who will make someone very happy. And whoever that person is, you should feel for them how you feel for Reed."

"I don't know. This hurts too much."

"Yes, it does. But if you'd moved in with or even married Dean, you would never have experienced this kind of love. Unfortunately, you chose a man who didn't want commitment. Now you need to find a man who creates these same emotions, but wants commitment."

In the last few months, she'd learned so much about life. First what a disappointment Dean had turned out to be and then Reed. Smart, intelligent, handsome with a knife that he would soon shove into her back, killing her business.

Lacey leaned back and wiped her eyes. "I don't know, Mom. I think for now I'm going to forget men for a while. Kerri is married, and I'm happy for her, but I don't think I want this kind of pain again."

Her mother frowned. "I understand. I just want you to be happy."

"I know. But passion hurts too much."

"How are you going to react to seeing Reed for the first time?"

Lacey took a deep breath and gave her mother a fake smile. "I'm going to smile and picture in my mind, me smacking him with my purse."

A genuine smile graced her mother's lips. "That's my girl. Maybe we should see about getting you a date."

"Absolutely not. No men. I want to face Reed alone," Lacey said, the thought of another man repulsive to her. She needed to be alone for a while.

"Okay. Amanda and I will attend. Plus the studio exec and his wife," she said, rubbing Lacey's arm.

"Just don't let me start swinging my purse." She didn't want to see Reed. Her heart was still an open wound and seeing him would only tear open the tissue.

Her mother laughed, the sound a welcome relief in the small room. "I can't make any promises. I could be the one doing the swinging if I don't like the way he's depicted my baby."

Lacey smiled at her mother. "Could be an interesting evening. Who knows? We may end it in jail."

Chapter Twenty

Lacey stared out the window as the limousine pulled up in front of Graham Production headquarters. She didn't want to get out of the car. She wasn't ready to face everything this film would do to her and her business.

The car door opened, she took a deep breath and stepped out onto the sidewalk, not sure she was prepared for this evening. Her mother followed behind her, Amanda next, and then Stan, the television producer who had arranged the limo, and his wife.

"Can't wait to see this film, Lacey," he said. "It's getting a lot of buzz."

"Great," she said, plastering the plastic smile on her face. She tried to have joy in her heart at the thought of her own television show. But that dream was fading and after tonight would no longer exist. Her only goal was to get through the night without seeing Reed. Her heart still hadn't mended from the wreckage he'd left.

They stepped inside the production company and were met by a secretary.

"Good evening. I recognize Ms. Morgan. Let me just check the visitors roster for your names."

Everyone gave her their name, while Lacey stood over to the side, gazing at the place where Reed worked. The company that would destroy her business and her life.

"Follow me please," the secretary said and led them to the reception area where a small bar was set up.

"Wine anyone?" Stan asked.

Lacey shook her head. "Sorry, I'm too nervous."

"I'd love a glass," her mother said.

Stan went to the bar, and his wife disappeared into the ladies room.

"Mom, please. No matter what happens tonight, you promised me you would behave."

She laughed. "And I will. Unless the film is totally bogus. Then I will get my hands on Reed Hunter. He could be a eunuch by the end of the night."

"Mom, my reputation can't handle a fight. Amanda is going to have to work magic just to hold off the press, until I can close the business."

"Have you told Stan?"

"I've tried and no matter what I do, it just never comes out right. I decided he would learn the bad news from the film. I'm sure the television deal is dead after tonight. Unless I'm going to be the female version of Jerry Springer, and that's not the type of show I want."

How did you tell the man who had worked so hard to find you a network that the film you both were excited about was only going to destroy you?

Amanda patted her on the back. "We're here with you. No matter what happens tonight, we love you and know you're a great relationship coach."

Her mother nodded. "We've got your back."

"And if during the film it gets bad and you want to leave, just give me the signal, and we're out of here," Amanda assured her.

Lacey sighed and glanced around the room at the people there to see her on film. Her stomach rolled, and she wanted to throw up. "Thanks for coming with me, guys. I don't want to see Reed." So far so good. She hadn't laid eyes on him, and she wanted to keep it that way.

Stan rejoined the group, and his wife returned from the ladies room. "Are you guys ready to go in?"

"Yes," Lacey said, her legs shaking. She wanted to get this night over.

They went into the small auditorium. The theater was filled with people in the industry and those who worked for Graham Productions.

They found six reserved seats near the front. After

taking hers, Lacey glanced around the auditorium and didn't see Reed. Part of her sighed with relief, part of her was disappointed, and a third part of her would have jumped into his arms at the sight of him.

That part she had under lock and key. Tonight, there would be no public displays of affection.

The curtains parted, and the lights dimmed while Lacey's heart started to pound. The feature film began, and Lacey's body started to shake.

Her mother reached over and took her hand. Amanda sat on the other side of her, and she also took her hand. Lacey's body shook from fear, her nerves completely wracking her body.

The film started with people leaving her seminars. They came out giving her rave reviews, and she relaxed a little. Reed appeared on the screen, his handsome face, filling her vision, her heart breaking all over again. She loved him and suddenly wondered if she would always love him.

"When I started this documentary, my intention was to show the world that people who didn't have counseling degrees were giving people advice about how to live their lives. I wanted to show relationship coaches were not qualified to help people change and make decisions about their relationships. Here is the story of Lacey Morgan, Relationship Coach."

The film depicted Lacey standing in front of a crowd, explaining to them what her job as a relationship coach entailed.

For the next hour, Reed showed her in seminars, laughing with her clients, crying over her clients, and she appeared as a caring human being trying to help people find happiness.

The couple that ended their relationship in her office broke her heart all over again as she watched the couple split-up on screen.

At the end, her clients talked about their experiences with Lacey, praising her for helping them realize why they couldn't find permanent relationships. How she helped them change.

Then her one problem client came on, and after Reed's interview, everyone in the theater burst out laughing at the craziness of the guy.

Reed's smiling face appeared on the screen. "This film became personal for me. Instead of finding that a relationship coach is someone who needs more education in order to help people find the relationship of their dreams, Lacey Morgan showed me how I needed help with my own relationships. I've been to Uganda, Haiti, and even Iraq, but very few documentaries I've filmed have affected me like this one. I learned I had no idea what it took to have a good relationship with a woman. Lacey showed me I needed to change."

He walked toward the camera. "If you know someone who always seems to find the wrong type of man or woman to date, then maybe what they need is a relationship coach to help them discover more about who they are. How can you have a good relationship, if you don't know what you want?"

Tears trickled down her cheeks, as she realized he'd shown her in a positive way. His film had proven how she helped couples, and instead of the trashing she'd expected, the film reflected her work. By the time the film credits started to roll, she was crying fully.

The people in the screening room burst into applause. Some of them turned to look at her, and she tried to wipe her tears away.

Her mother squeezed her hand. "That was beautiful, baby. I never knew what a great job you do for these people."

"Oh Mom, he made me look so good. He didn't betray

me."

Amanda squeezed her hand. "Lacey, your business is about to explode with clients. Reed has just taken you to the next level."

She sobbed. "I know."

Stan leaned over. "Pretty emotional moment. Reed Hunter has just made you a star."

"Thank you," Lacey said between her tears. "If you guys don't mind, I think I'd like to sit here in the dark a few moments alone. I need some time to regroup."

Amanda nodded. "Come on, Mom. Let's go out front and see if we can find Ty. I need to tell him thank you."

"Are you going to be all right?" her mom asked, clearly reluctant to leave.

"Yes, I just need a few moments."

The group stood and left Lacey sitting there, watching the credits roll on the screen. Sniffling, she thought of how Reed had taken her life and business and shown the world she was a human being who cared about people. He'd taken the worst and the best of her clients, and showed her resolving relationship problems.

In the film, he'd captured her love for her business, and in the process, she'd fallen in love with him all over again. Oh God, what did she do now? She loved him even more than when they'd parted.

~

Reed had stayed hidden and watched Lacey throughout the documentary. Even in the darkness, he'd seen her expressions and knew when he'd captured her heartbreak over the couple that had parted, her body had softened. She'd relaxed. And then at the end, he'd known she was crying.

He'd avoided Graham, but there he was before him, his face red, his body tense, rage reflected from his eyes.

"You're fired! Take your camera equipment, pack your shit, and get out of this company."

Reed shrugged. "Sorry, Graham, but I fell in love with Lacey, and I couldn't do what you asked."

"Graham," a woman came running up to him. "Oh Graham, honey, that was so good. I thought you hated Lacey's program, but to do a documentary on it. Oh honey, does this mean you're willing to try again?" Juliet stood before Graham, her blue eyes gazing at him like he was a God.

Graham looked from Reed to Juliet and then back to Reed, who could see the confusion on his face. He could see the man wanted to scream and yell and curse Lacey's business, but then, here was a chance of Juliet coming back into his life.

"Honey, of course this means I'm willing to try again. Sugar, I've missed you so much."

She flung herself into his arms and pressed her lips against his. "I'm so glad. Oh, Graham, what a lovely film. You couldn't have done anything better to get me back."

Reed smiled and gave Graham a thumbs up.

"Hang on a second, sugar," Graham said, not releasing Juliet, but watching Reed. "My office tomorrow morning at nine o'clock."

Reed shook his head. "Sorry, Graham. I've been fired. I won't be here." He turned and walked up the aisle. No way could he let her sit there another minute alone. Quietly, he hurried over to where she sat.

As he came up the aisle, she saw him, her gaze connecting with his. She swiped at the tears on her face.

"Hi," he said softly. "You came."

"Reed," she said shakily. "He fired you."

Reed shrugged his shoulders and pulled a handkerchief out of his pocket and handed it to her. "His loss. I'm thinking of going out on my own."

"But—"

He held up his hand. "Before you say anything about the film, I need to tell you the truth."

"I loved the film," she said in a whisper.

"Wait, hear me out," he said, frowning. He took a deep breath. "I didn't start this film out to make you look good. I had the worst of intentions. I meant to trash you just like you said. I was an ass and a jerk. But you changed me. You made me see the world differently."

"I thought you didn't believe in relationship coaches."

"I didn't."

"I thought you hated me and what I stood for."

He laughed. "I did. You changed my world. You made me see the life I was living was shallow and cold. You helped me to realize I was afraid of giving myself completely to any woman. You made me vulnerable."

He'd never felt so vulnerable as he felt at this moment. He needed this woman, like he needed his next breath. He wanted it all, and she'd shown him what he was missing.

"And now, how do you feel about me?" she asked softly.

"I hate you for showing me I was such a despicable ass." He paused. "I love you for changing me. I want to spend every day with you. I want to grow old with you."

She laughed at him. "Damn you, Reed Hunter. You're not following the twelve step program."

He took her by the hand and pulled her to a standing position, where he could wrap his arms around her. "Tell me what step I missed, and I promise I'll go back and do it. Tell me what I have to do to get you back in my life. You've made me a better man. I need you like my next breath."

His lips covered hers in a kiss that was full of love and hope and desperation. He'd missed her touch, her laughter, and the way she made him think bigger.

She'd changed his world for the better, just like she helped so many people.

The lights in the theater came on, and they came apart, seeing their friends and families standing in the doorway. They were smiling, and then they begin to clap. Softly at first, but soon the theater was loud with enthusiasm as people gave the couple applause.

Lacey blushed and leaned her head into his chest. "Marry me?" she asked.

"Just say when," he replied. "We can go tonight. Whatever you want, say the word, as long as you're by my side."

She hugged him to her, and Reed knew he'd come home. The permanent bachelor had found a woman he wanted to spend the rest of his life with.

Epilogue

Three months later, Reed took his seat out in the studio. His wife, his soul mate and lover was about to achieve her dream, and he had to be here to share the experience with her. She'd changed his life, and he couldn't imagine a day without her tender touch.

The music keyed, and she walked out on the stage in front of a live audience with a smile on her face.

Almost one year ago, he'd sat in an audience watching his wife, believing she was a fraud, but now he knew better. His wife had the ability to touch people, to help them see their problems in a new way and to help them change and grow. Look what she'd done to him.

And now, because of her support and belief in him, he was starting his own production company.

She smiled at him, and he felt so proud to be sitting here as her husband. Life was good.

"Welcome. I'm Lacey Morgan-Hunter, relationship coach. I'd like to begin by talking about the importance of passion in our lives."

God, he was a lucky man.

Thank you for reading!

Dear Reader,

Thank you so much for reading *The Relationship Coach*.

Whether you loved the book or hated it, I would appreciate it if you let everyone know by leaving a few words on your favorite vendor's website.

If you enjoy western historical authors, please join the Pioneer Hearts group on Facebook. This is a fabulous group of readers and authors who enjoy westerns.

Sign up for my newsletter at sylviamcdaniel.com if you'd like to learn about my new releases as soon as possible.

Reading one of my books is like spending time with me, and I just want to say thank you from the bottom of my heart.

Yours in Drama, Divas, Bad Boys, and Romance!
Sincerely,
Sylvia McDaniel

Books by Sylvia McDaniel

Contemporary Romance

Standalones
The Reluctant Santa
My Sister's Boyfriend
The Wanted Bride
The Relationship Coach
Her Christmas Lie
Secrets, Lies, and Online Dating
Paying for the Past
Cupid's Revenge

Anthologies
Kisses, Laughter & Love
Christmas with you

Collaborative Series

Magic, New Mexico
Touch of Decadence

Western Historicals

Standalones
A Hero's Heart
A Scarlet Bride
Second Chance Cowboy

The Cuvier Women
Wronged
Betrayed
Beguiled

Lipstick and Lead
Desperate
Deadly
Dangerous
Daring
Determined
Deceived

Scandalous Suffragettes
Abigail
Bella
Callie
Faith

The Burnett Brides
The Rancher Takes a Bride
The Outlaw Takes a Bride
The Marshal Takes a Bride
The Christmas Bride

Anthologies
Wild Western Women
Courting the West
Wild Western Women Ride Again

Collaborative Series

The Surprise Brides
Ethan

American Mail Order Brides
Katie

About the Author

Sylvia McDaniel is a best-selling, award-winning author of historical romance and contemporary romance novels. Known for her sweet, funny, family-oriented romances, Sylvia is the author of The Burnett Brides, a western historical western series, The Cuvier Widows, a Louisiana historical series, and several short contemporary romances.

She is the former President of the Dallas Area Romance Authors, a member of the Romance Writers of America®, and a member of Novelists Inc. Her novel, A Hero's Heart, was a 1996 Golden Heart Finalist. Several other books have placed or won in the San Antonio Romance Authors Contest and the LERA Contest, and she was a Golden Network Finalist.

Married for nearly twenty years to her best friend, they have two dachshunds that are beyond spoiled and a good-looking, grown son who thinks there's no place like home. She loves gardening, shopping, knitting, and football (Cowboys and Bronco's fan), but not necessarily in that order.

Look for her the first Tuesday of every month at the Plotting Princesses blogspot, and be sure to sign up for her newsletter to learn about new releases and contests. Every month a new subscriber is entered into a drawing for a free book!

She can be found online at: www.sylviamcdaniel.com or on Facebook. You can write to Sylvia at P.O. Box 2542, Coppell, TX 75019.

Since his mother abandoned him on Christmas Eve never to return, Colin McDermott has hated Christmas and sworn never to have children. But this year two angels are giving him everything he didn't want. A Santa suit, a child and a chance at love again. This is his last chance to learn the true meaning of Christmas.

Sneak Peek into The Reluctant Santa

"His soul is mine," Devon, the devil's angel, said. He watched the humans, who were oblivious to his presence, gathered in the sales office. One of the best things about being an angel was his ability to pop into just about anywhere and spy on his subjects without their knowledge. He could observe the humans as if were watching a play and even occasionally act as director.

A chill wind howled outside the downtown Denver office, heralding the arrival of winter and the holiday season. The perfect time of year to increase his soul count. Devon studied his next soul, a brown-haired young man with expressive brows and a quirky grin. Unbeknownst to him, the salesman's life meter was about to expire unless he made drastic changes.

"Devon," a voice echoed into the atmosphere before the being that irritated him the most shimmered into his vision. "Doing a soul count before he's yours?"

Slowly, an angel materialized, clad from head to toe in a white leather jacket and white knee-high boots fit snug over white leather pants. A gold belt around her waist, held a cross that signified sergeant, angel, first class. Her halo was tilted at a rakish angle. In earth terms, Gabriella looked hot.

"Whoever is in charge of your wardrobe, I like the changes they've made," Devon said, letting his eyes rake her until a searing heat reminded him he was crossing boundaries. "Please tell me they ditched the boring robes."

With a toss of her blonde hair, her blue eyes flashed, glinting silver as her brows rose. "My robes are hardly boring, but no, one of my cases is a motorcyclist. I'm riding shotgun today, trying to keep him from splattering all over the highway. The robes kept blowing up in my face, so I found a solution."

"Nice!" Devon shook his head and forced his eyes back to the human whose life he'd soon influence. "I thought your promotion at Easter took you out of the saving souls division."

Gabriella smiled as the air around her shimmered. Why didn't the angels from purgatory patrol get that shimmery essence?

"Devon, we work so…well together" she said, drawing out the word until he wanted to snap at her. He held onto his temper.

"We're all looking for ways to make quota this time of year. Only the strongest stay out of the pit, and every time I come up against you, I lose. But not this time. This one belongs to me," he announced, staring at the man whose only interest in life was making money. No family, no girlfriends, no friends—just work and money.

Gabriella tsked. "Now why would you want to send this poor man to hell for eternity? He just needs a little coaxing to choose the right path."

Devon sighed. "His time is about to expire. I'm here to collect his soul."

"Maybe," she said. "Unless, I can give him some guidance and save him from evil."

"Not this time. Heavenly angels may not be able to play dirty, but I can," he said, smiling at Gabriella. "And I intend to win this one."

Gabriella laughed. "Always so arrogant, Devon." She glanced at their human. "His case is challenging, but I'm certain I can help him."

She turned toward Devon, her brows rising. "Playing dirty landed you where you are now. Why should I expect anything less?"

"How I got here doesn't matter. I need this soul," he snapped. "You make your soul count or the big man sends you back to the pit to fight and claw your way back for another chance."

"And Colin McDermott needs to be saved," Gabriella said, swirling back to their subject. "I mean, look at the poor man. He has no idea his priorities are in the wrong place. He's a selfish, greedy man because he's unloved."

"Love!" Devon exclaimed. "You heavenly angels think loving someone solves everything."

Gabriella shook her head at Devon, her blue eyes darkening with some sort of power. "Even you deserved love, Devon. In fact, if I had been your angel, I would found someone to show you love. Hopefully, you'd have been smart enough to grab the lifeline."

"Well, you weren't my angel, and now I'm the big man's soul catcher."

"It's simple, Devon. Why would you want to lure more men into the darkness you already face?" she asked.

Devon clenched his fist, struggling to control the frustration that spiraled through him. Hell was not a place anyone planned on going. "The pit!" he said. "Let's just concentrate on the human."

"I already was." She contemplated Colin McDermott. "He's quite handsome with those long, sandy lashes and sparkling honey eyes. If I were human, one look and he'd melt my heart."

"Women on earth know he's not a good risk. I could wrap this case up before Christmas, if you weren't here."

"Too bad. I'm here to keep you from destroying him," she said, giving him a stern frown. "The poor soul has no idea of what he's about to face. I'm sure you've got some nasty surprises in store for him, some hard to resist temptations. But hopefully, with my guidance, he'll make the changes his life needs."

Devon shook his head. "No, by Christmas he'll be mine. Count on it."